The Alaska Strain

The Kielder Experiment, Volume 2

Rebecca Fernfield

Published by Redbegga Publishing, 2022.

Copyright

This is a work of fiction. Similarities to real people, places, or events are entirely coincidental.

THE ALASKA STRAIN

Second Edition. September 22, 2022.

Copyright © 2022 Rebecca Fernfield

Written by Rebecca Fernfield.

PROLOGUE

International Institute of Bio-Tech Advancement, Volkolak Island, Southwest Alaska

From her office at the heart of the research facility, Dr. Marta Steward watched the live feed with anticipation. As director of the programme she had ordered the team to procure a higher quality female and they hadn't disappointed. The woman was young and attractive, with slim waist, rounded buttocks, large breasts, and a pretty face, but she looked unwell, as though recovering from a bad hangover, or perhaps suffering drug withdrawal symptoms. Marta made a note to request that a 'clean' specimen be procured next time, then returned her attention to the screen.

Breath caught in her chest as the door opened and Max, or at least what had been Max, stepped into the cell. For several moments he hung back, sniffing at the air, then began his approach to the woman. Her screams weren't audible, but from the way she cowered in the corner, hiding behind the thin mattress, the only object of comfort in the cell, her terror was obvious.

"Put it down woman!" Marta hissed, frustrated as the woman remained out of sight. She made another note to tell Kendrick to remove the mattress next time; the woman's reactions were just as important to note as Max's.

Marta gave an exasperated sigh; something in Max's gait, the way he held himself, indicated failure. After another minute Marta was certain and cut the live feed to dead with an irritated prod at the keyboard; she had no stomach to watch the carnage that would follow yet another failed introduction. The screen returned to an image of herself, Peter Marston, Katarina Petrov, and Max Anderson against the backdrop of the Gothic façade of Kielder Institute. Taken on their first day at the newly refurbished building, their smiles were bright and hopeful. A moment of sadness, quickly extinguished, flickered within Marta. Max stood smiling, innocent, unaware of the terrible fate that awaited him, and she was struck by the realisation of how our lives progress, the incidents that make up who we are, and what path our life would follow, were totally random, inexplicable, and sometimes just bloody bizarre.

"Poor Max." Her focus moved to the Institute's portal on the screen. "But it won't have all been for nothing. I can promise you that. Peter will know what to do." She entered a password and accessed the hidden files labelled 'Project Kielder' then began to read through the notes before booking a flight back to England.

CHAPTER ONE

Volkolak Island, Kodiak archipelago, Southwest Alaska

As storm clouds gathered unnoticed, Christopher Miller positioned his mobile on the tripod, checked the angle, turned the video on, then walked back to the deer before raising the knife to shoulder height and slicing it down. Late afternoon sunlight caught the blade as it pierced the deer's flesh, and a mass of grey-pink and glistening entrails followed, spilling from the animal's belly into the waiting bucket. Detaching the innards, he inexpertly cleaned out the cavity as he talked to the camera. "You've got to take particular care not to nick the stomach." He laughed as though sharing a joke. "I've learnt the hard way that acidic bile leaking from any rupture will contaminate the meat." He hacked as steam from the deer's offal rose in the cold autumn air.

As he continued to narrate, with sunlight glinting on the water lapping at his half-beached boat, the muffled howl of a wolf carried from the wooded hills. Stopping mid-sentence, he cast a fearful glance to the trees and shivered as the hairs on his neck prickled. The creature was miles away, probably on the other side of the forest, but there weren't supposed to be wolves on the island—he'd checked. Gathering his senses, he turned back to the camera. "Did you hear that! Canis lupus or, in layman's terms, a grey wolf, sometimes also known as a timber wolf, but they're supposed to be extinct on this island!" The tension in each sentence was expertly heightened for maximum effect and, he hoped, maximum viewer engagement. He held the pose just long enough then turned back to hacking the deer.

His survival gear has been kept to the bare minimum, as advised, but he had brought enough tools with him to butcher the animal and prepped himself with multiple, at least three, video tutorials found on YouTube. The next day and a half would be a true test of his newly learned bushcraft skills and should put a stop to the armchair trolls who doubted him, plus he'd have the kudos of being among only a handful of celebrities willing to camp out in the Alaskan wilds.

With the carcass disembowelled, he switched the video off and turned the mobile's camera on. The stony beach was surrounded by a semi-circle of tall spruce that made a spectacular, dark green backdrop to the black-tailed deer hung by its legs over the makeshift slaughtering station. The deer's earlier reddish-brown summer coat would have looked more striking in the photo than its grey-brown winter coat, but coming here out of season would, he hoped, give his adventure an edge over the other survivalist celebrities. With the harsh Alaskan winter on the precipice of arrival, he'd be able to claim 'extreme explorer' status and shut-down the mocking haters for good. That was the plan, anyway.

He posed with one hand on the deer's leg, pressed the button, then checked the photo; it was out of focus. He tried again, this time with a comical, as opposed to manly, pose. *Nice!* He zoomed in on his face to make sure he had nothing between his teeth, took another photo in extreme close-up with the deer clearly seen in the near distance, then uploaded them both to his blog, 'Diary of a Wilderness Junkie'. He had wanted to add 'Celebrity' to the title, but Sally, his agent, had advised against it. Now to upload the video.

In the distance a siren wailed. For a moment he listened, trying to place the noise. As far as he was aware, the only inhabitants on the island were the staff who worked at the lodge and its guests, and this late in the year there was only a skeleton staff and six other guests. The siren stopped as abruptly as it started, and Christopher's focus was back to his mobile and uploading the video to YouTube.

Feed the beast. With a sudden wash of weariness his thumb hovered over the upload icon. Finding content to upload, making it interesting and attention grabbing, was becoming a chore, but Sally had warned him that if he didn't keep himself in the public eye he'd just be forgotten and, right now, after his last, very public meltdown, no one was interested in booking him. He'd show them though; diversifying into the explorer-cum-adventurer genre would get him back on track. He made a mental note to text Sally later, and tell her to call Roger, and get him making the calls. This time next year he wanted to be back in the celebrity limelight dancing on ice, or doing the waltz on Strictly, or better still, going into the Jungle; Ant was a great bloke, and perhaps it was finally time to call in that favour from Dec. That was a last resort though; he wanted to save the big guns for when his career was finally in the shitter, and he was sure it wasn't there yet—at least, not quite.

The wolf howled again, closer this time. "What the hell!" he muttered aloud and scanned the treeline. The bank of dark spruce remained silent. George, the owner at the wilderness lodge, had assured him that there were no wolves on the island, that they'd all been hunted to extinction more than thirty years ago when he'd bought the property and opened the lodge; it didn't do to have wild animals attacking the guests. These days, George had told him with a conspiratorial air, he wouldn't get away with it, there were policies about keeping a natural balance, but that was before the goddamned and interfering government had everyone tied up with laws. He'd leaned in then and said, 'You know what Volkolak means, don't you?' Christopher had shaken his head as George held his gaze. 'Werewolf,' he'd replied with emphasis and a quick glance beyond Christopher's shoulder as though searching the trees. 'But don't you worry, we killed them all off too'. He'd cackled and sauntered back to his workman's shed behind the lodge. Christopher had scanned the treeline and swallowed as his mouth had dried. The man was obviously bullshitting, but the atmosphere that pervaded the dilapidated lodge didn't need help to make it creepy, and, if the howl he'd heard in the night wasn't a wolf, just what the hell was it?

Logging on to his account he was met with a blue screen and the text 'You are in breach of community standards. Your account has been suspended.'

"What the hell!" His voice was explosive, ricocheting among the trees, and a bird catapulted from a cluster of shrubs close to the shore. The wolf, deep in the forest, seemed to answer with its howl. Logging off, eyes flitting from the screen to the trees, he tried again; *it has to be a mistake!* Again, he was greeted by the blue screen and message of exile. His hands trembled as adrenaline coursed through his body and fear dropped like a weight in the pit of his stomach; *if he couldn't upload his videos, then how was he meant to keep his career going?*

He repeated his efforts, each time with an increasingly stabbing finger. Each effort failed. He tried a final time, achieved the same response, and thumped a fist against the stump of a tree, regretting it instantly as pain shot through his hand.

As he sucked on a scraped knuckle, a flash of coloured movement caught his eye, and he focused on the treeline, narrowing his eyes to see beyond thick trunks and into the sunless forest; something had definitely moved.

CHAPTER TWO

Red light spread a dark glow across the room as Max uncurled from the foetal position. Outside he could hear the tack, tack of her shoes. Her voice mingled with a man's. A door opened then closed. A Tap, tap, tap filtered through the walls. His memory brought up an image of fingers on a keyboard, and a bright screen with dark marks he could no longer read.

He rolled to sit, the perpetual buzz of the tight collar ringing his neck an irritant. A growl burst from his belly, and he scraped fingernails along the wall. They dug deep into the plaster to the steel beneath. The area was shredded, the box littered with strips and chunks of broken board. The cycle was always the same; he shredded, scratching down to the next layer, barging shoulders against walls until they buckled. The collar buzzed. He would grow quiet, and his world would become black. He would wake to the stench of offal, or sometimes, living, pulsing, screaming flesh, and the wall would be complete again.

This time, wire mesh lay beneath the chalky board. His fingernails sliced through that too. The collar vibrated, sending a piercing wheedle to his ears, and a door clanked. This time he decided to play a different game.

Walking to the light-filled doorway, the stench of offal leaked from the open space. Particles of blood clung inside his nostrils, and his mouth watered. He crouched to eat and behind him the door closed.

Sometimes, as he ate, a panel opened, and the woman watched.

He reached for the meat, retracted his hand, then moved to sit against the wall, dropping his head between his knees and waited. *Katarina ... Katarina ... Katarina ...* The name rose to his memory. He whispered the word; it grated unformed over misshapen vocal chords. The panel slid open, and Katarina peered inside. He raised his head to meet her eyes and held out his hand as though begging. Talons, curved and grimy with the dark brown of old blood unfurled from his palm. "Katarina!" Scratched and warped, the word sat between them, and with a gasp, she closed the panel.

CHAPTER THREE

With his banishment from the social media platform forgotten, Chris searched through the trees, then along the shore, taking in the half-beached boat, and camping paraphernalia. The large pile included his blue, four-man pop-up tent, sleeping bag, comfort mattress, boxed supplies, stove, gas cannisters, and kettle, and the newly slaughtered and blood-stained deer hanging from the posts.

The area around the slaughter station was spattered red, and his belly did a watery flip as he realised that the blood, and the bucket of steaming entrails at the deer's side, would very possibly attract whatever meat-eating wildlife hunted in the forest. *Could be a bear? But weren't bears supposed to be hibernating by now? Did you check? No. But they do that now, don't they? Did you check? No! Idiot!* He scanned the area again, his scalp beginning to prickle, and took a breath. *Would Bear Grylls be afraid of something in the trees? No, he bloody wouldn't! Then you won't be either. And what about Ed-just-drop-me-naked-in-the-wild-Stafford? Huh? Would he be shitting his pants? No! So, stop titting about, and man-up Miller!* He took another breath to ease the tension tightening across his chest, reached for the bucket with one eye on the treeline, and decided against disposing of the entrails into the water; if an animal did come sniffing round, it was an opportunity! The punters loved excitement and danger, and there was nothing more dangerous than a bear coming at you. The video could go viral!

Chris took a step closer to his boat, fumbled with the controls on his phone, then took a panoramic video of the treeline. Narrating in hushed tones, his voice was laced with a carefully modulated modicum of anxiety. He swept the camera along the curve of the inlet, but nothing moved other than leaves pushed by the wind. As he filmed the area for a second time, he grew irritated at the lack of action, silently berating himself for being so jumpy. He maintained the act of tension, finishing the video clip with himself on screen, "Whatever is out there isn't making itself known!" He paused for effect, the camera held close to give a partial view of his face, focusing in on the trees as the microphone picked up on his rapid breathing. He zoomed out, his face now in full focus, and talked straight to camera. "It's time for me to set up camp." He flashed a dramatic look at the sky. "Light's fading." He turned back to camera. "And I don't fancy putting up the tent in the dark." He chuckled on screen, clicked 'stop' as he maintained a fixed, wry grin that he hoped was endearing, then thumbed 'save', and pocketed the mobile, confident the clip was a 'take'.

Within ten minutes, his compact pop-up tent was anchored on the beach just beyond what Christopher took to be the tide line. Once he had a fire going, his plan was to roast the butchered deer, and edit the videos during the evening ready to upload as soon as he could. He had already determined to make periodic videos through the night; footage of him being woken in terror, his eyes bright silver orbs in the dark as a wild animal - real or imagined - roamed around his camp, would make great entertainment.

With the sleeping bag unrolled, and a torch placed beside his bed, he crawled out of the tent to another howl, far louder than last time. "You're a lying bastard, George!" he hissed as he spun to check the area and pulled out his mobile, clicking the video to on. As before, the only movement was the lapping of waves on the shore, the odd bird flapping across the sky, and the sway of trees as they bent with the strengthening wind. He shivered, pulling his jacket a little closer, and narrated as he filmed every inch of the curved inlet, the crescent of grass beyond, and the trees that hugged it. "There's something out there," he said to camera, "but it's not making itself visible. It could be the deer's entrails that are attracting it so I'm going to dump those into the water, but my best line of defence is to make a fire." Phone in one hand, he dumped some of the entrails into the sea, zooming in on the spread of blood as it infused through the salty water, then collected driftwood for his fire. Much of the wood was too wet to burn, and he made a paltry heap from a few dried sticks whilst continuing his commentary. "It's not enough to keep the fire burning all night. I need to search for bigger logs."

Stepping beyond the beach and onto the grass, he made his way towards the edge of the woods, and a skewed, obviously dead, tree. Realising that filming was hindering his progress, he retrieved his tripod from the tent and mounted his phone to video the event. He pulled at the dead trunk. It creaked but was surprisingly sturdy. He grabbed a leafless branch, hanging on to it as a deadweight. It broke with a satisfying snap, and he made a loud grunt as he dropped to the ground and staggered backwards. He repeated the effort and broke off two more branches. Laying them in a tidy pile, he readjusted the mobile's lens, then ventured closer to the treeline, and another dead tree.

Something pink flashed between the trees.

Startled at the sudden flash of fuchsia, he stopped. Pink was not a colour he had seen since he landed in Kodiak, and then it was only the leggings of a toddler at the airport. At the lodge, George, his wife Carmel, and the staff who helped run it, all wore varieties of camo, black, green, or brown, and he couldn't imagine the guests, two corpulent men in their late fifties, and two newly arrived couples who talked about nothing other than the deer and bear they were going to track and kill over the coming two weeks, wearing anything but hunter's green. Someone was playing tricks on him, supposing him to be a fool! Christopher took a step back, then ran to retrieve his mobile from the tripod and made his way back to the tent with slow steps, camera held steady; whoever, or whatever, was in that forest, he wanted to make sure he had the evidence on camera.

A bird catapulted from a spruce several feet behind the treeline and flapped into the sky, its wings a silhouette against the sinking sun. Back at the tent, Christopher continued to narrate events as he reached for his hunting knife. Camera facing the trees, watching the screen as it filmed, he swept the mobile in a slow arc. Another flash of pink caught his attention. "There it is!" he hissed. He videoed its progress, filming glimpses of pink, then lost it as it moved along the crescent of trees. "It's bloody fast!" He panned the trees, unable to locate it. "Damn!"

The flash of fuchsia reappeared at the tip of the crescent.

Startled, he jerked to a stab of pain in his chest; there could only be fifty feet between himself and whatever was stalking him. As quickly as it appeared, it was gone, and the video rolled for another forty-six seconds, before Chris, realising that such inaction made for a poor show, and dismissing anything that was clad in fuchsia as being dangerous, switched the video off, and turned to scan the inlet and the sky. Waves slapped at the boat, and, in a sudden gust, wind rushed through the trees bringing a chill breeze across his cheek. In the distance clouds had gathered making the sky opaque. Chris had a vague memory of George mentioning something about a storm forecast which he had immediately ignored; storm warnings at home were constant, yellow this, red that, and they never came to anything—ever.

A vast bank of grey and rolling clouds hung in the distant sky and Christopher took out his mobile once more and began to narrate. Gravel crunched underfoot as he pointed the camera at the angry clouds. "Storm's coming!" Pebbles clacked underfoot as he turned to film himself against the dramatic backdrop of the oncoming storm. The sight that greeted him made his breath catch; the thing squatted at the edge of the beach.

"Get back!" he shouted, still filming.

Overridden with panic, he turned to run to the boat but as his foot caught on the pieces of driftwood he had hauled up the beach, he fell. The thing behind him jumped forward. He screamed, scrabbled to a lurching run, ran to the boat, threw the mobile to safety, then waded into the sea. Ignoring the shock of freezing water he grabbed the boat's side and pulled.

Seconds passed as he launched the boat and hauled himself aboard.

"You're a liar, George!" he shouted to the vast sky. He yanked the engine's pull cord. "A great big dirty liar!" The outboard engine roared into life, and he steered the boat to face the open sea. The thing squatted only feet from the lapping waves, watching as he left.

At a safe distance from the beach, he slowed the boat, reached for his phone, scrolled through the contacts to 'RACHEL B' and typed in the message 'WTF! Our secret. Will call later,' and attached the video.

Swept in from the east, clouds blotted out the sun, and cast a grey pall over the water. As he hit send with a trembling hand, laughing with glee verging on hysteria, the boat was rocked by agitated waves, and thunder rumbled in the near distance.

CHAPTER FOUR

Two days later

Opening her eyes to an unfurnished room, Melanie Jager lay in a state of semi-consciousness unable to process quite where she was. The place was unfamiliar, but that was not unusual; Melanie had lost count of the number of times she had woken in a strange room. At least twice someone had dropped something in her drink. Some tricks just weren't happy with taking what was on offer, what she was willing to give in exchange for eighty bucks, and on those two occasions the tricks had used her to fulfil their twisted rape fantasies. Idiots, if they'd just asked, she would have gone along with it, for another twenty bucks or so, but she guessed that having permission would spoil their fun; she would have given it a go and pretended; her acting classes wouldn't have been for nothing then.

The pain working through her body was a dull ache riding every muscle, but more intense in her stomach; she would need another fix soon. Lifting her head from the mattress something heavy sat around her throat. Through dulled senses, she felt her neck. A thick band of cold plastic ringed it. Senses alerted, she searched the room for a mirror, but each windowless wall was smooth and blank. Fingering the ring, feeling at the back of her neck, she searched for a buckle or a button, but there was none. The ring, like the room's walls, was completely smooth and emitted a low hum.

She checked her memory for evidence. Last night was hazy. Earlier on there had been a trick, a blowjob in his car; easy money and the guy had been polite. The rest of the evening was a blur of car lights and cold drizzle. She checked her body; fully clothed, her jeans still buttoned, her top un-ripped, she remained unviolated, at least for now.

She walked the length of the room; an oblong, twice as long as it was wide. She knocked on the walls. The sound was muffled which meant the partition walling was insulated. Her head throbbed. So, plasterboard, perhaps with insulation board between timber used to construct the wall. *See, Dad. I did listen.* He'd wanted her to become an apprentice, help him in his business, but she'd wanted the excitement of the big city; didn't want to end up like him and mom stuck in their boring lodge with their boring humdrum lives. She knew that was exactly how she'd end up, if she didn't do something about it, and when her mom had started to talk about what a lovely boy Jack Oskolkoff had turned out, and how his fledgling business was really taking off, she'd taken off the following weekend. The rest was history.

She ran a hand down the plasterboard, realising the walls were un-plastered and the joins between each board neatly taped. Whoever was working on the room was doing a good job, at least a neat job. A waft of bleach rose to her nostrils. She scanned the room. It was empty apart from the thin mattress. An air duct, which was also probably the heating unit, sat in one corner, and in the other was a camera. "Mel, what the hell kind of situation have you got yourself into?" With sudden clarity, she realised that the room was exactly the size of a shipping container, the same dimensions as the one her father had converted to a workshop. So, if it was a container, then one end should have double doors. She twisted to see. A black line ran down the centre of the far end of the box—the doors.

The ring around her neck emitted a low and monotonous buzz as she hammered at the doors; they barely moved under her efforts. Taking a step back, she forced her fogged brain to think, and noticed faint spatter marks on the plasterboard. The urge to run became overwhelming. *Stupid! Stupid! Stupid! You're an idiot, Mel. Just like Daddy told you.* Bleached-out spatter marks of arterial spray became obvious on the door and across several feet of the sidewall. The urge to defecate was intense and a dribble of urine leaked down her leg. *Stay in control! Yes, but you've been kidnapped by a lunatic, how the hell can you stay in control?* She scratched at the tape hiding the plasterboard's joins, then pulled at the ring around her neck. The tape was fast, just like the ring. Her mouth dried.

As she continued to scratch at the tape, desperate to pull off the plasterboard and break off a timber baton from the framework beneath, a low rumble rose to grating and something outside thudded against the container. To the sound of grinding hydraulics, the doors of the container began to open. Startled, she stood back. Brighter light shone through into the room, but as the doors opened to their full extent, and were anchored back to the sound of locking, she was only met with another bare room. At the other end were thick metal railings. Behind them the space was dark.

Like the container with the mattress, the new 'room' was constructed of plasterboard but this one had a sloping floor that descended towards the grilled opening at the other end, a corridor, identical to the 'room' she stood in, complete with bleached spatter marks. She stood frozen as her pulse throbbed, and listened.

A heavy, and unpleasant scent, wafted from the room at the end of the corridor.

Shuffling was followed by footsteps.

She swallowed. Something dark moved behind the bars, and then a pair of red eyes stared out from the shadows. The grille slid open, and she screamed.

AS MAX TOOK ANOTHER step towards the girl, Gabe Lewinski, second only in command to First Officer Kendrick Kingsley, was too agitated to sit, and stood with his attention completely absorbed by the drama unfolding on screen. The monitors that cluttered his desk flashed and beeped, returning their information of the players' vital signs. The female's heartrate was tripping at the higher end, the male's steady but rising; odd how fear and excitement had the same rhythm in the body.

An arm brushed his, and he became aware of his colleague. The man reeked of tension. Like Gabe, he was conflicted about the 'experiment' but, also like Gabe, he had parked his morals two years ago, trading them in for filthy lucre, and the path less travelled. Nowhere on this planet was there a job as fascinating, or probably as illegal, as this.

"Status?" Kendrick asked.

"The doors to the female's quarters have been opened. She's showing the typical signs of disorientation."

"Did she make it to the tunnel?"

"No, she hung back."

"The male?"

"Showing signs of movement. His heartrate is climbing, and his position has shifted. The door has been released and is fully open."

The monitors beeped. "Shut that noise off," Kendrick demanded. "I want to concentrate."

Gabe reached for the monitors and muted the incessant beeping.

"The lights are too low, Lewinski. I need a clear view of proceedings to make my observations." The light brightened. "Is this one clean? Doctor Steward said to get a clean one."

"She is un-fucking-believable. What? Are we supposed to give Jane Doe a drugs test before we kidnap her, or after?"

"It might make a difference."

He grew silent then said, "Do you think he'll kill this one too?"

"Too early to tell."

"If it looks like he's going to, can't we close those doors."

Kendrick remained silent for two seconds, then said. "No. There's no turning back. Once we set this in motion, there's no turning back."

The bank of monitors was set up to show various angles within the female's cell, the male's cell, and the corridor. Top of the range surveillance equipment had been installed, the cameras recognising movement and following the figures.

As the light brightened, the male's figure became clear, and he stepped into the corridor. The female's screen came alive with movement.

"Here we go."

Both men were silent as the male stepped forward.

"Get me a close-up of his face, I want to see every reaction, every nuance."

The camera zoomed in. A pair of red eyes stared into the lens as the male stopped and turned his head to stare at the moving camera.

"That always freaks me out."

"Just watch, Lewinski."

The woman was at the furthest recess in her 'room'. As the male progressed up the corridor, she grabbed the thin mattress and held it as a protective barrier.

"He's going slow. Perhaps this time will be different, but we should have taken out that mattress; Marta will be pissed."

Kendrick remained silent, completely absorbed by the proceedings, watching as the male's enormous talons sliced down.

"Shut it off! I can't watch this."

"We have to watch."

"Jesus!" Gabe said turning away from the screen.

"Too hot in the kitchen, Lewinski?"

"Something like that."

"Okay. He's done. Close the doors once he's back in his cell and get the cleaning crew in there."

"He hasn't ... eaten her?"

"No, just killed her."

"What a waste! What the hell is wrong with him? Marta will be pissed if we don't get some results soon."

"Talk to Katarina. She's the behavioural expert. It's up to her to figure this out. We just facilitate events."

CHAPTER FIVE

Birmingham, England

The mobile phone vibrated for a third time before Rachel Bonds reached across her bedside table and scrolled through the list of new messages; the first, an older message still unopened, was from old school mate and now D-list celebrity Chris 'Windy' Miller and was probably another whinge-fest about his failing career, the second was from her best friend Bianca, and the final one was from her mother. She clicked on 'MUM' and read the message: 'Happy Birthday, Darling! See you for lunch at Bellini's. Don't be late. Xxx'. Irritation at how she had allowed her mother to control her birthday yet again was followed by a wave of nausea, and Rachel remembered last night's bottle of red consumed in front of the television as she watched the late-night film. The tears had started after the second glass, and the bottle was followed by several extra-large gin and tonics. She had a vague recollection of a blurry Benicio del Toro strapped to a chair, or was it Anthony Hopkins? Maybe both?

Sunday night's alcoholic binge had followed on from Saturday's and the ache at the nape of her neck and temples intensified as she wondered how she would make herself look presentable enough to sit with her immaculate mother at the pretentious Bellini's. Rachel replied through dulled senses to her mother's text message, read Bianca's birthday message and promise of drinks later, and determined to read Chris Miller's message after taking a shower. Sagging back into her pillow, she glanced at the bedside clock; 8:46. She should be walking into the office right now, but since her last published exposé had gone so spectacularly wrong, she'd been told to take a leave of absence until the dust had settled, or more likely, until they'd had a chance to talk to HR and found a legal way of getting rid of her. The sombre face of the Human Resources director as he'd delivered the news, rose in her memory, and her vision blurred with tears.

The phone rang, breaking into her wallow of self-pity; Dexter Mason, her editor-in-chief. She sat up, coughed to clear her throat and, heart thumping, head pounding, answered the call.

"Morning Bonds."

"Good morning, Mr Mason." Her reply held a lilt that she hoped oozed confidence and said, 'I'm ready for the next assignment'.

"Bonds ..."

Griping pains ached through her belly at the hesitation in his voice; she knew what was coming. She forced brightness into her voice. "Yes?"

"I have an assignment for you."

He's not calling to terminate her contract! A silent fist pump was regretted instantly as the dull and throbbing ache intensified in her head. "Brilliant! ... I mean, thank you."

"You may not thank me once you've heard what it is."

"Oh?"

"But I've done my best for you ... given the circumstances."

"Oh." *Be more appreciative, Bonds!* "I'm up for anything, sir. Hit me with it."

"OK!" His laugh was forced. "We need a reporter to cover the opening of the new Lidl supermarket on Croxton Street."

"What!" The indignation burst from her mouth before she had a chance to hold it in check. "But ... but that's junior reporter crap! Sorry, I mean ... that's a piece that would be covered ... it's a piece-"

"Bonds ... as I said, I've done my best. I've talked them into keeping you on the staff, but ... you can look for a position with another paper, if you prefer. I can give you an ... honest ... you've written some great pieces in the past."

All efforts at politeness evaporated. "God damn it, Dexter! I'm an investigative journalist. I've got an MA in creative writing from Birmingham University, for Christ's sake! I've covered some serious shit. Hell, that paedophile ring-"

"Just stop right there!" Dexter countered. "There's no doubt you're a good ... capable reporter, but you've stepped on some big toes this time. We're just a small-town paper-"

"The Birmingham Herald is hardly a small-town newspaper!" she butted in.

Ignoring her outburst, Dexter continued, "... and we don't have the resources to fight this. Listen, we've done our best, but if you want my advice, you'll take this job and lay low until it all blows over. You're still on staff, you'll still get paid, so at least you'll be able to pay your rent and eat."

The heat of mortification rose in her cheeks. "Sorry, sir. I didn't mean to snap, it's just-"

"I know. I get it. Listen, try not to worry, your career's not over—yet."

"How about if I write under another name. I've got a lead on the Ashton Baileigh situation. Remember? I sent you an email last week—he's the MP for Perry Barr."

Silence on the other end.

"Mister Mason ... are you still there?"

"Yes, I'm still here." Dexter's voice was firmer now. "I need someone to cover the supermarket opening; a friend is pulling in a favour and, like I said, I've done everything I can for you."

Rachel recognised the veiled threat and sensed the rising irritation in Dexter's voice. To date, he had been supportive, avuncular even, and wouldn't send her on this job just to punish her. Would he? Humiliation stung as she replied. "Sure."

"Great. I'll get Sue to email the details. I wanted to talk to you first ... before I assigned it to you."

"Sure. Thanks."

"The opening is at ten. I want the article uploaded by eleven-thirty."

"Got it."

The line clicked to dead.

Five hours later Rachel sat across from her mother, the dreary report of the equally dreary supermarket opening uploaded to the newspaper's cloud file. Yesterday's alcohol consumption rode her in waves of nausea, and she took a sip of her drink whilst glancing at the bottles lined up behind the bar. Her mother sniffed and pursed her lips as she caught her glance. Rachel's eyes flitted to a woman at the bar and then to the door as she pretended not to notice her mother's disapproval.

White-blonde curls sat as an immaculately coiffured halo around her mother's head and Rachel regretted leaving her hair to dry naturally and then forgetting to brush it through before leaving the house. She coughed to clear her throat.

"You look tired, darling. Are you getting enough sleep?"

She replied with a surly 'sure' before taking a sip of her diet cola laced with a sneaky vodka shot.

"You should have had some water, darling. So good for the complexion; you look as though you need a good detox."

Rachel huffed. Sitting opposite her mother's judgemental gaze had shunted her back into resentful teenager mode.

"Don't slouch, darling."

Rachel took another slug of the hidden vodka. Her headache lessened and she shuffled to sit straighter in her chair. Her mother reached for the menu. Rachel reached for her phone, scrolled through her Facebook newsfeed for ten seconds, then switched to check her messages.

"I think I'll have the salmon. It's delicious, darling, and not too many calories."

The roll of fat around Rachel's middle, gained in the past month's comfort eating marathon, felt suddenly thicker. "Sounds good," she replied without taking her eyes from the mobile's screen. Her mother remained silent as Rachel scrolled through the messages. The silence continued as her finger hovered over Chris Miller's profile image with its cheesy and celebrity-laser-whitened grin. She might as well read his message now whilst they waited for their meal. She clicked the message. It reads 'WTF! Our secret. Will call later'. A video was attached and, intrigued, she pressed play.

"If you didn't want to come ..." Her mother's voice was laced with emotion. "... then you could have just said!"

Shit! A tear threatened to spill from her mother's immaculately mascaraed lashes. A band tightened around Rachel's ribs, and she sets the mobile down and reached a hand across the table. Covering her mother's hand with her own, the skin had a thinness she hadn't noticed before. The youngest of three, there was a large age gap between herself and her older brothers, and the sacrifices her mother had made; the promising career, the relentless school run that had eaten up so much of her life, the parenting that had anchored her to the house, the horror of being classified as a geriatric mother, the financial burden of another child when she should have been saving for a pension, had frequently been mentioned during Rachel's difficult teenage years. 'I was so close to getting my life back!' she'd overheard her mother confide to Aunty Jane, her mother's older sister, after yet another of Rachel's 'juvenile delinquent moments', as her mother so politely put her angry teenage outbursts, and what her father more crudely, and probably accurately, called 'being an arsehole'. With her mother close to tears because of her rudeness, shame settled on Rachel like a shroud.

"Mum, I'm sorry. This last month ..." She stopped, unable to tell her mother the truth about her broken career, and just how close it was to total destruction.

Chris Miller's voice rose between them in overly dramatic and tinny tones.

Her mother's eyes widened in anticipation as she continued to hold Rachel's gaze.

"I thought I was going to get a promotion," she lied.

Chris Miller shouted 'Fuck!'.

Embarrassment stung her cheeks, and Rachel fumbled for the phone as she continued to apologise, "But I didn't. I'm sorry for taking my bad mood out on you."

The light brightened again in her mother's eyes, and Rachel made an inward sigh of relief as the tension around her chest released.

Chris Miller screamed.

"What on earth *is* that, darling?"

"Just a video a friend sent me."

Her mother's response faded as Chris shouted another string of expletives and Rachel focused on the video's action. The camerawork was amateurish, jerking, and difficult to watch. Chris's face was central again, his narration dramatic, and then the camera scanned the trees behind the curving beach of a rocky inlet. The image blurred to vertical lines of black and green, and Chris's breath came hard as he ran. For seconds the image was of pebbles, then splashing water, then the grey and cloud-filled sky. Off camera, Chris grunted with effort, the image swung, and he continued to narrate with excitement.

"Can't you turn the sound down, darling? The whole restaurant is listening, and Pietro is throwing us dirty looks."

Her mother's request sat at the periphery of Rachel's awareness, unprocessed as she continued to stare down at the screen, absorbed by the footage. If this was staged, then it was brilliantly done. It ended with the start of the outboard motor then the camera focusing on the beach and an oddly deformed figure in fuchsia rags squatting at the edge of the water. "This is huge!" Chris said, talking once again to camera. "They're all in on it. They must be. Bloody liars. Goddamned bloody liars." As the wind caught at straggling blond hair beneath Christopher's camo beanie, an unearthly howl pierced through his tumbling words and the outboard's noisy engine.

"Bravo, Chris," Rachel muttered to herself. Whatever Chris Miller was up to, it was genius. "Fucking well done!"

"Darling!"

CHAPTER SIX

The band around his neck vibrated as he walked towards the open door. On the floor was a bowl and the stench of the bloody meat it contained was intoxicating. His stomach growled with the pain of hunger, his mouth watering. Sinking his teeth into the firm flesh, feeling the clotting blood running down his throat, would be an ecstasy. He squatted beside the bowl, every instinct urging him to sink incisors into the liver, kidneys, and heart that sat at its centre. He moved away, sitting against the wall, and waited for her to open the panel. The scent of blood an agony as he sat.

The panel opened and he met her eyes. This time she spoke. "You need to eat, Max."

The words were indecipherable, but the sympathy in her voice was clear.

"You'll starve if you don't eat," she crooned. "Come on now, Max."

Memories of the Laura, the One and the Only, the She, flooded his mind; She curled in their nest of ferns, sheltered from the wind by the branches he had gathered, her cheek nuzzling the first child that had slipped from between her legs, the second at her swollen breast, its mouth sucking at her nipple. Rage festered but he pushed it down, and instead held out a hand to the woman.

This time she held his gaze. "I'm sorry, Max. I don't know what you want."

He took a slow step forward, still holding her gaze. She didn't slam the panel shut like last time. He forced his tongue to form words, but only low and moaning babble filled the room. Frustrated, he snapped his jaws. Startled, the woman pulled back.

"Sorry!" He forced his tongue around the words. "Please!" The cage filled with unformed noise. "Please help me."

The woman's eyes glistened. "I can't stand this," she whispered.

"Katarina," Max tried again. "Help me."

"Oh, Max. I am so, so sorry." She wiped a hand across her cheek, the tears wetting her skin.

He chanced another step closer. Her scent rose above the stench of offal in the bowl. He slipped clawed fingers through the mesh. "Please ... help!" he repeated as he picked up particles of her breath and sweat. The scent of her fear rode the air between them, and his mouth watered as he noticed the throbbing pulse at the base of her throat. She placed a tentative finger on his and stroked with a downward movement from his knuckle to the tip of his fingernail.

"Oh, Max. What Marta has done ... it is all wrong."

He made a low mewl. She stroked his fingers. Tears rolled freely down her cheek. "You eat the food, Max, then go back to your room."

Her scent was overpowering and the need to sink his teeth into her veins as they throbbed with blood overwhelming, but he pulled back and returned to the dark room, leaving his food untouched.

CHAPTER SEVEN

Grimchester Zoo Cafeteria, England

With palms lukewarm and damp, Dr. Peter Marston wiped them down his green, zoo-issue, trousers as he sat in the cafeteria waiting for her. It had been almost three years since they were last together, and her call had been an unwelcome, sphincter-contracting surprise. He had only agreed to the meeting out of curiosity, and to get out of the office and away from the smell of gorilla, desert fox, lima, iguana, ground squirrel, porcupine, and – the list went on – warthog faeces. As fourth zoo veterinarian, a post he was vastly over-qualified for, his main duties were sampling the copious and continual stool samples sent in by the keepers anxious to check on the health of the animals in their care, but at least the job was low-pressure and gave him the headspace to continue his own research. Getting his papers published was the only thing keeping him going after the catastrophic failure at Kielder, and his subsequent inability to gain employment commensurate with his experience.

Of late, the amount of iguana faeces had increased disproportionately, and he suspected that their keeper, Marlon Briggs, a narrow-shouldered younger man with sandy hair and magnificent ginger beard, had the hots for him. Coupled with Marlon's stutter when talking to Peter, and the blush rising to his cheeks when he shoved another packet of poo into his waiting hand, Peter had become sure that was the case. Embarrassed by the man's attentions, but too polite to say anything in case he was wrong, Peter had continued to take the samples and be polite. However, the bunch of flowers that had arrived on his desk that morning with a mysterious card marked merely with 'M. x' had made Peter's hands tremble, and not with excitement. He would have to broach the subject and let Marlon down as gently as he could, telling him that his sexual proclivities were entirely on the straight and narrow. Perhaps, and Peter shuddered with fear once more, the meeting with Marta would help to get the message across; her attentions had always been friendly bordering on inappropriate, some would call it sexual harassment, and he'd been relieved when she'd zoned in on Max Anderson as her prey of choice. Sweat beaded at his temple as he remembered Max, and the 'accident' that had ended their careers, and he wiped at the liquid with his green, zoo-issue, shirtsleeve. After the flowers, Peter had determined that if Marta was as 'friendly' as she always had been, then he would reciprocate in the hope that the gossip would get back to Marlon.

His guts ached, and he wiped damp hands down his trousers once more. In the next second, she was there, standing in the doorway, pushing dark sunglasses from her face into her hair, the sweep of bright blonde a halo around her head. She looked every inch the high-powered executive in her dark trouser suit with its pinched-in waist. She stood in stark contrast to the mothers with their lumpy middles, saggy breasts, and baggy t-shirts standing in the line choosing which sandwich, 'jam' or 'ham', little Jace, or Jaycee could have in their picnic box, or the chunky zoo staff in their unflattering polo shirts. They were like nurses, he had thought, expanding in size to fill their uniforms as the months, then years, wore on.

The table knocked against his legs as he stood with a start, and the dirty coffee cup slid with its saucer across the melamine surface. Marta zoned in on him, raised a hand to wave, then strode forward, an Amazonian among pygmies as she called 'Peter!' with a flash of super-white teeth. Nowhere in the scientific community was there a woman quite like her, at least not to Peter's knowledge.

He thrilled at the look of genuine pleasure gleaming in her eyes as they met, and took her proffered hand, bending to the pressure as she pulled him in, and exchanged 'air-kisses' European style. Ease washed over him as his fears dissipated; she was happy to see him, had forgiven him for the mistake. She pulled back and locked her eyes to his. "Peter! ... It has been too long."

"Three years, Doctor Steward."

"Now, Peter, you know you can call me Marta!" Her teeth gleamed. "Let's sit," she continued and paused slightly before reaching for a chair.

"Sorry!" Instantly on the backfoot, Peter pulled the chair out, pushing it beneath her as she sat.

"Such a long drive from the airport. I have been travelling for hours to see you."

"Sorry!"

She coughed as though her throat were dry.

"Sorry! I should have asked. What can I get you to drink?"

She glanced at the board with its chalked products and prices. "Do they have Perrier here?"

Peter scanned the sign searching for the specific brand of bottled water. "No, sorry, but they do have other makes."

"It's fine," she replied with an air of martyrdom. "I shall have tea. You do remember how I like it, don't you?"

He searched his memory, remembering an image of her sitting in the orangery at *Kielder Institute*. On the table was a delicately patterned china teacup complete with saucer, a slice of lemon floating in the brown liquid. "Yes!" he said with triumph. "Black with a slice of lemon."

She nodded her approval, placed her over-large leather bag on the seat beside her, then stroked his hand as he took a step towards the serving counter. He offered a broad grin, warmth spreading; he was still one of them, part of the elite, despite his current difficulties.

Minutes later, black tea sans lemon – 'we don't do that kind of tea, here' – plus a café latte grande for himself carefully balanced on a tray, he manoeuvred back through the tables. Marta positively glowed as he returned; immaculate, relaxed, completely in control. Before her, flattened on the table, was a stapled sheaf of A4 papers.

"I printed it off, Peter, so that I could give it the attention it deserves."

"Oh?" he glanced at the pile as she returned the front page. It was his latest research paper, the one he'd had published in the *Journal of Bioengineering*.

"Your research is outstanding Peter. Congratulations!"

His shoulders broadened. "Thank you! I had no idea you read that journal."

"Ah, Peter, now you know I've always been interested in your work; it's why we were at Kielder together, remember?"

He caught his breath. Here it was—the accusations. He scanned her face; nothing but genuine admiration. His shoulders relaxed and the sudden tightness across his chest eased. "Well-"

"Your article on the application of next generation sequencing in mammalian cell engineering via Cbg8 protein transfection is fascinating."

A broad smile broke across his face. "If I had the resources to continue that research, I'm sure I could have the breakthrough that is needed. Here," he shrugged with a glance around the cafeteria, "my access is extremely limited."

She nodded as though in complete understanding. "And if I told you that you could have access to all the resources you need?"

"Well," he laughed, "then that would be incredible, but obviously-"

"And what if I told you that I have a laboratory waiting for you, with all the equipment, staff, and raw materials that you require?"

"Please, Marta, don't do this to me." A shadow of unhappiness fell over him like a shroud. "This job is all I could get after Kielder."

"Are you serious, Peter? You are wasted here."

"I know, but for some reason, despite the ... *problems* at Kielder not being public knowledge, I was unable to even get an interview with the major institutes and universities, and even when I did get an interview at a minor research centre someone else always took the post."

"Poor Peter!" she said leaning across the table and stroked his fingers. "Well, I'm not here to torture you," she raised her eyebrows with a smile.

"Oh?"

"No. I'm here to offer you a position, one commensurate with your experience and expertise. You're a genius in your field, which is obvious from this paper, and I need your skills on my team."

"Team, Marta?"

"Yes. I'm head of the International Institute for Bio-Tech Advancement. I can't tell you the exact location, but we're in southwest Alaska, somewhere near the Kodiak Archipelago. The work we're doing is ground-breaking, but we've got as far as we can." She held his gaze. "And we need someone to take us to the next level. We have top of the range facilities. You'll have a directorship, be in control of the project, answering only to me." She leant back. "What do you say, Peter?"

His jaw had dropped open and he snapped it shut as she continued to stare into his eyes. "Well ... I." Disquiet rumbled in his belly. Images of Max Anderson, the ... thing in the cage, the red light flickering its warning on her collar, flashed in his memory, and the smell of faeces, hot and muggy, seemed to cling to the membranes of his nostrils.

"The monthly salary is double what you earn here in a year."

"I-" The forest. The chop, chop of the helicopter. The blood-curdling howls. The gunshots. The sulphuric stench of rotting blood and offal. The screams. The squeeze of Blake Dalton's hand on his knee and his warning that 'they' would make it all disappear, along with Peter himself, if he wasn't careful.

"Your research will be published in any journal you desire. A professorship isn't out of the question."

He blinked, focussing again on Marta and her halo of bright hair. His heart tripped a hard beat against his sternum. "Yes ... Yes, I'll take it."

She reached into her bag and pulled out another sheaf of paper along with a pen. "Then sign here, and we'll have you on the next flight out to Kodiak."

CHAPTER EIGHT

The panel opened and Katarina smiled as Max stepped to the opening. He pushed his fingers through the mesh, and she stroked his hand. He placed his forehead against the mesh, and she leant in, their skin touching. The promise of ecstasy was almost too much, but Max pushed it down, focusing on the black box in her other hand. He snipped the dividing mesh with his fingers and peeled back the broken wire. She gasped as he stroked a hand across her cheek. With every ounce of inner strength, he replaced the wire and stepped back. She smiled and closed the panel.

CHAPTER NINE

Thin light broke through the gap in Rachel's bedroom curtains as she woke with a hangover for the third day in a row. She turned her eyes from the light and groaned, then reached for the bedside clock. It read 10:46. *Damn! Late again.* Although she didn't have to be in the office, she had determined to check her emails at the beginning of each working day and be dressed and ready to jump on any story that Morgan, or any of the other editors, threw at her. Sitting opposite her mother, feeling that sense of shame and failure descend like a damp cloth, had motivated her to stop wallowing in self-pity. There was also the lead she had on the underhand, very possibly illegal, definitely corrupt, goings on at a nearby nursing home owned by a clique of local councillors - quelle surprise! - that she wanted to follow up. She'd investigate it privately if Morgan wasn't going to give her the go-ahead, and publish it with another newspaper, under a pseudonym, if she had to.

Motes, eddying in the warming light, danced in irritated whorls as she sat up. Yesterday's difficult lunch with her mother was a haze in her mind, but the lurching pub-crawl with Bianca later in the evening, was a fug of alcohol-fuelled amnesia, and a bloodied graze on her knee, still wrapped in last night's laddered tights, and an ache across her right shoulder, were clues to some disaster of which she had no memory.

She reached for the glass on her bedside table and took large gulps of water. Though she had no recollection of placing it there, it was a trick her father, himself an old-school big drinker, had taught her. 'Rach,' he'd said after one particularly boozy Sunday afternoon, 'always take a pint to bed with you after a session'.

Her mother had raised an eyebrow over her own gin and tonic. 'She's only fourteen, Charlie! And I doubt she'll ever have a 'session', she's far too well-bred and sensible for that, aren't you darling.'

'Yes, mum,' had been Rachel's obedient reply though her cheeks had started to prickle with heat.

'Never too young to learn,' her father had winked at her then, an allusion to the secret pint of cider they'd shared during one of her mother's literary evenings out.

'And just for the record, it's a pint of water you take to bed, darling, not beer'.

'You're always right, my cherub,' her father had replied with a chuckle. The touch of irony in his voice wasn't lost on Rachel. 'A pint of water, Rachel,' he'd winked, pronouncing it as 'wa-tur'. Pulling on his north-midlands roots with exaggeration, was guaranteed to tweak her mother.

Rachel's phone beeped. A message from Bianca. It read, 'How's the hangover? Been sick twice this morning. Slept next to the toilet LOL!!!!' Another followed immediately after. "OMG! Can you believe Chris!!!'

"One exclamation mark does the job, Bianca," Rachel muttered. "Chris?" Her head throbbed. "What about Chris?" As she thumbed the phone's screen to reply, the fug of memory cleared, and she was back in the *Fox and Hound*, the fourth, maybe fifth pub, of the night.

They'd been standing with a group of Rachel's old school friends out on a reunion, and the chatter, jokes, and reminiscences had been flowing freely. Bianca had been surly at first, she'd been several years below them at school and only joined in the second year so had few memories to share. Jamie had brought her round though with the charismatic way he had with women, and she was soon laughing as loudly as the others. Talk had gotten round to a trip they'd all taken to Bakewell in their final year. Most of the kids had never seen a cow in the field, never mind sleeping out overnight in the middle of the Peak District and it had been hilarious to watch them attempt to erect the tents. Talk of Chris 'Windy' Miller had arisen and the source of his nickname—his unfortunate habit of letting-off throughout lessons as a younger child.

"Silent but violent!"

"They were more than that. He could clear a room in ten seconds. I swear he walked around in a fog of green gas at primary."

"He had a talent. That's for sure."

Rachel had laughed along with the others as Jamie had regaled further stories about her friend.

"He did alright for himself though. I saw him in Corrie once—not my cup of tea, but the missus told me he was in it, so I watched it—just the once though."

"He was in that hospital drama too. Holby? Casualty?"

"He's cocked it up though."

"Yeah."

Multiple heads nodded as they recollected the drama that had unfolded around Chris. His face had been on the front page for a couple of days before he had disappeared from their screens and plummeted into obscurity.

"He's out camping somewhere in the wilds," Rachel offered. "He sent me a video. I think he's cooking up some stunt to get back into the news." It occurred to Rachel that the reason Chris had sent the video was not out of friendship, but from self-interest. Who else would be more interested in his dramatic video than an investigative reporter? She sighed inwardly. Someone else trying to make a fool of her.

"Are you talking about Chris Miller, the actor?"

"Yes."

"He's dead."

"What?" All eyes turned to the woman.

"Yes, it was in the news."

"No, he sent me a video on ..." Rachel had taken out her mobile and thumbed through the messages. She paused as she noticed the date. "Three days ago!"

"They say he drowned. He was in Alaska, doing the whole Daring Dan the Explorer thing and his boat got caught in a storm. The US Coastguard have called off the search. Look." Finding the article on Facebook, the woman thrust the mobile in front of them.

Memory of the screen was blurred to Rachel, and a wave of cold that started from her scalp washed through her body. "Chris!" Opening the Facebook app, she searched for 'Alaska Coastguard'. The page for the Kodiak branch of the US Coast Guard popped up and she scrolled through. Several posts down the feed was one announcing the retrieval of Chris' boat and stating that the search for his body would be resumed after the current squall had abated.

Sickness squalled in her own belly. She clicked 'play' on Chris' video with a trembling hand and re-watched the drama. The screen was too small, so she rigged the phone to the monitor in her home office, a table shoved up against the living-room wall, and watched it there. As the drama played out, a creeping horror descended over her; if this was a hoax, then Chris 'Windy' Miller's acting skills had improved stratospherically. Fear leaked from the man, along with an undercurrent of wild excitement bordering on hysteria.

"They're all in on it!" he repeated as the inlet opened to the wider water. "George is a liar! A great big, fat liar!"

The camera turned once more to the beach and the flash of fuchsia. Rachel rewound the video to the first sighting of pink as it flashed between the trees. It showed someone running. The pink disappeared then reappeared. Christopher began to run. Pebbles, water, the side of a boat, the sky. The clouds swayed, the image blackened, then became clear and the figure in fuchsia came into view. Squatting on the beach, just beyond the lapping waves, was a dark figure in a tattered pink blouse. The image turned back to Chris. "Dammit, Chris!" Rachel rewound the video, caught a still of the squatting figure, then zoomed in. She rubbed her eyes. "What in God's name is that?" On screen, imperfectly seen, seemed to be a woman, a very hairy woman, naked but for the tattered shirt. Her face was hideous, reminding Rachel of a horror film she'd seen years ago. Long white triangles appeared in her mouth as she howled. Rachel squinted to focus—they appeared to be ... fangs! More disturbing than the long teeth, and naked, hairy body, were the eyes that gleamed red.

"Holy ... If those are prosthetics, then ..." There was no way Chris Miller was talented enough to a) act as convincingly as he did on the video, and b) pull off a stunt like this. She leant back in her chair, pushing away the thoughts that nagged her. *What if this was real? What if it wasn't a hoax?* Her mind travelled back to a series of disturbing documentaries she'd watched several years ago. One had shown a man seemingly covered in bark, they called him the 'human tree'. The 'bark' had been a viral infection of warts and, after years of horrific surgeries, one doctor had prescribed antivirals and they'd all cleared up. Another one showed a man with testicles that he had to carry around in a wheelbarrow. The similarities with a cartoon strip in the irreverent, and parentally banned 'Viz' had struck her as gut-wrenchingly tragic at the time. And everyone knew about conjoined twins sharing a torso, or head, so why not a woman covered in hair, a horribly deformed face, and overly long teeth; she was almost ordinary in comparison with the freak shows the television presented as entertainment.

She watched the film once more, picking out what evidence she could. Chris had sent her the video as 'their secret'. He'd wanted her to know, but no one else. Why? Because he was onto something. Perhaps something that he wanted her to investigate, and now he was dead, lost at sea, drowned in the freezing Alaskan water, and perhaps that wasn't a coincidence either! Rachel stopped the video with a jab of her finger and hurriedly made a call to Dexter Morgan at the newspaper, her mind in overdrive; *this could be it! This could be the story to get her career back on track.*

Two hours later, Rachel sat across from Dexter Morgan in his office.

"Chris Miller. I think he was killed!"

"Chris Miller, the actor?"

"Yes! He sent me a video." She pressed play and the room filled with melodramatic narration, shouts, screams, and expletives.

Five minutes later the video played on a large screen and Dexter seemed entranced by the footage. He paused at the image of Chris as he left the beach and steered his boat towards the incoming storm.

"Chris Miller is a notorious attention seeker, Bonds. There is nothing to suggest that this video isn't a hoax. It's a non-story. He drowned at sea, and that's tragic, but, and this is harsh, the man was a fool. He put his own life in danger and paid the price. Mother nature is an unforgiving bitch at times."

"But, sir, the thing on the beach-"

"I agree that the woman was … there … but she could be wearing a costume. As I said, I think the video is a hoax and Miller paid the ultimate price for his prank."

Rachel rose from her seat. "You're wrong."

"Pardon!"

"You're wrong. I've watched the film multiple times. Chris Miller just isn't that good of an actor. He discovered something out there and was killed for it … some conspiracy … we need to discover the truth."

"You seriously believe that?"

"Yes!"

"Then you're a bigger fool than I thought."

Their eyes locked and despite his seniority and imposing glare, Rachel held steady. "I'm going to Alaska."

Dexter threw his pen on the desk. It bounced and then rolled to a stop with a ting against the half-empty coffee cup at its centre before rolling onto the floor. Rachel reached for it with a huff as the band of her too-tight trousers pressed against her diaphragm. Leaning back in his chair as Rachel set the pen steady on the desk, he offered a muttered 'thanks', then said, "Bonds, are you drunk?"

"No!"

"I can smell it on you."

"It was my birthday yesterday."

"Drugs?"

"Hell no!"

"Then you're just stupid."

"No. I can see the story here. Granted, Miller was a self-serving, attention seeking D-list-"

"Zed."

"... Zed-list celebrity, but I believe his reactions on that video are genuine."

"It's a non-story Bonds, and not one that this paper is willing to fund. If you want to follow it up, then you'll have to do it on your own time."

Rachel rose to leave. "I will."

Dexter raised an eyebrow, his face a smirk. Rachel was unsure whether he was guarding admiration or just being disparaging. "And Bonds."

"Yes, Mr Morgan."

"Try to sober up before you get there."

CHAPTER TEN

Cars sat gridlocked at least one hundred feet below Marta's London hotel room as she listened with a sinking gut to First Officer Kendrick Kingsley, on the other end of the phone. His account of proceedings back in the laboratory on Volkolak was unnecessarily graphic, and her query as to whether the female had been in good health, was met with disdain, and not a little aggression. She replied in like manner, "Yes, I think you should give Jane-fucking-Doe a drugs test, and check for STDs whilst you're at it!" Assuring him that she was booked on the next plane back, she ended the call and threw the mobile onto the bed where it landed with a soft thud and disappeared within the duvet.

"Kendrick?"

"Yes!" She glanced at Blake Dalton lounging on the leather sofa. He poured himself another drink then sat back, one arm resting across its back.

"Another failure?"

"Yes!" She wanted to hiss and claw at the accusation in Dalton's eyes, but instead flicked at her blonde curls, and replied, "But each time we learn more, and get closer."

"Corbeur is getting antsy-"

"Sod, Corbeur! What does he know about how these trials work?"

"He reads the reports?"

"Yes, he reads the reports, but he's an arms dealer, not a scientist."

"Perhaps, but he's also the one footing the bill for the project, Marta. And, he has shareholders-"

"Shareholders! Is that what you're calling them?"

"It's an easy phrase."

She took a gulp of her wine, and undid the top button of her blouse, suddenly over-heating. "It's so hot in here!" She opened the window a fraction. The blare of the city was instant, and she pulled it closed. "Bloody racket! Where the hell is the air-conditioning in this place?"

Blake's eyes followed her as she strode across the room, and she revelled in the strokes of his gaze on her body, knowing that he was following the contour of her breasts to her slim waist and curvaceous hips. She undid another button on her blouse. The curve of a smile increased on his lips.

"Hot flushes, Marta?"

She bridled. The disappointment, and anger, instant. She knew exactly what he was referring to; more than once he had called her his 'sexy cougar', a nickname that she resented enormously given that he was only five years her junior, and Max had only been seven years younger. *That, Mister Blake-I-think-I'm-so-sexy-Dalton, was not the definition of a cougar! And she was definitely not going through the menopause ... at least ... no, there was no way! She was in the prime of her life, not hurtling towards becoming a brittle-boned old hag with a dried-up husk for a vagina*. "No, Blake, it's not a hot flush!" *Anyway, they could do wonders these days, and perhaps she could have some sort of ovary transplant—did they do that?* She regretted her words instantly as he laughed, eyes glittering with mirth, then took a slug of his whiskey, enjoying her discomfort. She flashed him a scowl. *And anyway, she was not the only one getting old; he had grey at his temples and was thinning out on top, perhaps she needed to remind him of that!* Perspiration glistened unseen beneath her blouse as her body continued to heat, and she yearned to be able to slip under a cool shower. Her mind focused back on Kendrick's report and the problems they were experiencing; p*erhaps IVF was the way forward, but then, how to get a sample?*

"What if we were to crossbreed? Using IVF would make things less ... messy."

"Crossbreed? With what?"

"Well, humans, obviously."

"Marta, that is insane, and totally fucking grotesque."

She was taken aback by his disgust. "Well-."

"No, fucking way. It's unethical."

She snorted. "Ethical, Blake? When did you grow a conscience?"

He rounded on her. "Breeding the weres is one thing, they're an abomination, but they're a new species created accidentally. I'm all up for breeding the ultimate specimens but crossbreeding with humans—just no!"

"Don't call them weres! It just sounds ... ridiculous." Her cheeks tingled, but she feigned indifference to his accusing eyes. "Anyway, it was only a suggestion, no need to bite my head off. I'm just thinking outside the box; we've tried sourcing locally, but the male isn't taking the bait."

"Not taking the bait? You said they were breeding like rabbits at Kielder!"

"The phrase I used was 'shagging like buggery', Blake, and yes, they were … they are, and there is evidence of … litters … but the male at the institute on Volkolak just shreds the females we source."

"Shreds? Females you source?"

"Homeless women, mostly from Anchorage, but sometimes Kodiak, although that is a little close to home. We present them to the male in the hope he'll bite them and begin to form a pack."

His face grew stony, and she expected a disgusted reprimand, but instead he said, "Just like at Kielder."

"Yes, just like at Kielder."

He took a slug of whiskey. "But he's eating them instead?"

"No, he just kills them."

"Odd." He took another sip of whisky, holding the cut-glass to the light. His mutter of "Perhaps I'm not the only one with a conscience," was barely audible. He raised his voice and said, "In our last conversation, we agreed that you would ship over some already infected females. So, why are you 'sourcing' females from the local population?"

"There are a number of reasons. The two females we retrieved were sterile. One was an older female, beyond the menopause, the other, an autopsy showed, had had a hysterectomy."

Blake's eyes widened with disgust.

Marta riled. "You can wipe that look off your face. This is the chalkface, Dalton! You know as well as I do that what we are doing," she lowered her voice to a whisper, "is entirely unethical. It is rather too late to grow a conscience."

His lips pursed. "You're mistaken, Marta. I'm not squeamish about what we're doing; I just don't want to hear about women's ... problems. I'd rather not have to listen to the grim details."

Pathetic! She took another sip of wine, enjoying the trickle of its smooth velvet as it slid down her throat. "As I was saying, one was post-menopausal, the other was without a womb."

"Jesus!" Blake slung back the remnants of his whisky and slumped back in the over-sized leather sofa. "You're a smart woman, Marta." She raised a brow. "How the hell did you let that slip past you?"

"Getting any of the ... specimens out of Kielder is risky-"

"Obviously."

"Well, finding one that is able to carry a chi ..." She stopped to correct herself. "Pups, isn't easy."

"You need a proven dam. Take out all the guesswork."

"That is the conclusion I have come to."

"If they're 'shagging like buggery', Marta, can't you just capture some 'pups' and ship them over to the station?"

"We have done, but to achieve the outcome the project demands, we need to breed in captivity. Dr. Petrov wanted to insert the micro-chips in-vitro."

"Whilst they're still in the womb?"

"Yes. It will cut down on any margin for error. They'll be completely under our control from birth; we can shut them down at the click of a button."

"There's a termination sequence programmed into the chips, so that the horror at Kielder won't be repeated."

"Indeed there is."

He sighed and became lost in memories for a moment, then said, "Ingenious."

"Dr. Petrov and I-"

Without waiting for her to finish, he asked, "What about a breeding pair—to cut down on the errors? Yes, that's what you should do; find a proven dam and her mate."

"There is only one alpha that I'm prepared to work with at the moment. We need him to sire the pups."

"Which alpha are you referring to? Aren't there several packs established at Kielder?"

"There are, but the only alpha I want to establish our packs with is Max."

"Max?" His eyes widened with genuine shock. "Subject Alpha 1 is Max? You've got Max on the island?"

She bridled at his reaction. "Yes, of course I've got Max!"

"But he was ... your colleague, and weren't you shag-"

"He's the perfect specimen. The leader of the alpha pack among the packs. The ultimate alpha male. You've seen the footage."

"Yes, but ... he was a colleague. I thought you may have taken one of the other males to work with."

She ignored his disgust and snorted with derision. "Blake, sometimes you confound me. You know what is at stake here, what money is being poured into this 'experiment', exactly which organisations are waiting on our product. I will only deliver the best, which is why we went to enormous trouble to procure Max. He is a perfect specimen, the leader of the alpha pack, and will be the founding father of the programme."

Blake shook his head. Marta's anger rose; they were in this together and him taking the moral high ground was ridiculous.

She rounded on him. "We're creating the ultimate dog soldier, Blake! A highly trained, expendable, apex predator completely controlled by the operator. We can't take any chances with the choice of specimens to breed; we can only use the best to establish the project."

"Are you kidding! Expendable! These 'dog soldiers' as you call them, will cost upwards of ten million dollars each."

"At this point, perhaps, but once we've perfected the technology and the breeding programme is properly underway, costs will come down."

"Still, expendable, is not-"

"Listen! They're not humans. They are the terrifying new face of biological warfare, a weapon to be utilised against an enemy, which is why we have so many interested parties."

He sagged back in the sofa and took a slug of whiskey. She allowed him the space to think; Blake was a reactionary, and sometimes it took him a while to realise just where his moral compass needed to be broken. A smile spread to his lips and Marta's own tension eased.

"You never cease to amaze me, Doctor Steward."

"Why thank you, Blake." She slid beside him on the sofa, resting her head on his chest, he stroked her hair in return. "The months after Kielder were traumatic, but what we created there-"

"What Max created there," he corrected.

"Seriously, Blake!" She pushed herself to sit, one hand on his chest. "It was you and I that recognised their application. Us who developed Max's unfortunate accident into something of commercial value and pushed it beyond the boundaries of tragedy."

"Sure," he relented and took another slug of whiskey.

His eyes were becoming bleary; she should have watered the alcohol down. She softened, taking a different tac. "What we're doing at the Institute, Blake, is keeping Max, and his work, alive."

"Oh, come off it, Marta," he returned. "Don't twist this around! You are not doing this out of a sense of philanthropic do-goodery for Max! You know as well as I do that the breeding programme will make each of us millions."

"Of course I know that."

"Then don't try and sugar coat it. To put it bluntly, we're weaponizing a mutant in order to feather our own nests."

"You make it sound so ... brutal!"

"It's the truth, Marta. We can at least be honest with each other ... can't we? When it's just you and me, I want us to be honest, just be ourselves."

Unsure if he was being serious, she rested against his chest, enjoying the warmth and the firmness of his flesh.

"Anyway, what about Marston? When will he be joining the team?"

"I saw him last week. He's booked onto a flight in four days."

"Good. Then that gives you four days to locate a proven dam and have it shipped back to the institute with him. Our sponsors are growing irritable at the lack of results, Marta. If we don't come up with the goods soon, they could withdraw funding."

A frown was quickly smoothed from Marta's brow. *There was no way she could let that happen!* "It's only a matter of time, Blake. Now," she said replacing her glass on the table and sliding a hand down Blake's thigh, "it's time for you to show me your goods." She laughed at her own joke as she rose. "Talk dirty to me, Blake. Tell me about the money."

He returned her laugh, took another slug of whiskey as she unclasped her skirt and let it fall to the floor, then began to explain – again – who was funding the 'experiment' and which organisations were interested in the product. She slipped her panties past her hips and unbuttoned her shirt. Blake watched her fingers undo each button. A bulge pushed against the fabric of his trousers.

"Tell me again, Blake, what percentage I'll get." She slipped a hand over the bulge, dipping searching fingers between his thighs. The bulge grew. Heat warmed her fingers. He pushed his hips forward. She pulled at his zipper and unbuckled his belt. He leant forward, nuzzling into her breasts, his face lost between the rounded flesh. She straddled him, grasped his hair, forcing him to meet her eyes. "Tell me again, Blake." She dipped to press her mouth against his, freeing his hardened flesh with her hand. "How much will be in my bank account?"

CHAPTER ELEVEN

Sipping at a short, and very strong, espresso at Birmingham airport's departure lounge, the fog of alcohol induced fatigue Rachel had lived in for the past weeks had cleared. Her digestive system had been 'cleansed' with copious cups of the detoxifying tea her mother had suggested, and her immune system fortified with a multi-vitamin, also at her mother's insistence. After a packet of fat-blocking pills had been silently pushed into her hands, Rachel had determined to cut back on the drinking, eat more healthily, and get her career back on track. If only to shrug off the disappointment that leaked from her mother like a poisonous fog.

Mobile in hand, she checked her boarding pass once more, then glanced at the information board. The gate through which she would board her flight to Kodiak, hadn't yet been opened, and she sat back on the cushioned bench in an effort to relax before pulling out the notebook especially bought for her research into Chris's disappearance. Inside were notes of the details she'd managed to glean from social media and his agent, Sally Pemberton.

Chris' blog, 'Diary of a Wilderness Junkie' had a photograph uploaded just prior to the video he had sent to Rachel, and she had matched the trees in the background, and the curved inlet on the image, to the beach and forest that had appeared on screen. There was also a clue - if it were real -

as to why the creature on the beach had been attracted to his small camp; the slaughtered deer hanging from what looked like newly sawn branches held together tepee style with what could be cable ties. The deer's legs were definitely held by cable ties as the thin black straps were clearly visible in the photograph. If the creature lived wild in the forest, then perhaps the sight, or smell, of the messily disembowelled deer had drawn her attention. Looking at the mess of blood and still dangling remnants of intestine, Rachel was surprised that a bear, or perhaps even a wolf, hadn't appeared on the beach. *Do they still have wolves roaming freely in that part of the world?*

That the creature on the beach was female was obvious from its hair-covered breasts, clearly visible mound of wildly curling pubic hair, and large clitoris sticking like a ripe damson from between its squatting legs. It was this exaggerated genital organ that added weight to the argument that Chris had been set up, and the 'thing' was someone dressed in an extremely well-made costume, albeit someone with a sense of humour. Although, and this added weight to the counterargument, she had been reminded of those apes with the red bottoms and cauliflower-like protruding sex organs and orifices, if an orifice could protrude, which it couldn't, being a hole! She'd grimaced as her train of thought chugged through images of monkeys and apes filmed at zoos and in the wild, naked and without any self-consciousness as they'd fornicated and touched themselves, sniffing fingers dipped into their own, or others, orifices.

"It just can't be real" she whispered to herself and forced her thoughts back to considering the creature. If it wasn't 'real' then it had to be a costume, no one had a clitoris that big, did they? Maybe they did. And the face. She gave a shudder. It had to be a mask, one of those clever, Halloween-style moulded masks that made your head itch and scalp sweat. Either that, or well-made prosthetics. Given that the body was so similar to a woman's, despite the exaggerated musculature, and genitals, the disfigured face had been a slap to the senses. Seriously messed up, with gleaming red eyes, it was as if an ugly dog with a terrible underbite had hit a brick wall, or a pug. *A true hellhound, or a were-pug!* She snorted at her own juvenile humour.

For some reason, she could no longer find Chris' *YouTube* channel despite searching using multiple terms, and so the sum total of her knowledge so far, much of it supplied by Sally, his agent, was that he had travelled to Alaska for a week of adventuring in a remote wilderness lodge. The idea, and here Sally was quick to point out that it was Chris' idea and not hers, was to jump on the current interest in survival, and gain worldwide attention as an explorer-cum-survivalist in the vein of Bear Grylls, Ed Stafford, and Mykel Hawke. Rachel had expressed her surprise; she wasn't aware that Chris had been in the forces as, to her knowledge, the current bevy of survivalist-cum-action-man explorers all drew on impressive military experience, some having been in the SAS or US Army Special Forces. Sally had confirmed that his experience was limited to two weekends at an adventure park in Sherwood Forest and a weekend of binge-watching survival videos on *YouTube*.

"... but he *was* an avid sailor," she'd said, "if what he told me was true, and I always took Chris' stories with a pinch of salt. He told me that he loved the ocean and that as a child the family had spent summers sea fishing in Scotland. I think he was a good swimmer too."

Rachel had a vague recollection of Chris bragging about the line of mackerel he'd caught on a family holiday in Oban, and winkles picked from rockpools at Beadnell on the Northumberland coast. That he was an 'avid sailor' was news to her, but they weren't exactly close, and the information only added to Rachel's intuition that Chris' disappearance was suspicious.

She drew a line down one page. On one side she wrote 'REAL' on the other she wrote 'FAKE' then listed all the reasons she believed that the creature was real, and then all those that suggested it was a fake. Thinking the problem through gave her a headache and, irritated at the lack of clarity she had about the case, she took another sip of espresso, sat forward, checked across the crowd of milling travellers, drummed her fingers on the table, and then knocked into the potted palm at her side as a briefcase swung into her shoulder and the corner caught a glancing blow across her cheek.

"Sorry!"

The espresso remained intact, and with a quick, 'It's okay,' she reached for her notebook, slapping it closed whilst offering the clumsy man a brief smile with eyes that didn't meet his.

The flight to Kodiak was spent continuing her research, scrolling through Facebook for any more posts about Chris' disappearance, but there was nothing other than the initial media reports and then US Coast Guard updates about the search which had now been terminated. His death had been a footnote ignored by the masses. "You'd have been disappointed Chris," she murmured as she continued to scroll through the newsfeed. Noting with relief that none of the footage he'd sent to her had appeared anywhere on the net, she smiled; her story, based upon her own unique and original investigation, with virgin footage, would be explosive. It could be the story they both needed to rocket them into public notice.

She clicked her mobile to off, then poured herself a glass of wine from the mini bottle supplied by the airhostess. After all the extra work she had been putting in, it was well-deserved. The geeky-looking passenger in the next seat was the man who had knocked into her at the airport, and she decided to introduce herself; perhaps the conversation would help wile away the hours.

CHAPTER TWELVE

The long-haul flight to Kodiak, had been just that, a long haul. The young woman that had bumped into him in the airport lounge, Rachel Bonds as she'd introduced herself, had coincidentally been on the same flight, and even more coincidentally, in the seat next to his. Several hours into the flight, a conversation had sparked up between them, one that he quickly regretted; the woman was searching for a friend lost at sea. Peter hadn't quite known how to respond other than with an 'I'm sorry for your loss' and tried to change the conversation to something he felt far more comfortable with, but she seemed disinterested in hearing about the diseases he could detect in scat.

The conversation had been a jumble of awkward gap filling as Peter desperately tried to remember interesting anecdotes about his time at the zoo, but his dislike of flying, combined with his unease about talking to an attractive woman twenty years his junior, and the concern he would wander into past, very much classified, projects, predisposed him to failure, and the conversation died twenty minutes later. The remainder of the flight was spent with the woman drinking a number of inflight bottles of wine, and him feigning sleep. His intention had been to use the flight as a working commute but, after the revelation that Rachel was an investigative journalist, his laptop and notes remained zipped in his case for the entire journey.

After making his way through customs, and collecting his bags, he stepped through the automatic doors and out into the crisp Alaskan sunshine. A sharp wind cut through the polyester mix of his V-neck jumper, and he immediately returned to the relative warmth of the arrivals lounge where he retrieved his coat from his baggage before stepping back outside. He checked his mobile and re-read the text from Marta; a private plane had been arranged to take him to the as yet unnamed island where the International Institute for Bio-Tech Advancement had been set up, and he was to wait for a chauffeur to take him there. During the flight, the fact that he had yet to be informed of the institute's address, other than that it was somewhere off the Kodiak Archipelago, had caused him a modicum of disquiet - *why the need for secrecy Marta?* - but he had pushed away the thoughts, reasoned with himself that even the Lego factory had metal shutters that eased down to protect their Research and Development department from industrial espionage, and focused on thinking through his next research paper. Marta had promised that his research would be published in any journal he desired, and he smiled as he recollected her words that a professorship wasn't out of the question.

As the plane had flown over the tips of the Aleutian Mountain Range, and the investigative journalist beside him had snorted in her sleep, the empty bottles on her open lap tray clinking as they rolled, he had allowed his imagination to carry him to an auditorium full of men and women in evening attire, cameramen focusing on his figure at the central lectern. The Royal Society's *Darwin Medal* held in his hand, he thanked his colleagues for their support during his research, as well as his doting wife, a stalwart behind the scenes, without whom none of it would have been possible. The fact that Peter didn't have a wife, had never been married, didn't mar the enjoyment of the moment - who knew what the future held? - and he basked in the imaginary glow before the pain of readjusting pressure as the plane began its descent hit his inner ear.

As Peter waited beneath the awning, his mobile beeped. The text read, 'Flight cancelled. Room booked at Karluk River Hotel. A taxi will take you to the airfield tomorrow. Dr. Katarina Petrov.'

"Katarina!" he blurted as he read the screen. The disquiet he'd felt earlier mushroomed to full-blown anxiety, but in the next moment he was pushed to the wall as the door behind him opened and a stream of people barged past. His phone dropped to the floor and, as he bent to retrieve it, a hand grasped it. Rachel from the plane. For a second, he scanned her face, checking that she hadn't read the screen whilst simultaneously berating himself for being so paranoid. She handed it back to him without a glance at the screen and offered him a smile. "Are you okay? You look a little ... distressed."

Peter eyed her, quickly hiding his distrust. "No, no!" He replied with a disarming smile, and his best 'I'm a professional and I can cope with this' voice. "Plans have changed. That's all. I was expecting a lift to catch my next flight, but it had been cancelled. I'm to make my way to the Karluk River-"

"Karluk River Hotel? Me too!" The woman beamed from beneath an oversized plum-coloured beanie. Her chin was invisible beneath an orange scarf knitted with the thickest wool Peter had ever seen. Bundled in an oversized ski-jacket, and pulling a huge suitcase, her face was flushed, her eyes a little blood-shot. She seemed to be overheating, although Peter was sure the redness of her cheeks was a product of the four mini bottles of wine and one gin and tonic imbibed during their flight.

He returned a guarded, "Oh."

"We can share a taxi," she replied with a large smile and pointed to the taxi that had pulled up alongside them. In the car she complained of 'sweating like a pig' before unzipping her jacket. The sweet aroma of her overpowering perfume, mingled with the scent of alcohol, rose like a warm fug between them.

BOTH IN HEAVILY PADDED jackets, hats, and scarves, the space inside the taxi was claustrophobic and cloying. Adding to that, Peter seemed nervous, and Rachel was now on edge. Any efforts to engage the man in conversation failed; his responses were stilted, and he appeared distracted. In an effort to distract herself from the awkwardness between them, she shifted her gaze to the town. After several minutes of non-descript shops and buildings, she noticed a poster for a missing woman, and was surprised when another for a second woman quickly followed. Both women look very similar; young, with pale skin, and long, blonde hair.

"Odd," she muttered wiping at the glass as her breath fogged it.

When a third appeared, she sat up in her seat. This woman had dark hair and was certainly not as attractive as the previous two. For there to be a third woman shown as missing in such a relatively small town as Kodiak surely must be unusual. Did Kodiak have a serial killer?

"What's going on here?"

Peter turned to her with a confused frown. "Where?"

"I've just seen a third poster for a third missing woman!"

"Oh," was his lacklustre response and he returned to staring out of his own window.

"Hookers."

"Sorry?"

"Sex workers, Ma'am." The taxi-driver explained. "The girls on the posters were hookers."

"All of them?"

"Yup."

"What do you think happened to them?"

"Well ... we had a fella a few years back, an out-of-towner who was sweet-talking girls into his car then taking them out into the woods ..."

"And?"

"I don't like to say, not to a lady, but when they found them girls, they'd been hurt real bad. They never did catch him."

"So, you think he's back?"

"Yup."

"How do you know he was an 'out-of-towner'?"

"Don't like to think it was a local boy. It's a tight community around here."

"Right. But often the killer is known to their victims," Rachel replied.

The man flashed narrowed eyes at Rachel then returned to focussing on the road. "Like I said, he was an out-of-towner."

"Right."

The remainder of the journey was spent in silence, and Rachel was relieved when, a few minutes later, the taxi pulled up beside the hotel. The driver removed her cases from the boot, along with Peter's, waited for a tip, then disappeared without a word.

"I think I upset him."

After Peter's disinterested response of 'Hmm' Rachel booked into the hotel, making no further effort to engage him in conversation, and closed her bedroom door with relief, and an exhausted sigh.

The room was surprisingly warm and comfortable. A honey-coloured pine wardrobe stood against one wall, and a large sleigh-style bed dominated the room. A sheepskin rug sat at its foot and a pair of heavy, woollen curtains hung at the triple-glazed windows. A large bowl of pot-pourri sat on the dresser beneath a mirror, and the room carried an odour of cinnamon and orange zest without the unpleasant chemical undertones of air-freshener.

Rapidly overheating in the stuffy bedroom, Rachel removed the layers of coat, hat, gloves, and scarf, then filled the small kettle placed on the dressing table. Two cups with saucers, and a wicker basket of packets of tea, coffee and biscuits sat at its side. Thumbing through them Rachel pulled out a packet of hot chocolate and, unable to get the posters of the missing women out of her mind, powered up her laptop whilst the kettle boiled, and ate one of the packets of biscuits as she waited.

A search through the local newspaper's online paper located articles about two of the missing girls. Their disappearances were spaced three weeks apart. There was no mention of any other missing women in either article. A search through the local police's social media accounts presented her with similar information, although on their Facebook feed she located three posts regarding the missing girls. Each confirmed that the women went missing during the early hours of the morning, and that two were prostitutes. Although there was no mention that the third woman was a prostitute there was a reference to a history of drug-taking. Apart from the initial post confirming the disappearance of the three women, there were no further posts, presumably because the investigations were ongoing. She took a sip of chocolate, hissed as the hot liquid burned her lips, then berated herself for getting off track. Christopher Miller's disappearance was what she needed to concentrate on. She returned to the local police's Facebook feed, searching for posts that dated to the period when he would have been at the wilderness lodge on Volkolak island. As with the women, there was one post proclaiming his disappearance, but unlike the women, there was another reporting the finding of his upturned motorboat at sea. There was no mention of Volkolak island.

CHAPTER THIRTEEN

Katarina copied the last of the reading across to Max's file, adding yet another day's worth of vital signs to make two-hundred-and-seventeen. She turned with a glance to the delivery panel where tranquillizer darts were administered if necessary, and decided, despite Kendrick's warnings, to have a final 'conversation' with Max; the observations, she reasoned, would be useful information for the project. With the file open on the 'Daily Observations' folder and its sub-division 'Behavioural Observations', she retrieved the remote control from her desk and clicked the button marked '1'. She squeezed the black plastic box between her fingers as the doors inside the suite of rooms, she can't bring herself to refer to them as 'the cells' anymore, opened. She tapped her keyboard, bringing up the live feed from inside the suite, watching as Max uncurled from his corner, and waited as the second door slid open. Light shone in the room from the strip lights secreted along ceiling and floor edging, and he shielded his eyes. A gleam of red shone at his fingers. Katarina pressed the switch to dim the lights and unlocked the heavy plate, sliding it to reveal the delivery panel. Here she removed the next level of security, a thick door of reinforced glass. Max stood on the other side, his eyes staring straight into her own. She stared back, her heart breaking with pity.

"Oh, Max." She stroked his fingers as they hooked around the wire mesh. He made a pitying whine, and she was reminded of her old dog Buster; made lame by an accident, the pain in his legs after they healed would make him weep in a similar way. She reached into her pocket, pulling out a piece of chocolate, one she had saved from her small ration last night as she'd watched Bridesmaids, the version dubbed with Ukrainian subtitles, for the seventh time. She offered Max the strip of chocolate, following the gesture with, "It is from my penultimate bar. There is no more after this. We have to wait another three months for new supplies." She smiled as he sniffed at her hand. "I have requested a whole box next time." He stared at her hand. "Take it. Is good. Ukrainian chocolate, from town where I live as child." She took another small chunk from her pocket, and bit into it. "See! Is for eating."

Max took the chocolate and placed it into his mouth. Silently, she shouted 'Yes!' If he was copying her, then perhaps, as she suspected, there was more of Max left than just the instinct driven monster that he appeared to be. Perhaps, given the recent changes in behaviour, his brain was healing. Not for the first time, her thoughts turned to a cure. She returned to her desk and entered the notes about Max's behaviour in the file and the thought struck her that perhaps if Max performed as Marta wanted and did sire a ... litter - some children - then perhaps, just maybe, she could be convinced to find a cure for him. Max whined, demanding her attention and she saved the information before returning to the open delivery panel. She didn't notice the missing security mesh.

There was no sign of Max.

She stepped closer, "Max!" she crooned. "Did you like the chocolate?" She listened but heard nothing. Perhaps he had gone back to his room? She took another step to the open panel, peering more closely into the darkened room. "Max, don't you want to talk to me anymore?"

She pulled the remote from her pocket and clicked the button to raise the level of brightness inside the room. Strips of light, set securely within the corners of the room behind reinforced glass, brightened, and the bare panels of the container's reinforced walls came into view. The room appeared empty. "Max!" she called. She waited. He didn't appear. Disappointed, she said, "Okay, I am going now. Is late. I go home. I see you tomorrow morninkkkh!" Steel fingers gripped her oesophagus, pulling her head, and then an arm, through the panel. As red eyes stared into her own, and pain exploded through her arm, she clicked at the buttons on the control, desperately searching for the button that would stop Max in his tracks. Instead the glass door began to slide shut, narrowing the space she had been pulled through. With a mighty punch, Max shattered the rolling glass and, with teeth bared, saliva drooling onto her cheek, he bit down onto her shoulder. Razor-sharp fangs scraped her clavicle. As she writhed in agony, arm dislocating, shoes kicking against the wall, he relaxed his grip, allowing her to slide back. Teeth still sunk into her shoulder, he squeezed his arm through the gap and took the controls from her hand. As she slipped to the floor, the infection already slipping into her bloodstream, a mechanical whirring filled the room and the outer doors to the container opened. Max stepped into the laboratory and, in one massive bound, stepped beside Katarina. In the next second, he hauled her over his shoulder.

CHAPTER FOURTEEN

As Peter hauled his suitcase down the hotel's steps, a second taxi pulled up along the kerb. He let the case bump down each step then wheeled it to the first taxi. He opened the door and bent to speak to the driver.

"Sorry, sir, but this taxi is booked for a lady; Miss Bonds."

With an embarrassed 'oh', and a silent groan, he shut the door; these coincidences were becoming tiresome.

Taking the second car, it pulled away from the kerb just before Rachel's did and as her taxi followed his through the streets, he realised she was making her way to the same destination as himself; the airstrip where he was to catch the flight to the institute.

Katarina's text message had been followed by one several hours later, giving him the time and location of the flight and informing him that a taxi had been arranged. He'd replied with a 'Thank you!' and 'Looking forward to seeing you again.' She'd replied with a juvenile smiley-face emoji that had made him smile. Apart from the gut-wrenching memories that thoughts of Katarina aroused within him, he was genuinely looking forward to seeing her, as well as questioning her about exactly what she was doing on the project. Her expertise was in animal behaviour, not reproduction. Disquiet sat as a queasy squall in his belly, but he dismissed it as worry about the flight, and forced himself to focus on a problem with his current research project he had yet to satisfactorily solve; it was a pointless exercise, once at the Institute the project would pale into insignificance in relation to his new role and the projects outlined by Marta.

As they reached the airfield's gates, Peter twisted to watch Rachel's car follow them through. Behind her was a third car. "Damn!" he muttered aloud before he had a chance to hold his tongue.

"Sorry, sir? Did you say something?"

"No, no, just remembered something I've forgotten."

"Do you need me to turn around? I can take you back to the hotel."

"No, no. It's fine." He checked around the airfield with its solitary hangar. A small plane sat on the runway. "Is this it?"

"It sure is, sir." The car pulled up to a door with peeling paint. 'Mackee Airways. Est. 2006' was painted on a bubbling sign. The weather-worn face of a copper bearded man with piercing blue eyes and a crop of thick red hair appeared at the door's glass panel then swung the door open.

"Looks like you've got a full deck, Mackee," said the taxi driver.

"Aye. I'm popular today!" He scanned the tarmac, stepping out from the office.

The man's broad Scottish brogue, on the edge of Kodiak Island, southwest Alaska, was like a slap in the face to Peter. Peter's gut dropped at his next words.

"They all going to Volkolak then?"

"Aye."

"Volkolak?"

The bearded Scot turned to Peter, "Aye, that's where the plane's going, with you on it, Mister …"

"Peter Marston."

"Aye, that makes sense." He turned to the woman. "And you must be Rachel." He turned to the third man. "And you must be Jean-Luc."

"That is correct," the man replied with a heavy French accent.

"But not Picard."

The man sighed. "Non! My surname is Macron."

"No relation to *the* Macron."

A heavy frown furrowed his brow. "Non!" he spat, then muttered, 'Imbecile' beneath his breath.

The Scot laughed. "Nae worry, lad."

Confused, Peter helped the driver to remove his case from the boot and joined the others as Mackee organised their luggage and then the large box that sat inside the Frenchman's trailer. The metal box bore more than a passing resemblance to a coffin, but at each end round holes had been drilled through the metal, giving further evidence of its construction; a wooden box encased in metal. As the box passed, Peter noted the locking mechanisms along the sides, and read the sticker placed just below the handle. In very small print, it read, 'Titan Blane Technologies'. On top of the box was another, much larger sticker that read, 'This Way Up' and 'Fragile. Handle with Care'.

Peter stared at the box, his heart beating hard. *Titan Blane Technologies* was the company Blake Dalton belonged to, the company that had funded the Kielder fiasco. With sweating palms, he looked from Jean-Luc to the box, and then to Rachel.

Were they all in on it? What the hell was going on? "What's in the box?"

Jean-Luc's eyes narrowed. Peter held his gaze, searching for the reaction that would give away any lies. "Mon frère," Jean-Luc stated baldly.

"No, it's not!" Peter blurted.

"Certainement! It is my brother," Macron rebutted. "Are you calling me a liar? Do you want to look?"

Mackee laughed uneasily. "Human remains is what's written on the paperwork." He glanced at Peter. "You a nervous flier, Mister Marston?"

Taken aback by Jean-Luc's aggression, and now mortified that he could be wrong, Peter muttered a repeated 'sorry' and felt his cheeks flush. But as he gathered his thoughts, and equilibrium, the pain in Peter's chest grew intense; he didn't believe Jean-Luc. Why would a coffin have ventilation holes? Rachel stared hard at him and not wanting to alert her to his distrust said, "Yes! Sorry! Yes, I hate flying."

"Well, you're in safe hands with us. No accidents for at least a month, and I only lost two passengers that time." Mackee's laugh wasn't joined by Rachel's or Jean-Luc's, and he quickly turned his attention to pulling the box to the plane's hold.

As the box passed, a familiar stench clung to his nostrils. Rachel gagged, covering her mouth, and turned away, colour draining from her face.

Stomach queasy, Peter turned from the sight of the box being loaded onto the plane. His mind wouldn't drop the question: if it *was* carrying Jean-Luc's brother, then why the hell had it got breathing holes drilled into its ends? Sweat beaded at his brow, and he walked with knees weakening to climb the plane's access ladder and take his seat in the cabin. Rachel claimed the opposite seat, Jean-Luc removed himself to two seats behind.

Fifteen minutes into the flight, Rachel stared at Peter with a frown and asked,

"Are you going to the wilderness lodge, too?"

No! Peter merely nodded then averted his gaze to the scene beyond the window.

She persisted, leaning forward, and whispered. "What kind of coffin needs airholes? And did you notice the smell?"

"No idea," Peter replied bluntly, unwilling to enter the conversation although he didn't believe Jean-Luc's explanation.

"And did you notice the label?"

He shook his head. "No," he lied. His head thumped.

"Oh." Rachel glanced out of the window, then returned to look at Peter with a wrinkled nose. "I hope he's not going to bury it near the wilderness lodge!"

Peter sighed and turned his attention to the scene beyond the window, hoping that Rachel would get the message that he'd really rather not talk. A rolling bank of grey clouds, almost black in places, filled the horizon.

CHAPTER FIFTEEN

A familiar excitement had grown within Max as he had bitten into Katarina's shoulder, and he had savoured each moment of the woman's pain as her blood had leaked into his mouth. Her heartbeat had dropped from a rapid tap, tap, tap as she had kicked against his grip, to a low, almost unfelt throb as he had carried her from the white space with its stench of chemicals. The room had smelt sharp each time the panel had opened. It was followed by their sweat, and their leaking stench of fear. Beneath that, the particles of the woman's sweat, and her dark places, swirled and eddied and he would breathe it deep inside his nostrils, inviting and sticky, ignoring the stench of blood from the bowl behind him. Now she was hanging over his shoulder, writhing. With massive strides, the woman's weight no hindrance to his speed, he sprinted through the woods, scanning the earth as he ran through the trees, the low buzz around his neck his next victim.

Stopping beside a large rock overgrown with lichen, ferns long and curling around its base, he lay the woman down. She bucked, thrusting her chest upwards, twisting onto her belly, curling, then uncurling. Max stooped to grab a large rock half-buried in the loam. It filled his hand. Dirt sprinkled over the woman's back as he raised his arm then slammed the rock against the thick band of plastic ringing his neck. Pain rocked his head, but he raised the rock again, leaning up against a tree, pushing one side of the ring against its bark, and smashed. Blood trickled down his clawed fingers, running over the long black hairs as the band fell to the ground. Lights flashed. He scooped the shattered plastic from the ground, grasping it with a handful of pine needles and dirt, and tore at the wires dangling from the shattered case. The light died.

Picking the woman up, he carried her deeper into the forest, running beside a trickling stream, then jumping across its narrowest point higher up the hillside. The sweetness of life, its pulsating, throbbing lifeblood, carried on the air as skittish deer hid behind ferns. There were bigger animals too, their stench rich and strong. He ran until he reached a rocky outcrop, the woman limp in his arms, and turned to scan the horizon. Far below, the squat buildings of the prison were nearly invisible in the fading light. An orange light flashed. A vehicle moved. An alarm sounded. Another vehicle followed as the first disappeared into the trees. He clasped the woman to him, dipped his nose to her neck, inhaled, then fought the urge to sink his fangs deep into her flesh and tear.

At the highest point of the hill, he found what he needed, and lay the woman on the cave floor. Treading back into the woods, he collected an armful of long and curling fronds. Returning to the cave, he lay the fronds on the cave floor and crouched on muscular haunches to watch the change. The woman bucked, twisted, crawled, then, on all fours, emitted a low growl from deep within her belly. Throwing her head back, her skull almost touched her spine. Dark hair flowed down an arched back, her face grotesque with pain and the new bones deforming beneath her skin. Growing bones pushed against her tailored shirt, each vertebrae a poking hillock. Infected cells warped, strengthened, and bloated, and the muscles across her shoulders split seams and tore fabric. Shoes lost as he had carried her, horned toenails gouged through black socks. A down of dark hair spread across her cheeks and forehead, darkening along her nose as it elongated and widened. He moved to the cave entrance, mesmerized as her teeth elongated, and her jaws opened in a scream of agony. Their eyes locked, the blue of hers now an opaque and bloody red. She slumped to the forest floor, unconscious. Max took her by the arms, dragged her back inside the cave, and lay her on the bed of ferns, before stepping back out and returning to the forest.

CHAPTER SIXTEEN

The sea was a blanket of lapping grey-green waves covering every inch of surface to the horizon. Above the dark line of the horizon was a band of clear blue, but above that the sky was heavy with dark clouds. Rachel checked her watch; Mackee, who also turned out to be the pilot, had told them that the flight would take no more than forty-five minutes. With another thirty to go, they seemed to be heading straight for a storm. She tightened her belt just as turbulence rocked the plane and, in a moment of absolute clarity, realised the utter insignificance of her being. She was a tiny speck riding in a vast sky, itself a tiny dot in an incomprehensibly enormous universe. Buffeted by the wind, she was a fragile body of flesh and bone at the mercy of invisible currents ...; *why hadn't she asked about parachutes? Did they even have them on this type of plane? No, stupid! They have life jackets. Calm it, Bonds.* Pushing down the panic, attempting to maintain the calm reserve she had made such an effort to cultivate since deciding on this new venture, she checked for a life jacket beneath her seat. Relieved when she touched the folded jacket, she relaxed, then took a quick look at Peter; he was wearing the over-padded jacket purchased this morning from one of the shops in Kodiak. The tag still hung from his collar. "Peter!"

He ignored her.

"Peter!" she said, louder this time to combat the noise from the engine. His response was a startled and annoyed frown, as though he had been pulled from deep thought, and she offered him a smile to ward off his irritation, then tapped her shoulder. He shook his head with a questioning frown. She pointed to his shoulder then reached across to pull at the tag. Embarrassment spread across his face as he gave it a tug and pocketed the card.

"Thanks," he mumbled, then returned to staring out of the window.

Rachel took the opportunity to watch him; there was something about him, something off. He was on edge right at the start, at the airport lounge back home, but since she'd told him about her mission to Alaska, and her job, he'd been positively allergic to her. And now, this slender man who looked like a typical undernourished, bespectacled nerd who'd spent his youth playing *Dungeons and Dragons* rather than out on his bike or playing football, was on his way to a wilderness lodge. He just didn't look the type to go kayaking, or bear hunting, which were the main attractions of the place according to its website. She flinched as she noticed his stare reflecting back at her from the plane's window, and quickly looked the other way. But, she mused as she sat back in her seat, still feeling his glare at the back of her head, he did look like the type to watch the wildlife, go out bird-spotting, or collect fungi or lichen, that kind of thing, and he had mentioned that he worked in a zoo sampling poo, which was basically just poking through bags of shit. She relaxed; that must be it, he was a wildlife tourist; he'd go for walks and take photographs of birds, perhaps animal droppings, certainly with the amount of luggage he had, there could be a camera and tripod stashed in there.

She pulled out a pack of peanuts, and a mini-can of gin and tonic, and sat back to try and ignore the gathering storm clouds in the east and stop her mind churning.

The plane lurched, bumping her against the seat, and the mouthful of gin and tonic she was about to take from the tin spilled down her chin, soaking into her polo-neck sweater. She grimaced, held the can tighter, and tried again, enjoying the soothing fizz of the tonic's bubbles and the smell of juniper.

Ten minutes passed without a word between the passengers and her thoughts had passed from Peter Marston to Jean-Luc. Since Mackee's painfully bad efforts at humour, she couldn't think of him without adding 'Picard' to his name and it was unfortunate that he bore more than a passing resemblance to that particular captain of the Enterprise. She searched her memory for the actor's name, but came up blank, and turned her attention to the man. He was tall, and muscular, and the khaki combat style trousers, and dark green hunting vest worn beneath his thick outer coat, left Rachel in no doubt that he was ex-military, presumably on a hunting trip with the required permits. Along with the metal coffin, which inexplicably bore the label 'Property of Titan Blane Industries', he had a case which she was sure held a rifle, and a large canvas holdall. She took another sip of her second gin and tonic, then drained the can. A warm buzz spread from the back of her head, and she enjoyed the sensation before a thought occurred; the box looked industrial, and *Titan Blane Industries* didn't sound like a company that would produce coffins. She checked her watch; only another five minutes to go before they reached Volkolak Island.

Taking out her phone, Rachel typed *Titan Blane Industries* into the search bar, surprised at how strong the signal was considering how far from civilisation they were; at home she had to stand on the landing to get more than two bars. The response was almost immediate and directed her to the company's website, but as she clicked on the link, the plane jolted. Her hand knocked against the seat, and she lost her grip on the phone. It skittered beneath the seat.

"Damn!"

Unfastening her belt, she noticed a distinct thumping coming from beneath her feet. She straightened, looked around, checking to see if the others had heard it too; Marston sat slumped in his seat, his eyes closed, seemingly oblivious to the turbulence and the noise, and Jean-Luc remained stony-faced. Their eyes met, his bald pate gleaming in the light shining through the window but gave no indication that he had heard the thumping. Rachel straightened in her seat.

Thump! Thump! Thump!

He must have heard it this time! She swung to Jean-Luc. Alert now, he made a concerted effort to avoid eye contact, and instead focused on something unseen in his hand. View blocked, Rachel rose above the headrest, and attempted a surreptitious glance at his lap. He held a black box with a screen very similar to a handheld games console. As he noticed her efforts, he shielded the screen, and she dropped back into her seat.

Thump! Thump! Thump!

This time, his brow wrinkled at the noise.

"You heard that didn't you!" He ignored her and continued to focus on the box. She stepped into the aisle as the thumping continued. "What is it? That noise." Turbulence rocked the plane, swinging her into the side of the seat. "Jean-Luc!" He continued to ignore her. "What was that?" The plane bumped again, then tilted, throwing her back as she grabbed the headrest.

Marston opened his eyes, woken from sleep but now alert as the plane was bounced again by turbulence. "Hear what?"

"It is just the turbulences," Jean-Luc placated. "Sit down, or you will be hurt."

"No, the thumping. There was a thumping noise, under the floor."

Rachel noticed the widening of Marston's eyes, and the flicker of fear that passed across his face. Noticing her watching him, his eyes flitted from Jean-Luc, and then to the plane's wings. "The engines look alright. I can't see any smoke."

"There is a storm coming. It is just turbulences," Jean-Luc repeated.

Thump! Thump! Thump!

This time Marston trained his eyes on Jean-Luc, and Rachel noted the intensity with which he watched the man's reaction. "That doesn't sound like turbulence, Mister Macron."

"Peter is right. The thumping doesn't sound like it is coming from outside. It sounds like it is directly beneath us." She paused for a moment. "What is beneath us?"

The thumping continued and was followed by a thud as the plane tipped to the right.

"It's in the hold!" Rachel exclaimed. "I bet it's that coffin sliding across the floor and hitting the sides. It must have come loose."

The men stared at each other. Jean-Luc broke the silence. "Yes, perhaps it has come loose, but there is nothing to worry about. We will land very soon."

The plane hit another wave of turbulence, and Rachel was thrown back. Grasping a seat, she steadied herself and sat back down as the pilot's thick Scottish brogue filled the cabin as he explained that they were experiencing turbulence and requested that they remain seated until they landed. As he asked them to fasten their seatbelts, a flash of lightning was quickly followed by an enormous rumble of thunder and the plane's windows were suddenly drenched with rain, rendering the scene outside opaque. Cabin lights flickered and the plane's engines stuttered. Another flash of lightning was followed by a boom and the plane rocked, suddenly banking to the right. Startled, Rachel screamed, and Peter shouted.

Jean-Luc rubbed at the window as the plane made a sudden drop and steep bank to the right. Rachel screamed again as she was thrust sideways, her body straining at the belt. An odd silence filled the cabin, and Jean-Luc shouted, "Le moteur! The engine it is gone!"

The plane continued to drop, twisting in a steep decline. Above the shouts came the stuttering whine of the remaining engine. It spluttered. Whirred. Seemed to correct itself. Then stopped. The noise in the cabin reduced to silence and then erupted again as the plane took a nosedive and filled with louder screams. The seatbelt squashed Rachel's innards, bruising her hip bones, but she was oblivious to the pain. With all thought gone, she screamed until the plane hit water.

JEAN-LUC MACRON'S EARDRUMS vibrated with the woman's screams until the impact of hitting the water fractured his cervical vertebrae and severed his spinal cord. Paralysis was instant, and death quickly followed as his lungs filled with the salty Alaskan sea.

THE THOUSAND DOLLARS Gerald Mackee had begrudgingly spent on bringing his plane up to current safety standards twenty years ago, had just saved his life. As soon as they hit turbulence, he had slipped the annoying shoulder harness on and clipped it to locked; he always kept his lap belt secured, whatever. The plane had hit the water, and he'd been shunted forward, but the harness had kept him secure, bruised, and with a broken clavicle, and from the pain in his hips, perhaps a fractured pelvis, but alive. The waves, and the life vest he'd grabbed after impact, had done the rest, and he'd bobbed to the shore in agony before the sea had a chance to either drown him, or freeze him to death.

He lay absolutely still, icy waves lapping at his feet, the greyed-out, storm-filled sky above him. The pain across his shoulders and pelvis was immense, but the cold stroking every inch of his flesh seemed worse. He tried to move and failed. He shivered, knowing that if he didn't get up soon, hypothermia would succeed where the sea had not. He made a tentative effort to look to his side. There was no pain, and he turned his head to scan the area; an inlet of large pebbles and larger rocks, backed by grasses leading to the typical trees of the Alaskan shoreline.

Digging elbows into pebbles to haul himself out of the water Gerald screamed as pain shot through his right shoulder and pelvis. Minutes passed, his core temperature dropped, and he shivered, tiredness becoming overwhelming. Realising he had reached a hypothermic state, he renewed his efforts and edged up the beach. As his feet left the water he sagged back to rest; *if only he could close his eyes, and sleep.* With eyelids closed, the cold seemed to ebb, and he slipped into a dream. The noise of stones clacking, knocked together by feet walking close by, woke him. *Thank God! He was saved!* Opening his eyes, he knew, as he stared back into a pair of blood-red eyes, that he had already died and gone to hell.

The creature descended, jaws wide, and teeth, bone-white and needle sharp, sank into his shoulder.

CHAPTER SEVENTEEN

Cold suffused every cell in Rachel's body as she moved from a blank darkness to consciousness. Brightness flickered and she squeezed eyelids tight to block out the light. The cold bit, but beyond that there was pain, and a heavy weight somewhere on her body. Water lapped at her face, running up her nose, and she spluttered, raised her head, and spat. Snorting water, she swallowed, boked at the saltiness, and coughed. Opening her eyes to the light, she quickly closed them, then peered through her lashes at the sky. From around her came the sound of lapping water, and waves rushing over shingle.

Through a fog of memory, she realised she was alive, and pushed against stones to sit. The pain in her leg was immense and, as she sat, blood mingled with the water. She shivered and shuffled back from the sea until it no longer lapped at her feet. Breathless with the effort, and the pain searing her leg, she scanned the area. A curved and stony beach sat in a crescent. Behind her a thick bank of pine trees rose up on a hillside whilst before her was the vast, life-ending sea.

Movement among the waves caught her eye, and Jean-Luc's metal box bobbed on the surface. She watched, mesmerised by its sway as it disappeared then reappeared on the waves, edging closer to the shore with each movement. A memory of Chris and his video stirred. The footage was amateurish and clumsy, and she'd mocked it as a style he was trying to perfect to fit the 'found footage' genre until she'd realised that perhaps he was, in fact, scared shitless. The video showed a curved inlet backed by a bank of trees. She scanned the beach once more, following the same line as his video had done. The curve of the beach was the same, the bank of trees was the same, and, as she made a one-hundred-and-eighty-degree turn, blue tarpaulin billowed with the wind. Chris's tent!

She attempted to pull herself up, but the pain was too much, and she sat back down with a thud. Torn jeans blossomed with blood. Gathering her nerve, she stared at the wet stones on the beach then inspected her injured leg. Peeling back the edges of her torn jeans revealed a deep and jagged wound at the centre of her thigh and protruding from the cut was the tip of a grey shard. She sucked air between her teeth; she had seen this kind of scene before, most recently in 'World War Z' where Brad Pitt had a massive shard of metal straight through his side, metal that had also been plane debris. She knew what to do. Taking hold of the shard, she gritted her teeth, expecting the pain to be overwhelming, and pulled. A slice of metal no longer than the tip of her index finger, slid out. Horrified that the shard had penetrated her body, but surprised at how small it was, and how easily it came out, she threw it down. It landed beside the water, and waves washed away the blood.

Bobbing on the water, the box was now only five feet from the shore.

She pushed up again, this time managing to stand, and took tentative steps towards Chris's tent. The sides flapped and billowed. To the left, only a short distance from the tent was a bucket and the remnants of what had been the deer she'd seen on the film. Whatever flesh had covered its bones was now almost entirely stripped from its carcass, and it lay strung up like a gruesome, occultist's warning. Behind her the box crashed against the beach, the metal clanking on the stones as it rolled with the waves. She scanned the horizon for evidence of any other debris, but the sea was clear.

Scattered about the entrance to the tent were a number of items including Chris' backpack. She pulled the flap back. Inside, although ruffled and obviously disturbed by some small mammals, Chris' sleeping bag was laid out on a thin roll-up mattress. In one corner was a box of cooking utensils, complete with firelighters, lighter fuel, and matches. In another box was a stack of plastic food boxes, each one filled to the brim with cereals and protein bars. There were two boxes of long-life milk, tea bags, a kettle, a mug, and plates. The remains of a bread loaf was evidenced by the crumbs left scattered over his sleeping bag and the shredded paper bag it had been wrapped in. Whatever Chris had been doing here, roughing it wasn't quite what he was prepared to experience.

Sinking down to her knees at the entrance, not wanting to wet the sleeping bag and fleecy blanket she could see poking out from inside, she pulled the large holdall pushed up against the side of the tent's inner layer. Inside were clothes: thick socks, pants, a thermal vest, long johns, spare jeans, and walking boots. There was also a micro-fibre towel, deodorant, teeth-whitening toothpaste, a toothbrush, as well as mouthwash, a mirror, hairbrush, concealer, beard shampoo, condoms, and half a tube of haemorrhoid cream complete with applicator. Her nose wrinkled with disgust, but she took the towel, wrapping it around her dripping hair, then stripped off her wet clothes, throwing them onto the stony beach outside before turning the lamp on, and zipping the tent shut. She shivered as she replaced her own clothes with Chris' thermal vest and socks - she couldn't bring herself to wear his pants – then turned her attention to the still bleeding leg. Finding a small first aid kit in his rucksack, she placed a sterile dressing over the wound then wrapped it with a bandage. Blood quickly seeped through. Taking another bandage, she unrolled it and tied it as a tourniquet, another technique she had seen on film, and hoped that it would slow the flow of blood. It may need stitches but sewing it up would be a step too far, even if she could find a needle and thread.

With the wound dressed, and the blood slowing, she pulled on his jeans. Chris was a slender build, Rachel more curvaceous, and the pastries, crisps, and alcohol overindulged in the months since her career took a nosedive, had found a new home around her belly and hips, but the zipper did up, and the muffin top that spilled over the waistband was camouflaged by the baggy hoodie that she pulled on over a layer of t-shirts and thermal vests.

Dressed, she sat with head reeling, still only barely able to comprehend the last hours. She checked her watch, but the face was cracked, and water sat beneath the glass, the hands unmoving. Removing it, she dropped it at the side of the mattress. Despite the layers of clothing and thermal underwear, she shivered, so pulled the micro-fleece blanket around her shoulders. *Wine. What she needed was a large glass of wine, it always took the edge off, but alcohol seemed to be the one luxury that Chris had denied himself.* She reached for the box of supplies and brought out a chocolate bar. It showed a bear on its back legs to a backdrop of pine trees. A cluster of nuts sat at its feet. She bit into the chocolate, savouring the taste, clutching the blanket around her, unsure of what she should do. She mentally scanned through the survival shows she had seen. Images of Bear Grylls scaling a steep rockface and Ed Stafford, naked except for a skirt of leaves he had made as he caught fish in the pond he had created in a stream, came to mind. She sighed, pulling the blanket tighter, and wondered if Peter, Jean-Luc, or the pilot, Mackee, had survived. She took another bite of chocolate, chewing on the nuts and caramel at its centre, and pulled the fleecy blanket tighter. Should she stay put and wait to be rescued, or try to make it on foot? But on foot to where? Chris had arrived, and left, by boat. Sure, but the lodge was on the island on the other side of the forest, her research had shown that. Plus, it wasn't a huge island, just twenty-nine miles by thirty-seven. It was time to put her rudimentary orienteering skills, those learnt at one of her three Girl Guide sessions, to good use. She scrabbled through Chris's belongings but sat back with a disgruntled sigh. "You have Corn Flakes, and Frosties, chocolate bars, and Peanut Butter Cups, but you don't have a map, or a compass, or a pencil and paper! Bloody hell, Chris Miller, you were a twat!"

"Hello!" The voice from outside the tent made her heart skip a beat.

CHAPTER EIGHTEEN

After recovering from the embarrassment of being overheard, thankful that it was not Chris Miller himself come back from the dead, Rachel had unzipped the tent with an emotion tantamount to joy.

"Peter!"

His face had been grim, his lips blue with cold, his face colourless.

"Peter!" She had repeated and stopped herself from flinging her arms around him because a) he didn't look the touchy-feely type, and b) she didn't want to get wet and cold again.

Thirty minutes later, they sat inside Chris Miller's tent, sharing a cup of black tea, and eating bowls of his cereal. Peter had exchanged his wet and salty clothes for the remaining pair of jeans and fleece. His padded coat had been thoroughly wrung out, and was now hooked over Chris' makeshift slaughter-station, drip-drying. The deer's carcass had been deemed unfit to eat and unceremoniously tossed into the sea. The metal box was now stranded half-way up the beach, left there by the receding tide.

Through a mouthful of super-sweet 'Frosties', she said, "It's too late to try and find our way to the lodge now."

"Do you know where it is?"

"Kind of. I was doing some research, trying to piece together Chris' last days and hours, so I know that it's on the other side of those trees." She pointed a thumb at the tent wall.

"That's one hell of a hill to climb! Isn't there a route around the edge?"

"I have no idea. I just know that the lodge is on the other side of the hill."

"More like a mountain."

She glanced at her socked feet and then to the pair of walking boots tucked beside the mattress. They weren't a good fit, would probably cause blisters, but they were at least dry. "Well, we could stay here. I'm sure the coastguard will be searching for us by now."

"That's if anyone has noticed that we're missing."

"Why wouldn't they?"

He shrugged, the glum façade dropping down once more.

"It's getting stuffy in here. If we're going to stop, we might as well make the most of it," she smiled, pulling out a large bag of marshmallows from the box of supplies.

Peter's face brightened, and then he laughed. "That box is like the bloody Tardis!"

She chuckled. "It is. I don't think Chris was the off-grid, live-from-the-land, kind of guy. So, shall we?"

He offered a questioning frown.

"Make a fire and toast marshmallows?"

His smile broadened. "Yes, let's."

Thirty minutes later, orange flames danced within a stone circle, burning through logs, and kindling from a pile collected by Chris.

"Let's make it a big one," Peter said throwing more logs into the circle. "It'll keep away any nasty beasties."

"Nasty beasties?" Rachel asked with a laugh.

"Bears, wolves, and other horrifying predators," Peter said with exaggeration.

Rachel shivered and nodded her head. She had no idea about 'wolves and other horrifying predators', but according to the lodge's website, the island was popular with hunters, and it claimed to have procured a record number of bear-hunting licences last year due to an explosion in the brown bear population. Peter threw another log on the fire. Sparks flew, eddied, then disappeared. Between them they pulled up two larger logs as seats then sat before the fire, each with a marshmallow on a stick.

"I've never had toasted marshmallows before. My mum always said they'd rot my teeth."

"Me neither. What we really need are crumpets."

"Ooh! Now you're talking. I love toasted crumpets with real butter."

"My Granny used to sit beside the fire of an evening and toast them for us," Peter beamed. "Once the council put gas into the property, it was never the same. You know, sometimes progress isn't so great. Evenings lost all their charm after that." He sighed then looked out to the sea. Dark blue and grey beneath the darkening sky, it was once again placid. "The storms here practically come out of nowhere."

"Hmm," Rachel bit into a blackened marshmallow.

"Hot?"

"Uhuh! Bloody hot."

"Exactly. It's crumpets all the way for me." Peter pulled his own marshmallow from the flames, placing it beside him to cool."

Rachel took a sip of long-life milk from the carton. "I think that's what happened to Chris."

"Death by marshmallow?"

"No!" Rachel laughed. "The storm. It caught him by surprise."

"Chris is the man who left this camp?"

"Yes." Rachel remembered the odd-looking woman who had been at this very beach and gave the shoreline and bank of trees behind them a quick glance. There was nothing untoward among the trees although the lowering sun had deepened the darkness between their trunks to black. She swallowed. If they had to stay here tonight, at least she had Peter for company, surprisingly good company. She returned her gaze to the older man, appreciating for the first time his aquiline nose, the flash of grey at his temples, which she now realised gave him an air of the silver fox, and smiled. His eyes were a bright, and intelligent, blue. "So, Peter, before you worked at the zoo ..."

Her words faltered as his eyes widened, a startled deer.

"Did you ... were you a ..."

He cocked his head as though trying to hear something, then held a finger to his lips. She zoned in on the noise. A tap, tap, thud, was followed by another thud, and the sound of metal clanking on stones. Movement caught her attention and drew her eyes to the metal box still sitting on the beach. It rocked. Peter turned to follow her gaze and groaned.

"It's not Jean-Luc's brother, then." As Rachel stood, a howl curdled the air. She twisted to the sound, catching Peter's look of dread, then returned her attention to the box. The thudding continued, more insistent this time.

Another howl, and the hair on Rachel's neck prickled. "I guess there *are* wolves here as well as bears, then. It didn't mention them on the website."

Taking one of the longer branches that lay half in and half out of the fire, she used it as a torch and walked to the box. To the background of howls, she shivered. Water lapped at the box. "The tide's coming in." She turned to Peter who hadn't moved from his spot beside the fire. "Help me drag it up the beach," she called. She forced the torch into the ground then tried to lift the box, but it was too heavy. A shitty stench wafted to her nose as it escaped through the drilled holes, reminding her of Aunty Sheila's Labrador after a walk in the rain; the geriatric dog, fat and cancer-riddled, with a mouth full of rotten teeth, over-indulged and spoilt by her childless aunt, had stunk even before it had become wet, but afterwards, the stench was overpowering.

Each side of the box had a handle for carrying, and beside one was a small flap, and beneath it a key. "The key's here!" She pulled the key from its clasp.

"Don't open it!"

"But it'll drown!"

"You don't know what's in there. It could be dangerous!"

She bent to the holes, peered inside, but saw only black. "I can't see anything, but something's alive in there. I knew he was lying!" She placed the key in the lock and twisted. "We can't leave it to die."

It released with a click.

"Rachel!" Peter called. "Don't!"

Another howl erupted from the hills.

The thudding in the box returned, followed by a long and electronic beep.

"Did you hear that?"

"They sound closer!" Peter replied looking across his shoulder to the hills with their thick blanket of massive pine trees.

"No, the beep. Something inside beeped. Maybe it's something mechanical?"

She moved along the box, unlocking five of the six locks. At the sixth she faltered. The thudding, howling, and beeping had stopped.

With a crunch of gravel beside her, she twisted to Peter standing no more than two feet to her right. He held a large branch in his hand as though holding a baseball bat.

"Lock it back up, Rachel," he said through gritted teeth.

"No, Peter, whatever's in here could die."

"Perhaps that's for the best." He took another step closer as she placed the key in the final lock.

"Of course it's not! I thought you liked animals? You work in a zoo."

"Yes, I work with animals, which means I know exactly how dangerous they can be."

"But ..." Rachel faltered, pulling the key from the lock, then replaced it. Peter raised the branch.

She raised an arm in defence. "Don't hit me!"

"It's not for you! It's for that thing!" Peter gestured at the box. "Haven't you wondered why Jean-Luc lied and said it was his brother?"

"Yes! No. Well ... I guess it's a rare animal, or something the lodge doesn't have a permit for."

Peter sighed and lowered the stick. "It's not for the wilderness lodge."

Rachel frowned. "Then what's it doing being shipped to Volkolak island?"

Peter filled his lungs, then said, "It's for the Institu- ..."

"Institute?" Rachel finished. "What Institute."

He didn't reply.

"There isn't one on the island. I did research; there's only the lodge here."

"It's a ..." Peter faltered again.

Pulling the key from the lock, Rachel took a step away from the box. "So ... an institute. And how do you know about it?"

"I don't."

"But you just said that the box was for the institute."

"I was wrong."

"That doesn't make sense." Rachel's frown deepened and she watched his face closely. "So ... do you know what's in the box?"

"No."

"But you seemed pretty sure that whatever is inside is dangerous." She gestured to the stick in his hand. "And you were going to batter it, if it got out."

"I'm not at liberty to say."

"Not at liberty! What the hell is going on here?"

"I'm not at liber-"

"That was a rhetorical question!" Her eyes bored into his through the torchlight. "So, the Institute ... are shipping some rare animal out here. It's for animal testing. Is that it?"

Peter bit his tongue. He couldn't tell her what he suspected, for one thing, he could be wrong, and any information would lead to more questions, and he couldn't let her know about Kielder, or admit to being part of a programme that officially didn't exist.

"I don't know."

Rachel persisted. "Is the animal in there dangerous then?"

Peter didn't respond, but Rachel continued. "It must be dangerous, because you almost shit yourself when you heard the noise coming from the box."

Thud!

Peter quivered. "Lock the box! It could be a bear, or even a wolf! You've heard the howls. Perhaps you're right about the lodge importing animals for hunting."

Thud!

"Lock the box!" He grabbed for the key.

She jumped, jerking the key from his reach, her leg brushing against the edge of the box.

Thud!

The box rocked.

"Rachel!"

He took a step back as the lid began to lift. "Get back!"

Thud!

As Rachel twisted to the noise, the key held aloft, the lid lifted and from the dark interior a pair of red eyes shone.

CHAPTER NINETEEN

With sudden blow from behind, Rachel was pushed aside as Peter threw himself onto the lid. It slammed back into place with a thud.

"Lock it! Lock it! Lock it!" he screamed.

Peter's body rose along with the lid and a foul stench wafted from the gap as Rachel scrambled on her knees and, using her own weight to force the lid into place, pushed the key into the first lock.

"Lock the other side!"

She scrambled around, stones and pebbles spraying as she hauled herself to the other side of the box. The lid lifted. Fingers, clawed and covered in coarse, dark hair, slid over the edge. She slammed her weight against the lid. The thing inside screeched and the fingers pulled back.

"More weight here, Peter!" she said as she pushed the key into place. As Peter shifted his weight, the key slid into its hole, and the lid was locked down.

With hands trembling, Rachel moved around the box, securing each lock. Thudding mingled with the creature's angry growls and then a scratching, tearing noise.

"It's trying to break out!"

Grasping her arm, Peter yanked her back. "We've got to get away!"

Despite her fear, Rachel remained close to the box, transfixed by the angry growls.

"Oh, my God! That was terrifying. Did you see its eyes? They looked so red in the firelight, but I was right, Peter."

"What!"

"It's a wolf, or maybe a bear. I saw its claws, and its fur is brown." She took a step back, heart still pounding. "The lodge ..." she took a moment to catch her breath. "I was right! The lodge must be importing bears for their hunters. They bragged about the bear population exploding and being able to get a record number of hunting permits, but it's all a lie!" Her smile broadened. "This will make a fantastic story! And ... oh, my God!"

"What?"

"I'll bet this is why Chris is dead!"

"But I thought he drowned at sea?"

"They never found the body! And I bet the creature on the beach was a hoax to try and scare him away." It suddenly all made sense. "Yes! The lodge are importing animals illegally. Chris discovered it—he even mentioned that they were all 'in on it' in his video."

"Video?"

"Yes! I've lost my phone so I can't show you, but he sent me a video. He was on this beach, but he got spooked by a creepy looking woman. God, she was ugly. Covered in hair. She even had fangs. I just knew that Chris didn't have the acting skills to fake it!"

"What happened? On the beach?"

"Well, he set up camp," she gestured to the tent. Peter nodded, encouraging her to continue. "And he was making videos about his time here, you know, Daring Dan the Adventurer, Celebrity in the Wild, that kind of thing. He was desperate to get his career back on track – that's what his agent told me. Anyway, he sent me a video. It was shaky, like some sort of found footage deal, and, at first, I just thought he was doing his usual attention seeking thing, but when he disappeared, and then was reported as missing at sea, I watched the video carefully. He was terrified, that much was obvious, genuinely terrified. Something was stalking him, watching him from behind the trees. He videoed it running. You could see a flash of fuchsia—that was what was really weird—the fuchsia; no animal wears a fuchsia shirt, but it was so fast. He lost track of it and then caught up with it again on the beach."

"And? What did it look like?"

"It was ridiculous, really. It had this torn pink shirt, just the collar and one shoulder were still intact, but the rest of it was naked. It ... you could tell it was a female ... if you know what I mean, but it was hairy all over and I think it had fangs. Whoever did the prosthetics was brilliant, but then the camerawork wasn't great, and the image was kind of fuzzy, but it was enough to scare the shit out of Chris. He legged it to his boat and sent the video to me once he was at sea, and that's the last he was heard of."

"Did you show the video to the police?"

The question seemed odd to Rachel, an accusation. "No, it was too late by then. The US Coast Guard had already called off the search. I showed it to my editor, but he didn't believe it was real."

"But you did?"

"Yes!"

"And you thought you'd come and investigate it yourself."

"Well ... yes."

"And get a great story out of it too." Peter's voice was flat, his words a statement.

"Well ... listen, there was nothing I could do. The search had been called off, but I thought there was more to the story than just a D-list celebrity trying to claw his way back into popularity, and ... and it would make a great story—it will make a great story. I just have to find out who is behind it all. The woman was a hoax. I bet if we make it to the lodge, then we'll find the costume. It will be proof that Chris' death wasn't just an accident."

"It sounds like it was, even if he had been spooked back onto his boat. The weather around here is treacherous."

She nodded. "Perhaps, but there's something else going on." She gestured to the box. "Obviously." The thudding had quieted, and the clawing stopped. "I think the bear has given up. Maybe it's weak and gone back to sleep."

Peter offered a noncommittal, 'maybe'; the fear that had been etched into his face only moments ago, now smoothing away. "But you're right; it must be a bear."

Rachel turned back to the box. "It must only be a young one though, that box isn't big enough for a big one."

Peter only nodded and made noises of agreement then mumbled, "We should set up a watch if we can't leave here tonight. I'll go first."

STARS SAT BRIGHT IN the sky as Max returned to the cave. Across his shoulder was a deer, the throb of its heart slow, missing beats, stopping. He dropped it to the ground outside the dark entrance. The scent of her was strong, she had been in this very spot, perhaps scuffling back as he approached. He sliced a talon down the deer's belly. The mist of rising heat twisted into the cold night air, the stench of its offal sticky and delicious. He grasped its liver, and bit down, the organ still attached to the body. The noise of her shuffling came from inside the cave. He swallowed the liver, a smile pulling back over his fangs. He reached for the heart. It gave a final throb as it left the safety of the cavity. Taking the first bite, he listened to her move towards the cave's entrance, then swallowed the rest. She growled. He ignored it, and took a kidney, holding it in his hand, the steam rising from glistening membranes. The woman grunted, growled, and shuffled forward, her figure outlined at the entrance to the cave. She took another step closer. He growled, snarling at her with bared teeth. She disappeared back into the cave, and he finished the kidneys. Squatting next to the eviscerated carcass, he sat on his haunches, a pain that erupted from his chest building from the deepest hollows of his body and raised his face to the moon. *Laura ... Laura ... Laura ...* The name scorched into his mind, burned at his soul. He howled, filling the air with a sorrowful wail. "Lauuuuraaaaa ... Lauuuuraaaa."

The female sat the entrance again, and he pushed past, allowing her to leave as he curled on the bed of ferns. She scurried out, crouched over the carcass, and leant in to devour the innards, turning to stare at him with fearful eyes.

He would claim her later.

CHAPTER TWENTY

Despite the gnawing cold, and his best efforts to stay alert, sleep had claimed Peter in the darkest part of the night. There had been no repeat of the thudding from the box, and even the howls that had stirred dark memories, and made his flesh creep, hadn't recurred.

He woke to Rachel's gentle snores and the sound of waves whishing on the inlet's stony beach. Coat done up, feet thrust into unlaced boots, he unzipped the tent with a slow hand, and peered outside. The last stars of night were still visible in the sky, but dawn had brought a thin grey light. The trees that curved around the inlet sat as a dense wall, dark and pregnant with foreboding. The fire lit last night had grown stone cold though untouched by the rising tide. The box remained silent, ominous with its promise of horror. Peter swallowed, then emerged from the tent, determined to overcome his fear, light the fire, boil water for tea, and have a plan of action for their escape ready before Rachel awoke. His heart beat a rapid tattoo as he stood in the light, a sharp breeze nipping at his cheeks.

Almost certain that the strange woman on the beach that had tracked Chris Miller wasn't a hoax, he realised that their safest route to the lodge would be by sea, but without a boat, or even a raft, survival in the icy water would be impossible. He glanced to the forest of pine trees; they towered and spread, undulating over the hills for as far as he can see. If there was something in there, something from Kielder, then trying to cross, without any means of self-defence, and even with a means of self-defence, would be a suicide mission. He decided that the best course of action, at least for today, was to wait for a rescue party. He took small branches from the pile they had gathered yesterday and prepared the fire as he mused. The Institute would be missing them by now and, even if Marta wasn't concerned about the missing plane, or its passengers, she would most likely be very concerned about the missing cargo. The beep Rachel had heard was likely a tracking device, like the ones they had attempted to tag the creatures with at Kielder, so it wouldn't be long before a search party, complete with tranquilizers or whatever other methods they now had for dealing with their subjects, would arrive.

MAX WOKE TO THE NOISE of birds and the gentle thud of Katarina's heartbeat as she lay curled with her back against his belly. Hot breath rose as a mist, and the cave was filled with their scent; he could taste the sticky particles of her sex; it rose from the dark, warm place between her legs. He pushed his nose into her neck and inhaled then bit down on her shoulder, sinking long incisors into the soft flesh. She yelped, her body stiffening. He maintained his hold, her blood trickling into his mouth. As he withdrew his fangs, she scrambled to her feet. Red stains bloomed across the remains of her white shirt, split over newly contorted bones and muscles. She crouched at the cave entrance. He sat on his haunches and waited, her scent from their mating last night clinging to him. A deep ache rode through his belly as he waited. She tore at the remains of her shirt to expose a fine covering of dark hair swirling over her shoulders, down her sides, running as a V to her navel, and then spreading across her thighs. As she crouched, the smell of her genitalia rode the air. She was ripe. Ready. Playing the game.

Eyeing him with blood-red eyes, she moved across the cave to crouch beside him. With skeins of hair around his fingers, he pulled her to the bed of ferns, the need to take her primal. Inhaling the musky scent of her dark place as he parted her legs, he sank deep inside her tight heat. Clamping around him, it sucked with each powerful thrust, and he howled as he emptied into the warmth of her dark place, and the life-giving seed swarmed as it searched for its prey.

The sun rose above the dark outline of the forest as Max stood at the entrance to the cave with his woman, Katarina, crouched at his side, and dug fingers through her hair as he looked out over the forest. To his left he could see the shoreline with its curving inlets, and to his right a plume of smoke coming from a clearing. Particles of scent that were not her, tickled his nose. His belly growled and a new need rose; the need to sink his teeth into hot and steaming innards. A flash of blue beyond the trees caught his attention. His fingers curled tighter around Katarina's hair, and she yowled, crouching closer to his body, rising to follow his hand. He growled, pulled her to follow him, then sprinted into the forest, darting between trees, jumping over worming roots, and clambering down steep slopes with ease. Katarina, slower, followed his lead, snapping and yelping her excitement.

On the wind, above the scent of pine and rotting leaves, of deer and bear, was a scent that made his mouth water; a

Screamer, the ones that ran and screamed and tasted so, so fucking delicious. He jumped across a slip of running water, jumping high above its flow, grasping an overhanging branch, and jumping to the other side, landing with a thud. Behind him, Katarina tumbled to a stop, yowling as she lay beside the water. He yapped, growled, leapt back, hauled her over his shoulder, and jumped the running stream, throwing her down with force, and a growl, then turned back to the forest and ran to their scent.

The Red One, the man from the sea, followed.

PETER'S BOWELS TURNED watery as the thing in the box mewled again.

"What the heck was that?" Rachel's head appeared from the tent, and then she forced her body through the gap, stumbling out onto the stony beach.

"That," Peter said making no effort to keep the fear from his voice as he pointed.

"The box?"

"Yes."

The mewl was followed by a muffled and weak howl that petered out to a scratching whine.

"Do bears howl?"

Peter turned to Rachel with an incredulous frown. *You're that dumb?* "No, they don't. They growl."

"Then ... it's not a bear in there."

"I think we can be sure of that."

She stared at the box as though waiting for it to speak. The thing inside mewled again.

"It sounds a bit like a dog, so I guess it's a wolf."

From the distance a howl rode on the wind.

Peter's sphincter contracted. "Oh, Jesus!"

"So, the lodge is importing wolves?"

"I think we should consider getting into the water …"

"I bet they don't have a permit for that!"

The howl repeated, another creature responded.

"Rachel, we need to leave—now!"

Halfway up the hillside a flock of birds ejected from the trees, flapping into the sky as though catapulted.

"Well, we can go across the hill, but it's a hell of a way to walk."

At the periphery of his awareness was the growling hum of something mechanical.

"We have to get in the water!"

The metal box rocked.

"We'll freeze to death!"

The thudding resumed along with the unbearable scratching of nails against metal.

"I think it's trying to get out. Perhaps the pack is coming to find it?"

With a sudden moment of clarity, Peter realised that the irritating buzz he could hear was the noise of an outboard engine. As he swivelled to the direction of the sea, a boat came into view.

"Thank God!"

The boat, a dark-grey dinghy with an orange stripe along the side, steered towards the beach. Rachel ran to the water's edge, waving her arms. "We're here! We're here!"

As a growl erupted from the box Peter followed, standing at her shoulder as she waved her arm. On board there appeared to be three men. Each was dressed in black, their outlines blocky. As the boat moved closer, it became obvious that the men weren't from the Coast Guard, or the lodge. Rachel jumped up and down beckoning for them, guiding them to where she stood.

The boat mounted the beach, and two men jumped ashore as the other killed the engine. All of them were armed, and Peter recognised the uniform of Titan Blane's security guards.

Rachel took a step back as they approached. "Who are they? That's not the uniform of the US Coast Guard."

"It's not," was Peter's laconic reply.

"Doctor Peter Marston?"

Rachel stared at him with an open mouth.

"Yes."

"We've been sent to retrieve you and the cargo."

"And this is Rachel Bonds." Peter said with a quick step towards Rachel, blocking the man's advance. "She's an investigative journalist."

The man's gaze flitted from Peter to Rachel. The man, obviously ex-military judging by his demeanour and build, the way he expertly handled his weapons, and picked up on Peter's hint, quickly hid the flicker of concern at the mention of Rachel's occupation and turned. "We were told to come and look for survivors." As he spoke, the other two men approached the box.

"Be careful!" Rachel called. "There's a wolf in there." They ignored her and continued to inspect the box. As the first of the two made adjustments on a handheld device, and the second loaded a small gun with a dart, the third man placed an arm around Rachel's shoulder and attempted to lead her to the dinghy. She was on edge, perhaps sensing Peter's discomfort. He tried to respond naturally as the man asked if there were any other survivors.

"We haven't seen anyone else. Have you spotted any debris?"

"The animal in the box is still alive," Rachel butted into the conversation taking a step towards the metal box and the two guards attempting to lift it. Peter was relieved that they had tranquilised the creature without Rachel noticing. "We think it's an illegal wolf being imported by the lodge's owners. We should call the Coast Guard and report it."

"We're working with the Coast Guard, Ma'am. A wolf you say?" The man asked with what appeared to be genuine surprise, then shouted to the guard. "Dane, can you check on that animal? Lady here said it's an illegal wolf."

"Already did, boss. It's a dog."

"No, it's not!"

"You saying my colleague is a liar, Miss Bonds?" He glared at Rachel then turned back to his men. "Get it on board and let's haul on out of here."

"Do you have blankets? Aren't you supposed to have thermal blankets or something when you rescue people? Who sent you? You're not wearing a service uniform. I was expecting a helicopter."

The man gritted his teeth and replied. "We're on Special Ops in the area. The US Coast Guard asked us to cover this mission, Miss."

"Oh ... special ops?"

"Special Operations."

Rachel made no effort to hide her curiosity and after scanning the men's uniforms and equipment, asked, "What Special Operations?"

Peter sighed, relieved that the uniforms carried no identifying logos.

"I'm not at liberty to say, Ma'am."

"Oh."

Rachel continued to question the guard as the box was hauled onto the boat and, after stuffing as many belongings into Chris' bags as she could, she joined them on the now full dinghy.

CHAPTER TWENTY-ONE

Sam Brewster woke to the distinctive notes of a wolf's howl. *George was a god-damnable liar!* She jabbed a fingertip into her husband's muscular back. He grunted in his sleep, "What!"

"Did you hear that?"

"No. Go back to sleep."

He snorted, immediately asleep. She pursed her lips in irritation; even after sixteen years of marriage, his ability to sleep at the drop of a hat, or as soon as his head hit the pillow, irked her enormously. The howl repeated. Her heart thudded, but not with fear. She threw the covers aside, swinging her legs over the bed, alert for further noises, and peered out of the window and into the blackened forest. There were definitely no wolves on Volkolak Island, despite its name. There were bears, black-tailed deer, and a host of other mammals, but no wolves, at least no legally acknowledged wolves. Pulling on her sloppy joggers and Jerry's extra-large hoodie, she walked through to the cabin's living-cum-dining area and flipped her laptop open. The screen flashed to life, and, after only moments, the browser re-opened on the last page she had been reading—the *Department of Fish and Game*'s guidelines on hunting and permits. She typed in the URL for the lodge's website, scouring each page for mention of wolves. There was nothing other than a brief mention of how it came to be called 'Volkolak' – something about a previous owner's desire to keep visitors away that was possibly linked to his belief there was gold in the hills and a statement that 'No wolves have been on the island since 1986 when the island was made into a hunting ground for brown bear and blacktail deer by the current owner George Wilson'. A wry smile crossed her face; the old coot made them extinct so he could run his business. That would explain the dusty wolf pelts above the fireplace in the entrance hall to the lodge.

She opened a new tab and began to search for any mention of wolves being reintroduced to Volkolak. Her search returned nothing. She checked the Government's web page for their *Department of Fish and Game*. Again, there was nothing on their site. Widening the search, she typed in 'new wolves Alaska', and then 'reintroduction wolves Alaska', and finally 'hunt wolves Alaska."

Finding no information about the reintroduction of wolves on Volkolak, and sure that George wouldn't allow them back on the island, given his detestation of the creatures, she leant back in the chair with a smile; all the evidence suggested that there *were* wolves on Volkolak, unregistered and illegal wolves, and that meant only one thing to Sam; an unlimited cull. The *Department of Fish and Game* could go suck on one and stick their 'One bear only' hunting permits where the sun don't shine; she was going to hunt the wolves down from dawn till dusk without anyone telling her to stop. She strode back into the bedroom and jumped onto the bed beside Jerry.

"What're-"

"Jerry! Jerry! Get up!" she said, barely able to contain her excitement and prodding his shoulder for added effect.

"What is it?" he asked finally sitting up. She straddled him, hands cupping his full beard. "We are going hunting!"

"Of course we're going hunting," he returned with a bemused smile, his hands sliding to cup her full buttocks. "That's why we're here."

"Yes, but we're not hunting bear."

He squeezed her buttocks, pulling her hips closer to his. "We are," he said through a face full of warm breast. "I got the permit."

"Nope," she said as he took her breast into his mouth. "We are going to hunt wolves!"

He released her nipple. "Wolves? There aren't any on Volkolak."

"There are. I've heard them. They're not supposed to be here, but they are. And do you know what that means?" She pushed her hips over his growing hardness. "Do you?"

He moaned as she rose then lowered herself over him. "Right now, I don't care." He cupped her breasts as she began to rock.

"It means we can kill as many as we want." She rocked her hips rhythmically. "It means we can kill a whole fucking pack!"

In a quick movement, he flipped her to the bed, anchoring himself with one hand around the bedpost. "Sure, babe, but first ..."

Thirty minutes later, showered and dressed, they sat at breakfast with their long-time friends Suzy and Caleb. All four sat tight-lipped as George, the lodge's owner, along with his wife, Carmel, a tiny oriental woman at least thirty years his junior, served a breakfast of hash browns, scrambled eggs, bacon, sausages, and toast.

"All okay for you folks?" he asked with a slight frown.

"Just fine," Jerry returned with a smirk. Sam tapped his leg beneath the table; the last thing she wanted was for George to cotton on to the fact they knew there were wolves on the island. They had all agreed to keep exactly what they intended to hunt today a secret; nothing was going to stop them enjoying their day of unrestricted hunting. Sam had already imagined the wolfskin hides pinned above their own fireplace at home or laid out as a rug in front of the fire. Being a woman who took pride in being able to turn her hand to anything, from fixing a gearshift to sewing her niece's prom dress, she also wanted to turn her hand to making a pair of wolfskin moccasin boots, or at least slippers.

"What're your plans today?"

"We were thinking about heading up to Eagle Point." The hill, with its distinctive rocky promontory, several miles from the lodge, was an area that George, Sam realised, had guided them away from.

A frown quickly furrowed George's brow. "If you want to get your bear today, then you'll be needing to be over at Halo Bay," he said as he placed a plate of scrambled eggs in front of Suzy. "That's where they're at. Best hurry though; won't be long before they're all hibernating, and your permit is only good for this year."

"Sure." Jerry agreed too quickly, and with a bemused, bordering on paranoid, frown, George retreated to the lodge's kitchen along with his wife.

Suzy picked up the conversation they had shut down as breakfast was served. "Are you sure you heard wolves, Sam?"

"I am. And if Caleb heard them too-"

"I sure did!"

"Then I'm positive there are wolves on this island."

Jerry threw his napkin down after wiping it across his mouth. "Then," he said in hushed tones, "let's get going."

All four pushed their chairs back, uncharacteristically quiet, their excited chatter spoken in hushed tones. As the room emptied, Carmel scurried through to clear the plates and George watched from the doorway.

Ten minutes later, an outboard engine hummed as Sam climbed into the passenger seat of the 4x4 that would take them away from the lodge and deeper into the island's thick forest. She pulled out a map of the island, scouring each marked promontory. "Eagle Point is marked with caves, I'll just bet that's where the pack is."

Leaning over to the map, Jerry agreed, started the engine, then manoeuvred the car to leave the lodge's parking area. Overhung with trees, it was edged by the forest, and the sense of being swallowed played with Sam's anxiety. Walking through the wilds, challenging herself to the next adventure, was what Sam lived for, what had gotten her from semester to semester for the last five years since she took up her position as lead teacher in the school's English department. The increased workload hadn't been a surprise, but the stress and pressure that went along with her new role had, and she had transitioned with a lurch from being in love with her career to barely hanging on with broken fingernails. The last straw had come two months ago when, after months of banging heads with another colleague, her mental health had taken a nosedive and she had her first panic attack in the middle of class. Forced to take time off for stress, she was slowly recovering from burnout.

The holiday on Volkolak was supposed to be her final treat before going back to work. She was loving the holiday, but truly terrified of going back to work and, for the past few mornings, she had woken from a dream where the pupils and teachers at the school were bearing down on her. The howling wolves, and the plans to track them down, had come as a welcome distraction, but the same sense of drowning, of being overwhelmed, had caught at her as the car had backed up from the dark bank of towering pines.

CHAPTER TWENTY-TWO

The boat ride to the lodge took less than thirty minutes but seemed far longer with the metal box laid at his feet. Through the roar of the boat's engine, and Rachel's stream of questions to both himself, and the other men on board, Peter listened for any sign that whatever was in the box was waking, certain that Rachel did not believe Dane's lie that it was a dog. She quizzed him, trying to catch him out, no doubt practicing her investigative techniques, which certainly needed honing – there was nothing subtle about her efforts of interrogation – until he began to ignore her and stared out at the horizon. Having gained no information whatsoever about who they worked for, or what was really in the box, she turned her attention to Peter, quizzing him about the Institute. He cursed himself for mentioning it, and remained tight-lipped, the fear of reprisal from Marta far more powerful than any concern that he was being rude.

The dinghy pulled up and onto the beach as a large, bearded male of about sixty years of age strode from the lodge. From his purposeful stride, and waving 'hello', he was obviously expecting their arrival. Behind him, a small woman with dark hair, carrying a bundle, followed, running to match the much larger man's stride. The woman held a folded blanket, which she threw across Rachel's shoulders as she stepped from the boat. They greeted her like a queen, and Peter felt sure that Kendrick had radioed ahead to warn them.

"Miss Bonds! Welcome to Volkolak Lodge. I'm George Wilson, the owner, and this is Carmel, my wife." The woman made a small bow in deference. Rachel made an awkward curtsy in return. "We're so sorry that you've had such a terrifying time getting here." He turned to the small woman tugging at the blanket in an effort to wrap it even tighter around Rachel's shoulders. "Carmel, honey, take Miss Bonds to her room and run the lady a bath." The woman nodded and tugged at Rachel's hand. Rachel didn't budge.

"Peter?"

A large hand grasped his elbow. "Peter is coming with us. We need his help with the dog, Miss Bonds."

Peter nodded, surprised at the force in the hand around his elbow.

"Will you bring him back?"

"He'll be back before sundown."

"Peter?"

"Don't worry about me, Rachel. Go inside. It looks like you'll be well taken care of. I'm sure I'll see you later." Relieved that he wouldn't have to keep up the pretence once they left the shore, the lie slipped from his tongue with ease.

As Rachel was ushered up the stony beach to the wooden steps leading to the lodge, asking questions about when the police would arrive to take her statement, and what security measures they had in place against the wolves, George placated in soothing terms about hot baths and glasses of wine before a log fire. Kendrick powered up the boat and turned it around to face the sea. Storm clouds had gathered on the horizon and a pearlescent glow had spread across the greying sky. In the distance a wolf howled, and Peter noted the flash of fear that flitted across Dane's face as they momentarily locked to Kendrick's and then glanced back at the forest.

"Goddamn those wolves!"

"Keep it under control, Gillespie," Kendrick said as the boat swung to follow the island's coastline.

Peter remained silent as the boat hugged the coastline, focusing on the horizon rather than the gathering storm or the dark forest, and forced himself to ignore the coffin-like box that sat at their feet.

"Not much further, Doctor Marston," Kendrick reassured after nearly a quarter of an hour had passed. A fine mist had begun to fall, and the sky had become an angry grey. "We should make shore before the storm hits."

Peter shivered as memories of his icy plunge into the water surfaced. "I hope so! I've only just got warm," he replied in an effort to lighten the mood. Kendrick merely nodded in return then focused on steering the boat. Another inlet appeared. It also was a crescent surrounded by a bank of trees but there was evidence of industrial activity where massive tracks had gouged and scarred the earth. An earth mover sat silent, its huge bucket resting on the beach. A short road wound up through the trees to a clearing on the hillside where a compound of container-sized buildings, camouflaged in dark wood, had been built. Several plumes of smoke rose from the compound. "The Institute?"

"Yes, sir."

Peter gripped the boat's side as it was run aground, and quickly jumped to the stony beach. A sulphuric and shitty stench invaded his nostrils. He rubbed his nose and took a breath of fresh air as cold and salty sea spray spattered his face as the wind whipped at the waves. A hand grabbed his elbow as Kendrick urged him to move forward and the metal box landed with a thud just feet away. Inside the creature growled.

"I thought it was supposed to be knocked out," Dane said with a flash of fear in his eyes.

"It is."

"Then why is it awake?"

"What did you give it?"

"The stuff in the syringe."

"Which was?"

Dane pulled out the empty bottle and showed it to Peter. 'Thiodrental Sodium' was printed on the vial. "That's not strong enough!"

"It's just a dog."

Peter stared at the man with incredulity, then turned to Kendrick. "Does he really believe it's a dog in there."

"We don't have clearance to divulge the contents of the box."

"Ten millilitres of thiodrental sodium, particularly a dose that has been administered with such a short needle will not allow adequate sedation of one of the ... weres."

"Doctor Steward doesn't want us to call them weres."

"Shut up, Dane!"

Peter frowned, closed his eyes, and blew breath through his nose, the sigh of a frustrated martyr. "What you must do is use twenty-five millilitres of the drug and administer it via intramuscular injection at the ventrogluteal site. That is the best option for a rapid absorption of the drug."

"In the ass?"

"Yes, using the buttocks allows you to use a longer needle with a larger gauge and penetrate deeper into the muscle with a larger dose. What exactly is in the box, Kendrick?"

"I'm not at liberty-"

"For crying out loud! I'm one of the scientists who worked at Kielder."

After a moment, Kenrick admitted, "A were."

"Yes, yes, but what age and sex? Male, female, adult, juvenile?"

"Adult female."

A howl rose from the forest and the men turned to the trees.

"Jesus, that shits me up!"

"I've radioed ahead. Johnson should be here any time to collect. We're fine if we stay near the water."

Perturbed by the men's fear, Peter asked, "The wolves ... weres ... are they ... in the forest?" Kendrick remained silent and didn't meet Peter's gaze. He was going to lie.

"No."

"No? Then what's howling out there and why are you so afraid? Men like you don't get edgy because of a wolf in the forest."

Kendrick's jaw tightened and he locked eyes with Peter. As another maudlin howl erupted from the box, he made no reaction, but when it was quickly followed by a responding howl from the forest that sounded even closer, he couldn't disguise the flicker of fear.

"Tell me!" Peter demanded, anger making him bold.

"Fine!" Kendrick returned. "We've had two security breaches."

Peter groaned, fear rising in his gullet as he listened to the man's explanation of how the adult female had managed to escape, but how they had quickly retrieved it and 'locked it down'. *The woman on the beach!*

"And last night ... the alpha, an adult male-"

"Yes, yes, I know what an alpha is!"

"Last night the alpha escaped."

"Trashed the lab and took Doctor Petrov with him."

"What!"

"We don't know that for sure."

Dane frowned. "We do. It was on the security film. And we're not sure where Doctor Petrov is."

"Katarina!" he whispered, the hairs on his arms rising. "Doctor Petrov sent me a text yesterday. All seemed well at that point."

"He must have bitten her after-"

"Zip it, Gillespie," Kendrick snapped. "We have no evidence he bit her."

"There was the blood. It was everywhere: on the walls, the floors, sprayed across the desks ..."

"Yes, but he could have taken her ... to eat later." He turned to Peter. "I've read the notes from Kielder, and watched the video footage, so I think it most likely that he killed Doctor Petrov and took her with him as a food supply."

"She looked dead in the film, and the footage showed a massive wound in her throat—no one could survive that."

Except that they can! Mouth suddenly dry, Peter swallowed. "The ... subjects have extraordinary abilities to rejuvenate, so it is possible that, despite Doctor Petrov's injuries, she is still alive."

"Alive, but that means she will be one of them."

"Yes. Did you watch the footage from the initial ... accident ... in the laboratory at Kielder?"

"No, only from the woods."

"Well, it clearly showed the first female recovering from a massive wound to the throat; her flesh healed as she ... as the infection spread. So, there could be two subjects, one female, and one male, in the forest." Dread settled over him as his memory was flooded with images of Max staring at him from the edge of the forest, the male and female villagers that had once been human jumping around him like demented beasts. No! Not like—they *were* demented beasts, monsters thirsty for his blood and hungry for his flesh. He shivered again and nausea began to curdle in his belly. The thing in the box thudded against its walls, and a low growl turned into a long and wailing howl. A howl returned from the forest.

"We have got to get off this beach!" Peter insisted. "It's best if we get back on the water."

Mobile phone in hand, Kendrick thumbed the screen then tapped to call. As he listened, he watched the woodlands, his free hand fingering the automatic rifle slung across his chest. A bird catapulted from a tree halfway up the hillside, less than a mile away from their position.

"Do you have tranquilisers with you?"

Kendrick walked back to the dinghy. "Yep," he said as he swung a long, black case down onto the beach.

"Then can I suggest you load the gun, or guns if you have more than one."

"We've got one each. But any problems, and the automatics will obliterate the fuckers!" A gleam of excitement sat alongside an edge of fear. "This is a Heckler and Koch HK16. It can fire up to nine hundred rounds a minute. We used it to kill Osama. The weres won't stand a chance against it."

The pain of tension increased across Peter's chest, his breath harder to catch. The throb of his pulse painful at the base of his throat. "But you said you'd watched the footage from Kielder!"

"We have."

"Then you'll know that guns and bullets are next to useless against them!"

"The mistake they made at Kielder was using hunting rifles. This," he patted his rifle once more, "will obliterate them. Their flesh will be so torn up, their own mothers wouldn't recognise them."

They wouldn't anyway! "I appreciate your point," Peter said at the edge of panic, "but tranquilisers have been the only effective way ..." Peter's words were ignored as a large flatbed truck rolled through the gap in the trees and swung to a stop at the head of the beach. Five more black clad men jumped out and ran in unison. The truck made a quick three-point turn, ready to leave. The next minute was a blur of instructions and orders as first the box was lifted from the beach with Peter being marched at its side, and then both were pushed onto the flatbed. Before the last man jumped on board, and the box strapped down, the truck, with a roar of its engine, moved at speed away from the beach and through the gap in the trees.

The light dimmed as they passed between massive spruce at least one hundred feet high. The men stood, or knelt, their rifles loaded, their focus on the trees, their orders to 'shoot at anything that moved'. Wind whipped Peter's thinning hair and the trees passed in a blur. The thing in the box remained silent, and the only sound was the thud of Peter's pulse and the truck's engine. The forest was ominous in its stillness. Nothing moved as they sped past, and even the wind didn't seem to reach the forest floor. Peter scoured the space between the trees for any sign of movement. Beside him a guard swung his rifle as though following something, then changed direction.

Thud! Thud! Thud!

The box began to rock, sliding against thick belts strapping it to the truck's floor.

Thud! Thud! Thud!

One of the men twisted to the box and kicked it. A howl erupted.

"Jesus, Kurt! What did you do that for?"

"I hate those goddamned things!"

A howl responded.

"Idiot! Now look what you did!"

"What *I* did?" He kicked the box again.

"Quit it, Kurt!"

An angry howl responded from inside the box. A stronger howl, more insistent, returned from the forest.

"Shit!"

Without warning, gunshots fired, and then a volley of bullets sprayed into the forest. Peter ducked then peered over the edge of the flatbed. Bark splintered and ferns shredded as something flitted from trunk to trunk, disappearing then reappearing as a flash of dark flesh. Barely seen, glimpses were caught of a heel or shoulder, a partial back, moving closer with each second. Wood splintered as the creature passed behind another tree. It stumbled, disappeared behind a cluster of fronds, then bounded up, and ran with a limp.

"Got it!"

Several seconds behind the first, unseen by the men, a second figure ran; a larger, more muscular figure.

"The alpha is behind!" Peter's voice was lost among the men's frantic shouts and the firing rifles. "The first one ..." His breath caught. A third creature, also an enormous male, this one tinged auburn, kept stride with the alpha. "... is a decoy!"

Unheard, he watched as the large male moved with an easy, powerful grace, from tree to tree, but just as Peter gained Kendrick's attention, the truck careened off the road, down a short track, and flew over the grilled entrance to the Institute. Massive gates swung shut behind them and locked with a clank. A low buzz emanated from the fence as the truck slowed to a stop.

"I got a hit!"

"Holy shit!"

"Woohoo!"

The shouts of relief, and exclamations of exaggerated horror, replaced the silence of the forest and the pounding of Peters' pulse. He remained squatting, peering back through the electrified gates to the forest beyond. Nothing moved, but as he turned to face the men, a huge alpha, its power obvious from the size of its thighs, torso, and shoulders, stood between two massive spruce trees and stared at him with red and angry eyes.

"Max!" he whispered.

CHAPTER TWENTY-THREE

Katarina at his side, the Red One squatting only feet away, Max dug sharp claws into the tree's thick bark and climbed. She whimpered. He threw her a short growl, then continued to haul himself up the trunk. From his vantage point he saw into the compound and watched as the men jumped from their truck. A wailing howl carried on the wind, and he scratched claws along the bark, leaving deep gouges in the wood's creamy flesh. He savoured the sound, listening to each mournful note, and returned it with his own call. "Lauuuraaaaaa!" The truck, along with the box, disappeared through the trees and into a large building. Doors closed behind it, locking her, the One ... the Laura ... She ... away from Max. "Lauuuraaaaa!"

A low growl curdled in his belly, rising to his chest as pain. She. The One. She was here. In there. A low moan escaped dark lips overhung with sharp incisors. He grunted. She. "Laura!" he whispered, forcing a thick tongue around the syllables. "Laura!" He squatted on the branch, inhaling the last of her scent, watching the black figures scurry then disappear, and waited. The dark was the time to find Laura, break her from the box, crush her to his chest, smell the sweetness of her dark place. He snapped his jaws, frustrated, grunting at the shining sun, and waited for the moon to rise. The female at the base of the tree mewled, then made a tentative bark. He grunted back, and she cowered, lowering red eyes to study the forest floor.

"DID YOU HEAR THAT!"

"Of course I did."

"Sure, I know you did, but hell, that is close!"

"Are you sure it's a wolf?"

"What else howls like that?"

"I don't know, but it had an odd tone to it, like ... hell, like it was a man's voice being a wolf."

Jerry laughed. "A man being a wolf?"

"Do you mean like the Shaman? There's a strong shamanic tradition among the tribal people in this area, and the Sammi from Norway still believe they can transform into animals, including wolves."

"It's a wolf. It's got to be."

"Sure, but perhaps we should consider other options. I mean, there aren't supposed to be any wolves on this island. George was adamant that he culled the last ones that were here decades ago."

"Perhaps some found their way here, from other islands?"

"Like swam here?"

"Yeah, could be."

"More likely they've been reintroduced without George knowing."

"They couldn't do that, surely?"

"You know what the government departments are like. If they want to do something, they just go ahead and do it, people be damned!"

"Sure, but wolves? That would just be dangerous. They'd be too worried about being sued."

"Sure, I'll sue them if one bites me."

Jerry snorted with laughter.

CLIMBING DOWN THE TREE, Max landed with a light foot, the urge to sink his teeth into steaming innards suffusing every cell in his body. As he had squatted in the branch, yearning for the Laura … the One, locked away from him behind steel doors, the scent of sweat, and breath, and sticky orifices, had reached him, caught on the wind. The scent had caught the membranes in his nostrils, trickling down his throat with sweet and irresistible temptation. He had listened then, turning his ears to the west. The sound of voices, male and female, could be heard in the distance.

With a growl at the red male, and a yap at the female, he had grasped her hair and tugged, and all three had set off at a sprint, following the voices and the scent, picking it back up when lost.

CHAPTER TWENTY-FOUR

Close to the top of the hill, and with stiffening muscles, Sam lowered herself to a smooth boulder half-buried in the earth and surrounded by ferns. After two hours of walking, much of it uphill, her legs ached, and the overly heavy rucksack, packed with ammunition, their lunch and a flask of coffee, two bottles of water, a spare pair of socks, a first aid kit, and her secret stash of chocolate, weighed her down. She only had herself to blame though; she had packed it with extra ammunition, and then added some more. Jerry had advised against such a heavy load, without offering to share the burden, and she had replied, with not a little resentment, that they needed the supplies, or they would go hungry, and that the extra ammunition was to ensure the day was a success; running out of ammo would be embarrassing as she'd already promised to 'bag the entire pack' in front of Suzy and Caleb. Jerry's ungentlemanly response had been to tell her that if she packed it, she could carry it. Her repost had been that she'd 'bag' Jerry too if he didn't stop being such a 'dick'. An offer of sharing the burden unforthcoming, Sam had silently ruminated on all the times Jerry had let her down. They were, she had concluded, legion.

So far, the hunting expedition had been a disappointment as they had not seen, nor heard, nor picked up any of the wolves' tracks. This area though, with its recently trampled 'run', looked promising. And there was a definite odour to the place; a den couldn't be far away. She pulled out the map to pinpoint their location. From lower down the hill, she could hear the voices of Jerry, and Suzy. Surprised at the distance now between herself, and the others, she wanted to shout at them to be quiet, and tell them that they would alert the wolves to their presence, but that would defeat the object, so she sat in silence, several feet from the pathway, hidden among the overarching fronds of several very large, and lusciously green, ferns, and smeared a little more earth across her cheeks. The pathway, as far as she could tell, led to the top of the hill and a promontory of dark and jagged rock.

A rustle of leaves and twigs cracking in the undergrowth, alerted her to something nearby. With slow movements, she picked up her gun, then remained as a statue whilst scanning the area from the left to the right of her peripheral vision. Alert to the rapid thap, thap of feet running through the forest growing closer, she focused on the sound, raising her rifle, ready to shoot. The noise came towards her, from up the hill, and to her left. She swung the gun in that direction. She released the safety catch; it made a small click that she hoped didn't alert whatever was running – hopefully a wolf – close by. From behind her position, came the louder crack of undergrowth splintering. She froze, listening only to the noises, aware of her own breathing, trying to remain unnoticed. The flash of a figure, of … some *thing* among the trees … a figure that had the shape of a man, but couldn't *be* a man, ran lower down the hill, its arms and legs pumping hard, its pace too fast for her to follow, as it appeared, then disappeared, among the trunks. Fifty feet away branches high in the trees shook and bounced, the movement far too heavy to be the wind, or a squirrel. Behind her something moved, so close she could hear its breathing, then crashed past her, the sound of its feet as it sprinted down the hill fading to silent only feet from her spot.

She sat unmoving as another of the creatures passed her in a flash of rich auburn. Closer this time, she watched with jaw dropped open as the man ... beast ... wolfman ... ran past. Clothed in a tattered long-sleeve top with one half entirely missing, the red-haired creature disappeared as quickly as he had appeared. His jeans were still belted to his waist, but great rents had been torn in the fabric as though, too tight, his massive thighs had burst from the legs, the hems at the ankles still intact. His arms pumped fast, and in the seconds that the image of him running became imprinted on her mind, she noted the broad and muscular shoulders, defined biceps, massive pectorals, and long arms with huge hands ending in curved talons. Incisors had grown long in an elongated jaw, covered in long auburn hair with flashes of bright copper that spread over his forehead, temples, cheeks, and chin. On his shoulder, beneath the hairs, the skin was tattooed with a spray of oriental flowers inked in reds, oranges, and blues. Watching his back in her peripheral vision as he disappeared among the foliage, huge and muscular buttocks sat atop delineated thigh muscles that a speed skater would be proud of.

She closed her mouth, opened it to speak, remained silent, and attempted to process what she had seen. There were no wolves on the mountain, at least not the traditional kind, but there were ... creatures. Her thinking-self refused to speak the word her instinct wanted to blurt, and she began to doubt what she had witnessed. What she had just seen couldn't be real, couldn't actually have happened. She shuffled slowly forward and scoured the ground where the huge ... wolfman – *there, she said it!* – where the wolfman, had run. A fern lay broken, its stem snapped, on it a copper hair was caught. She sniffed at the air as she began to reach for it, changed her mind as the sour odour of the wolfman reached her nostrils, and sat back on her rock. In the distance a scream was cut short and for the first time in her life, Sam experienced the paralysing force of absolute fear.

In the near distance she heard Jerry's voice. For a second, relief coursed through her, then a need to warn him, and then his voice was accompanied by Suzy's laugh, a laugh Sam recognised from their single days, a laugh that put Sam on alert, and saw her raise her gun to eyelevel. Less than a minute later, as Sam remained stock-still on the rock, in her safe place within the ferns, gun pointed, Suzy appeared, and was quickly followed by Jerry. In the near distance, a tree bowed with the weight of something climbing among its branches.

As the tree's leaves shivered, and the thudding of feet stopped, Jerry's arm circled Suzy's slim waist. He allowed her to step forward, gripping her waist from behind as he helped her over a boulder in their path. His hands were massive around her hips, the fingers covering her belly. As she stepped up onto the boulder, he cupped a buttock. Sam's lips thinned, her jaw clenching, her finger a gentle pressure on the gun's trigger. Suzy responded to Jerry's groping with that flirtatious giggle Sam was so familiar with. An adjacent tree bowed, but not with the wind. Sam gave it a side glance and fingered the trigger. *Warn them, Sam!* Jerry glanced around the space - *a furtive glance!* - then stepped up close to Suzy's back, slipping his hands across her front, sliding one below her belly, the other up to fondle her breast. Suzy giggled, then rested her head on Jerry's chest, her eyes closed, obviously enjoying his touch. Something thudded to the forest floor. A tree, only feet away, shuddered. *Warn them, Sam!*

With the pair in her sights, Sam opened her mouth to shout a warning, but Suzy turned to Jerry, and slipped a hand between his legs. *Horny little bitch!* Tears welled in Sam's eyes, blurring her vision. Jerry gave the trees, shrubs, and ferns another furtive glance, then lowered his head for a passionate kiss. Pain hit Sam as a stone to the belly as she recognised Jerry's foreplay routine. It never changed; full-on kiss on the mouth, followed by a sliding of the hands to the buttocks, back up to the breasts, nuzzle the neck, then hands to the lady parts. A tear rolled down her cheek as Jerry's hand slipped down the front of Suzy's briefs. A branch cracked. Something yapped. The woman giggled, then closed her eyes as Jerry delved deeper, his knuckles angular against the fabric of her jeans as they see-sawed. *Bastard!*

Movement between the trunks behind the pair flitted in Sam's peripheral vision but, by the time she had moved her head to check, there was nothing but the browning pine needles that covered the forest floor and the clusters of ferns. Turning back to her husband, the pair had parted, Suzy is looking back along the path. *Looking for your husband, Suzy?* Sam remembered the scream that had been cut short. *Caleb!* Jerry took a sniff of his finger, wiped it against Suzy's back pocket, then pulled her to him for another passionate and groping kiss, but she was distracted, pulling away from him, and peering through the trees.

"No, Jerry! What if someone sees?"

Too late, bitch!

"There's no one! Sam's gone on ahead. She's way up there," he pointed to the top of the hill with a fling of his arm. "And Caleb is ... well, he's way back there." He flung his arm in the other direction, the flush on his face, and the bulge in his jeans, registering his frustration. He grabbed Suzy's arm. "Come here, babe." He grabbed her hand and rubbed it against his crotch. "I'm ready for you. Let's go behind a tree, they won't see."

Suzy's giggle was short-lived, and she swivelled to another crack of branches.

"What's that?"

"How the hell should I know?" Here he was, the rude and impatient Jerry that Sam knew so well.

"It could be Caleb!"

"We're in a fucking forest. It's full of-" Jerry stopped, his attention suddenly alert and focused into the trees.

"I need to find Caleb." Suzy stepped back onto the track they'd followed up the hill. "This place is starting to give me the willies! Where's Sam?"

Sam wanted to shout, 'Yoohoo! I'm here, your best friend and the woman whose husband you're cheating with, bitch!' but instead, she remained silent, with Suzy clear in her sights.

In the next second, as Jerry turned to a noise that seemed to come from all directions, a dark and monstrous figure leant out from behind a trunk. It disappeared within the second, but in that moment the image was scorched onto Sam's mind and made the pain of her husband's betrayal evaporate. Lean and muscular, with a large penis nesting in a mass of curling black hair, its power was obvious, but it was its face, with an elongated nose, and jaw complete with bone-white incisors, rows of pointed teeth, and blood-red eyes with hugely enlarged pupils, that suffused every cell in Sam's body with terror. Seconds later, the beast reappeared closer to Jerry and Suzy.

Still oblivious to its presence, Suzy called, "Caleb!" When her call was met with silence, she made a louder call. "Caleb!" Still no reply.

Sam fingered her trigger. *Warn them, Sam! Shoot it, Sam!*

Jerry finally turned his attention to his wife. "Sam!"

Entirely still, Sam watched as the creature moved from tree to tree. Branches snapped underfoot, and Jerry twisted to the noise. Sam swallowed against a drying mouth, keeping her breath steady and silent. *Shout! Warn them that they are being hunted.* She shivered. *Don't move. Breathe quiet. Warn him ... Quiet breaths ... Stay calm ... Don't ... move.*

The thing took a step closer, moving out from behind a thick trunk. *It licked its lips! Actually licked its lips!* It sniffed at the air. *Smelling their scent.* Sweat dampened her armpits. *Stay calm. Don't sweat. Stay still!* She continued to breath in small and steady silent breaths, desperate to stay calm, and stop the reek of fear that would envelop her if she panicked. As she watched the creatures circle her cheating husband and ex-best friend, instinct told her to be quiet, to disappear among the ferns, to make herself mouse-like and inconsequential.

As Jerry took a step closer to Sam's position, calling her name, the creature struck. Pouncing from the undergrowth, it jumped with claws outstretched at Suzy. Landing on her back, she was thrown to the floor. Sam watched in horror as before Jerry had a chance to turn, the creature had sliced through Suzy's throat and dragged her back into the forest.

The scream of warning stuck in Sam's throat as the creature returned, another at its side—this one a female. In her hand was the lower portion of an arm, a fat arm with the remains of a distinctive dragon tattoo. *Caleb!* The male launched itself at Jerry as he opened his mouth in a surprised 'O'. His face contorted with confusion and then horror, but no scream or shout erupted as the creature pounced, one hand slammed against Jerry's open mouth as the other sliced down his torso ripping through fabric. Jerry landed with a thud under the force of the creature's full weight. Hand still over Jerry's mouth, the creature ripped at his torso, tearing away layers of jacket, shirt, t-shirt and finally flesh. Frozen in terror, unable to take her eyes away from the horror playing out in front of her, too terrified to make a sound, or even breath, Sam watched as the creature delved inside her husband's ribcage, pulling out his heart. Jerry's legs stop kicking as the aorta split.

Minutes passed, and the burn in Sam's thighs and biceps grew intense, but she sat completely still, gun still pointing, and waited for the longest minutes of her life until the creatures moved back into the woods. Jerry's body lay where it had fallen, heart by his side. She lowered her gun, and slowly eased herself to the forest floor and reached into her backpack for her mobile phone. Not daring to speak, she sent a text to the lodge. Hands trembling, palms sweating, she tapped each letter as quietly as possible whilst maintaining a slow and quiet breath to quell the rising overload of utter panic. Listening intently to the noises in the forest, and interrupted by constant glances at the trees, she typed. 'SOS!!!!! Trapped at Eagle Point. Werewolves! Jerry and Suzy dead. Caleb – she baulked at the memory of his severed arm - dead. Please save me!' She re-read the message. Deleted 'werewolves' and replaced it with 'Attacked by wolves' then pressed send. She watched the screen. The signal buffered and then 'MESSAGE SENT' appeared. With a repressed sob, she bit her bottom lip, and glanced with blurred eyes at the vast expanse of forest that rolled down the hills to the lodge.

CHAPTER TWENTY-FIVE

Thirty minutes after Peter's dramatic entrance through the Institute's gates, and still reeling from the knowledge that Katarina had been attacked and taken into the forest by Max, he sat in a small suite of rooms allocated as his apartment for the duration of the project. The intermittent tremor in his right hand that had begun several months before his flight to Alaska, was even more pronounced, but he was determined to confront Marta about just exactly what was going on at her new Institute.

The room was a division within a windowless box fitted out hotel-style with a narrow hallway flanked on one side by the bathroom, and on the other by a wardrobe, leading to a bedroom complete with double bed, comfy chair with coffee table, and television above a set of drawers topped with a small kettle. A tray held a cup and various bags of coffee, tea, and milk. There was even a welcome chocolate on his pillow and a handwritten note from Marta herself which must have been penned before the fiasco with the plane. It read,

'Peter,

Welcome to the International Institute of Bio-Tech Advancement!

I trust that the journey was pleasant and that you are not suffering too badly from jetlag.

These are exciting times for bio-technology, and I am confident that your knowledge and expertise will take our project to the next level. We are pioneers in our field, Peter, and I am thrilled to have you along for the journey.

Once you have settled in, please notify me of your arrival and I will arrange induction and familiarisation, and then take you on a tour of the facility myself.

Marta'

Beneath her name was a number. He reached for the telephone beside the kettle and dialled. To his surprise it rang and a business-like, if slightly anxious, voice replied. "Peter! Thank God you are alive."

Taken aback, he replied, "Marta?"

"Yes, of course it is me, Peter. Who else?"

"Sorry, I didn't expect you to answer so quickly."

"I'm sure you're all in a dither-"

Irked by her choice of vocabulary, realising that her need to belittle him was undiminished, he replied with a forceful tone, "Well, not quite a dither, Marta. I am however, deeply disturbed about proceedings thus far."

Silence for a moment, and then, "Oh, Peter. You are such a grump."

"Grump? Marta, I-"

"Kendrick tells me that you are in fighting spirits and that you remain unphased by your experiences, and 'proceedings thus far.'"

"Are you serious, Marta? Has Kendrick debriefed you on quite what occurred on our rescue from the beach?"

"Yes, and it is all under control, Peter." She replied with the hard edge of certainty Peter recognised, and his determination to confront her receded. "I'll collect you from your room in ten minutes, Peter, and then we can discuss the project."

"Are you seriously-."

"Ten minutes, Peter."

His reply faded to a mumble as she cut the connection and he replaced the receiver, lost in a whorl of deja-vu. He clamped his lips together, staring at his face in the mirror, loathing the image reflected back. *Spineless! You are utterly spineless, Marston.* He took in the hair greying at the temples, the eyebags puffy from lack of sleep, cheeks that were beginning to sag, and the first signs of a jowl hanging beneath a chin and jaw that was once taut and well-defined. *Here he was again, at the behest of Marta Steward, incapable of resistance. The woman was a force of nature against which he had no defence.* He rubbed his chin as he turned away from the mirror—*perhaps a beard would help.*

Ten minutes later a knock on his door announced her arrival and he was surprised when the door opened to an anonymous but stern face. "This way Doctor Marston," the guard commanded and, without waiting, turned to walk back along the corridor. Peter followed, quickening his pace to keep up with the man's rapid stride. Peter noted the rifle slung across his chest with unease. "Is that really necessary?" he asked, catching his breath.

"The rifle?"

"Yes."

"Yes, sir, it is."

"Right."

The end of the corridor reached, double doors were pushed open, and the men strode through into a larger, though still compact, room. At one end was another pair of double doors, but along one wall was a single door with a small glass window reinforced with mesh. Peter attempted to look inside as he passed. A quick glimpse showed it to be a laboratory, complete with extra-large animal cages built along each wall. A central table with several computer monitors, and keyboards sat at the centre. A sharps bin sat on the counter beside a sink at the far end. A large white board was hung with a ring of thick black plastic, the device seemingly linked via cable to one of the computers. Apart from the black ring, the laboratory was a replica of the ones kitted out at Kielder, although the cages there were smaller.

They're bigger here, Peter!

He swallowed.

She's at it again, Peter. No, she can't be. Kielder was too horrific.

He wiped away the sweat beading at his brow.

Perhaps she was trying to find a cure? What, and keeping the news as a surprise for you?

The explanation for the extra-large cages, the heavy security, and the animal in the box, was too grotesque to consider. Instead Peter focused on thinking about the notes he'd made about the new project Marta had contracted him to set up and manage. It was utterly tiresome that all his carefully written and researched notes had been lost along with his laptop and were now probably at the bottom of the sea, but he wanted to be able to make a good first impression despite the losses. Thoughts intruded.

She's just shifted the operation to Alaska.

No! It's impossible, and Marta just wouldn't do that. It's unethical.

Oh, Peter, you are a bloody fool.

Shut up! Just shut up!

After making their way through several short corridors, each with a side door opening into another room, Peter was led outside to an open space with a huddle of buildings at its middle. The buildings were clad in wood with a narrow window just beneath the ceiling. These buildings, he noted with rising tension, had two layers of security; a heavy outer door led to an antechamber, and the outer door had to be secured with a code before the inner door would open. Peter shivered, this level of security at any institute was not something he had experienced before, and the only place he had come across an inner door that wouldn't open until the outer door had been secured was at a zoo to stop the animals escaping. Peter had the creeping concern that here, in this inner sanctum, it was to prevent the animals from getting in.

Once through the antechamber, they passed along a narrow corridor and then a final locked door to an open space. At its centre were a group of tables and comfortable chairs, and Peter noted the steam rising from a delicate china cup sitting beside a mug. The room smelled of coffee and a perfume he recognised as Marta's. A door opened and Marta strode forward.

"Peter!" With a smile that couldn't hide the fatigue in her eyes, she beckoned him. "Come into my office. Oh, and bring my tea will you, please? I've made you a coffee. I hope it's how you like it." She threw him a huge smile before turning back to her office. Without question, though irked by her command, he took the tea in its delicate bone china cup and saucer along with the milky coffee, into her office. Dwarfed by the massive leather chair, Marta sat behind her desk, thanked him for her tea, then took a sip as though they were relaxing in a particularly pleasant tearoom. Her red-rimmed eyes closed.

"Marta-"

She held up a hand, stopping his flow of words. "Peter, before you say anything, I have to assure you that we have everything under control here, and that the project is on track as planned."

"Marta." He waited until he had her attention, and her eyes were locked to his. "Marta, have you brought ... any subjects from Kielder to this island?"

Her lips narrow. He waited for the lie. "Yes."

"Oh ..." *Think Peter!*

"But I can assure you, Peter, that everything is under control."

"Although an alpha has attacked Katarina and taken her into the woods!"

"It is all under control, Peter! Kendrick is retrieving them as we speak, and we've learnt our lessons from the events at Kielder. We weren't prepared. Here," she gestured to the office, "we are. Only last week we had a security breach, and one of our female subjects managed to escape," she held up her palms as though to ward off his ire, "I know, I know, but we have put new protocols in place, and the female was brought in without any damage having been done, as will the alpha and Katarina."

"You mean before she had a chance to kill or infect anyone."

"Exactly."

Peter shook his head. "Or anyone found out," he stated.

"Well, there isn't really anyone here to find out, but yes."

Before Peter had a chance to explain that the escaped 'subject' had not only been seen but recorded on a video that was then transmitted to an investigative journalist in England, Marta continued, with, "Each of our subjects is implanted with a tracker; it records their heartrate, oxygen, and hormone levels, along with their location. We have also taken the precaution of giving the employees trackers too, although they're not implanted." Her smile was triumphant.

"How many subjects do you have?"

Ignoring his question, Marta continued. "Like, Katarina, the female had been an employee, but she had managed to get bitten by one of the younger cubs-"

"Cubs?"

"We've brought some younger specimens across."

Peter struggled to comprehend exactly what Marta was saying. The ramifications were too awful, too unbelievable, to consider. "Younger specimens ... from Kielder?"

"Yes. We decided that acquiring a range of ages would be the best way forward, although what we really need is to capture them at the very first, embryonic, stages."

"To find a cure?"

Marta's brow furrowed.

"For Max?"

Her brow smoothed. "Certainly we can attempt to find a cure for Max, once the project has been established."

See! She's not working on a cure! He began to delve into a subject that his mind had refused to accept. "I was told that I would be involved in a breeding programme, Marta."

"And you will be."

Peter's eyes narrowed. "I'm beginning to suspect that the programme I will be working on is not the one I signed a contract for."

Marta flashed him a tight smile. "There have been some changes in our plans since we last spoke."

"Marta, just what is going on here?"

She remained silent.

"I think I have the right to know."

Her eyes didn't meet his.

"Marta?"

"Project Kielder."

"I knew it! As soon as I saw that damned box at the airfield, I knew it." He gritted his teeth whilst exhaling, an angry frown directed at Marta. "I was just stupid enough to think that perhaps you were working on a cure! Imagine that, Marta. I thought you wanted to help Max!"

"Oh, come on!" she blurted, then under her breath but loud enough for him to hear, she muttered, "The lies we tell ourselves!" She paused then continued with her gaze directed at him. "Well, a cure isn't out of the question. Obviously, there are serious, ethical-."

"Ethical!"

"... ethical considerations, Peter, as regards what state Max will be in once 'cured'. The effects of the virus have been dramatic to say the least, and it may be the decision of the board that Max should remain ... as he is."

"Disgraceful!"

"Pish!" Marta's lips thinned and her eyes focused on her teacup. Peter took advantage of the chink in her armour.

"Surely, Marta, it is your moral obligation!"

Marta laughed, her gaze once again fixed to his, her eyes merciless. "Morality, Peter, is more honourable in its absence than in its observance where bio-technology is concerned. What we're working towards will revolutionise the field, advancing its application far beyond what we ever imagined possible."

Peter tried a different tac. "The projects were meant to cure disease, Marta."

"No, it never was."

"Yes!" he insisted. "The projects that Max was working on were both ethical. He would never agree to his work being used to this end, Marta. Never!"

"Well, he shouldn't have allowed himself to get bitten then, should he!"

Marta's frown was petulant, her eyes unflickering steel and Peter realised in that moment that he was staring into the eyes of a bone fide psychopath, and one with absolute determination not to let anything get in the way of her success. Considering for a single second that Marta was interested in working on a cure for Max's condition was beyond naïve, and mortification slid over him like a pall, and rose as anger.

"You should have blown that place to smithereens, Marta!"

"Why on earth-"

"At the very least castrated the males and sterilised the females. It could have been done; there is a substance that when administered orally renders the recipient sterile, at least it does with females from what I know. Tests haven't been carried out on males though we have evidence that the Nigerian government are using it on a particular section of their female population as part of a sterilisation programme."

Marta frowned. "On humans!"

"Sadly, yes."

"That equates to genocide, and you call me ruthless."

"I haven't said that you were ruthless."

"Not during this conversation, no, but in the past ..."

Ignoring her petulance, he said, "We have to stop the spread of this 'disease' Marta! Max ... we need to find a cure for Max, and Laura, and Lois and all the others."

"There aren't that many left."

"In Kielder?"

"Yes, in Kielder. Once the population was established, there really wasn't much in the way of sustenance in the ... compound, and they turned on each other."

Peter's nose wrinkled in disgust. "So ... they ate each other?"

"Precisely. We have a core nucleus, only the most powerful and healthy remain. Perfect for us to work with."

"Work with?"

"Yes, the aim of the project is to develop the strongest specimens. We intend to implant the micro-chips in-vitro, although now that we have lost Katarina, a replacement will have to be found."

"You cannot be serious."

"How else are we meant to continue with the programme? Thankfully, I do have contacts with a number of other colleagues."

"No! The breeding programme? You cannot be serious!"

"You're beginning to sound like a more annoying version of John McEnroe, Peter. Of course, I'm serious! You don't think for a second that your renumeration and re-location package would have been so generous otherwise, do you?"

"But-"

"Are you trying to tell me that you thought that your overly-generous salary wouldn't entail working on some – how shall I put it? – controversial projects? If you believe that, then you are only lying to yourself."

"I shall only work on the project I have been contracted to!"

"Read the small print, Peter. We have the right to change the subject to be tested ad nauseum."

"No! I won't do it."

"Seriously, Peter, you are forgetting quite who you are dealing with. Apart from arousing the anger and retribution of Titan Blane, Mister Corbeur, and the numerous partners waiting on our product, do you really want to go back to testing stool samples ... for the remainder of your career?"

Peter remembered the squeeze on his knee as Dalton Blake had threatened him but rallied against Marta. "Well, something will come up."

"Really? Who do you think it was that secured you that post in the first place?"

"Are you telling me that you had anything to do with me getting that job, Marta?" Peter sneered; she really was an egomaniac.

"No, but I will tell you that it was me who made sure you didn't get anything better."

Her smirk cut through his bravado and a tremble took hold of his fingers.

Their eyes locked.

"Remember Earlham Institute?"

He nodded, remembering the rejected application form.

"And what about Roslin?"

"Yes," he hissed remembering the smarting mortification he'd felt when he'd opened the email rejecting his application; he'd thought the interview had gone so well.

Marta reeled off a list of prestigious jobs that he'd applied for after leaving Kielder, and then the lesser roles he'd been rejected for. Sickness swirled in his belly. "That was you?" His voice was hoarse.

Her smirk broadened. "Yes! Do you see now, just how much you need this job? No one, and I mean no one, will employ you again if you leave here now. I will make sure of that. You'll struggle to get a job stacking shelves at Tescos, never mind another lab job sampling gorilla shit, if I so choose. And there is always the prospect of finding that cure for Max ... presuming you are still here to carry out the research, of course."

Peter's resolve to challenge Marta, and demand to be taken off the island immediately, dissolved.

"Now, I need to know exactly when the specimen we shipped over ovulates so that we can arrange a mating with the alpha."

Peter couldn't help a poke. "When you retrieve him from the forest?"

Her glare was icy, and she ignored his jibe. "I expect that information on my desk by morning. Have I made myself perfectly clear, Doctor Marston?"

"Crystal."

"Good, now finish your coffee and I will take you on that tour of the facility as promised."

CHAPTER TWENTY-SIX

Crisp sunlight filtered in through the glass panels of the lodge's entrance doors as Carmel mopped the floor. Cut from trees logged on the island more than thirty years ago the wood shone like warm honey, and the space had a glow that she was proud to have helped restore; she had plans for the other rooms in the lodge, and the cabins in the grounds, over the winter months.

Above the entrance, the pelt of a grey wolf stretched out across the boards. Her efforts at cleaning it had created dust clouds that made her cough and sneeze, and George laugh; the ugly thing was as stiff as a board, and the nails with which it was pinned to the wood, rusty and impossible to remove. The walls were hung with a mixture of tribal rugs collected by George on his travels during his younger days, and photographs showing images of hunters. They stood in groups, or alone, but all wore khaki jackets, and huge grins. Dead bears or deer lay at their feet. A much older photograph, faded with time, showed George squatting beside a row of wolves laid out along the ground, all shot, he had told her, by himself. The story went that when he bought the island with his first wife, it had been infested with wolves. At first, their presence hadn't bothered him, but when a pack had started to pay the property more attention than was healthy, and his boy, only a toddler then, had been dragged off one morning by a female, he took action.

The pelt on the wall was the very one that had attacked his child he told Carmel with pride. A picture of the boy, now a grown man, showed him with rifle in hand, and a wolf at his feet, and hung beside his father's.

The story had sent shivers down her spine, and each time she left the lodge to walk along the beach, she would keep to the water's edge and away from the forest that seemed to want to swallow the land. When she had agreed to move to Alaska after a brief on-line romance, her friends had begged her not to go, and her mother had been heart-broken, but Carmel had trusted that George was a good man, packed her bags and left on the flight from Bangkok with no intention of returning. George had turned out to be a good man. He wasn't perfect, but he had been true to his promise, and they had been married, and she now had a home to call her own, and a share in the business.

In the past week though, since the first wolf's howl had been heard, she had seen a different side to George. He seemed to be on edge, wearing a permanent frown, and nit-picking at the smallest thing. On two occasions he had made her cry, and she wondered if the honeymoon period was over, and this was how their life would be from now on. Any questions about how wolves had returned to the island were met with a stare of incomprehension and denial that anything had been heard, and Carmel had begun to think that perhaps she was only dreaming the noise, given that it had woken her in the night.

After the first howl had broken into her sleep, she had told George. He had become angry and told her not to be stupid, then seeing the tears well in her eyes had softened and told her that it must have been a dream. 'You'll see,' he had said, 'it's just a dream, honey. Now, don't you worry your pretty little head about it.' He had placed a large hand on the back of her head and planted a soft kiss with fat lips on her forehead. A wave of irritation washed over her at the memory; George was a good husband, and even told her that he loved her, but he treated her like a doll he was too scared to play with in case it got broken. 'Go along, now,' he'd said with a hug of her shoulder. 'There's nothing to worry about. I bet tonight you won't hear a thing'. But she had, and that was the day that the man, Chris Miller, had taken a boat loaded with supplies, and a tent, and then disappeared.

George had been edgy the following day, but it wasn't until he heard the howling for himself that his temper had really begun to fray, and he had taken to cleaning his large collection of guns and walking along the beach paying particular attention to the trees. She'd heard him arguing too, on the telephone, and also with Michel the bush pilot who was working for the lodge this year as a general handyman. He too seemed on edge, and Carmel's nerves had become stretched. The arrival of more guests helped take her mind off the men's irritability but had only served to make George's temper worse.

The lodge phone vibrated on the desk used as a reception area, and she retrieved it, hopeful that it would be a prospective guest asking for details about the lodge in readiness for next year's season. The envelope icon sat on the screen—a text message. She searched for George, then decided to read the message herself, hoping that he would realise how much effort she was making to improve her English reading skills; she wanted to be a help to the business, not a hindrance.

The text was from Sam Brewster, the blonde woman who went out hunting that morning with three other guests. Carmel had immediately warmed to Sam, who treated her as an equal, unlike her lustful husband who had appraised Carmel's figure with his eyes on their first meeting, then patted her bottom as he'd followed her up the stairs. She hadn't wanted to make a fuss, George needed happy guests, ones that would spread the word about the lodge, and perhaps come back again, but his touch had instantly sent her back to the tourist bars in Phuket where she had worked for too, too many years. *Was that it? Could he see who she really was? She was working so hard to be a respectable wife!* She clicked on the message, and read it with difficulty, sounding out each syllable, struggling to translate the alphabet to her native Thai

An hour later, with only a garbled understanding of the message, unable to find George, and with growing unease, she replaced the phone on the desk.

CHAPTER TWENTY-SEVEN

Accompanied by Kendrick and his rifle, Peter stood across from Marta in the laboratory assigned to him. Between them sat a table, and on the table, the metal box. Kendrick held the key. The door of a large and reinforced holding cage was open. The room was suffused with a medical taint of chemicals with undertones of a sulphuric and shitty odour.

"The first females proved to be infertile. We had to retrieve another one, but we've made sure this time it is a proven dam. We've managed to tag the majority of the remaining specimens at Kielder."

"You should have exterminated them, or, at the very least made them infertile."

Marta threw him a scowl. "As you know, Doctor Marston, making them infertile is the opposite of what we need. Laura's progeny will be a new species, the likes of which has never been seen on this earth before—a human hybrid. The perfect apex predator."

"The perfect apex predator, and you've brought them here, to Alaska?"

"We chose this location because it is surrounded by water – you know that they hate water - which means if we do have a security breach, then the weres are trapped on the island."

"And we're trapped with them."

"Well, yes, but we have security protocols, devised by Kendrick," she flashed him a deprecating smile, "in place for such an eventuality."

"It sounds like you've had experience, Marston."

"One of Marta's breaches."

She bridled and flashed Peter a scowl. "We've learned excellent lessons from that ... security issue."

"Are you referring to Kielder, Doctor Steward."

"Yes, Marston," she snipped.

He quickly averted his gaze, making no eye contact with Kendrick; the look on Marta's face enough to tell him he had overstepped the mark.

"As you know, Kendrick, Kielder was where we made the discovery, and carried out our first efforts at 'containing' the creatures. It was a trying time."

Peter bit his bottom lip, describing the carnage that took place at Kielder, and the annihilation of its inhabitants as a 'trying time', was the most grotesque understatement he had ever heard.

Peter couldn't help prodding. "And you say you've overcome the security issues? What about the girl who escaped last week?"

"Our protocols ensured that she was retrieved before any damage was done."

"But that's not true." Peter pushed again, remembering Rachel's story. "She wasn't captured before harm was done."

Marta's brow furrowed. "Kendrick and his team retrieved the female before she had a chance to kill or infect anyone. I would call that a success."

"True, Marta, but unfortunately, she wasn't captured before she was seen and her presence videoed, and that video sent to an investigative journalist in England." Marta's eyes widened as Peter continued. "Rachel Bonds, the young woman that also survived the plane crash, is here to find out what happened to her friend, a British celebrity who sent her the video of the werewolf tracking him before he disappeared."

Marta's frown deepened to a scowl, and her grip tightened on the corner of the desk as she leant against it. Peter put out an arm to steady her; she batted it away.

"Don't touch me!"

"Forgive me! For a moment I thought you were going to faint."

"Don't be ridiculous! This woman, the investigative journalist, where is she now?"

"At the lodge, still determined to discover exactly what was in the metal box you shipped out here. She's not convinced it's the dog that Kendrick and his team fobbed it off as being."

Marta threw a glance to Kendrick.

"But she is convinced that the lodge's owner is importing wolves illegally, for the hunters."

A smile crept onto Marta's face. "Is she now, then that is useful."

"But she was asking some rather searching questions about Titan Blane. It was stamped all across the box. Luckily, she had no internet access at the time, but now she's at the lodge …"

"It will only be a matter of time before she starts digging again. We can't let this get out. If she uploaded that video, it could spell serious trouble for the project; our sponsors expect absolute secrecy. I expect you to deal with this Kendrick."

The man's face hardened, but he nodded then left the room.

CHAPTER TWENTY-EIGHT

Pulling her hair back into a tight ponytail with a band found beside the bed in her room, Rachel took a moment to peer outside the window. The sun's brightness reflected from the waves that lapped at the cove. Two small boats sat halfway up the beach, but only one had an outboard motor, and both looked weatherworn. Further along, past the wooden steps that led from the lodge's veranda to the beach, sat a rack of kayaks and a neglected black clapboard shed with gaps between the wooden slats, and sides that leant to the right. The place looked similar to the fuzzy images on the lodge's website, but those showed buildings far less shabby.

Condensation trickled down the window, and she wiped her hand across the glass, picking up a trail of black mould on her skin. Spattered on the glass it was thicker along the edges and filled the corners, and the taint of mildew pervaded the muggy air in the bedroom. Her pillow had a distinct yellowish tinge that she suspected was sweat from numerous guests, and from the bathroom a nastier odour, seeped. Altogether, the wilderness lodge carried an air of dilapidation that was a surprise after the welcoming warmth of the entrance hall and the lounge she had first been ushered into.

As she looked out to the water, imagining Chris bobbing along on his boat, buffeted by an angry sea, she heard the hum of a heavy engine coming to a stop and then a door slamming shut. Peering through the glass in an effort to see who it was, she only managed to catch the glimpse of a black-booted male as he disappeared beneath the veranda's roof. The glass in her window shuddered as the doors below slammed shut and then the deep tones of men's voices rose from below. She recognised the bluff tones of George, the lodge's owner.

The voices were still muffled as she stood on the landing and as she made her way down the stairs, listening intently whilst attempting to seem natural, the office door opened.

"I was assured that the work being carried out was safe!"

"It is. Just keep the girl inside."

"I've got four guests out hunting today. What am I supposed to do about them?"

"We have a team already out and the Director is organising retrieval. If we come across the guests, we'll advise them to report any sightings, and come back to the lodge."

George stepped into the lobby, following the black-booted man.

"But-" George stopped mid-flow and glanced upwards, the man followed his gaze, catching sight of Rachel with a frown. Too late to hide, Rachel took another step down the stairs as though she hadn't stopped to listen to their conversation and smiled. George's frown quickly smoothed as the friendly lodge owner persona resurfaced.

Since arriving, Rachel had realised that the 'George' mentioned in Chris' video was most likely the same 'George' who owned the lodge, and she was determined to find out exactly why Chris had called him a 'liar' and just who he was in cahoots with. Taking the last step down the stairs, Rachel pushed for more evidence. "Is there a problem?"

The uniformed man stepped back through the doors and disappeared down the step at a run. Stepping past George, she watched as he jumped into a waiting truck. Each seat was taken in the vehicle and the barrels of automatic rifles were clearly visible.

"Was he from the institute?" she asked swivelling to George.

"Institute?"

"The one on the island."

"There is no institute on this island."

"There is!"

Their gaze locked.

"I own this island, miss, I'd know if there was an institute on it."

"But I heard the man-"

"A group of hunters. They lost their dog. It's not friendly so they've advised anyone out in the forest not to go near it."

"Oh, but he mentioned a 'director.'"

"It's just what they call the head honcho. He organises their trip every year."

"Oh."

"Can I get you anything miss? You're a little late for breakfast, but Carmel will be more than happy to supply some fresh pancakes. I think we've still got some wild berry compote left. She made it herself." The conversation about the dog was forgotten as he described in detail how Carmel had picked the berries herself and made them into a delicious compote. "And there's not even much sugar in them. I tell you, Miss Bonds, my Carmel is a wonder. Such a kind soul, and hard-working too."

Rachel had nodded freely, softening a little towards George; he obviously doted on his much younger wife. She desperately wanted to ask about Chris, but bit back the words and instead asked if she could have a cup of coffee, and perhaps a round of toast, if it wasn't too much trouble. George replied with "No trouble at all" and called for his wife. Rachel stepped to the door.

"No!"

Startled, she pulled her hand back as though burnt. "But I just want to get some air."

"You can't go outside."

"What?" Rachel peered through the glass. The sky was a bright blue, without threat of any storms. "Is there a storm coming, or something?"

George covered his frown with a smile. "No, it's just that we've had a few problems with bears this morning."

"Bears?"

"Yes, ma'am. There's a big old brown bear and her cubs out in the woods just behind us, and this morning they were roaming around the property. Those she-bears can be dangerous when they've got cubs with them."

"Cubs! Oh, I'd like to see those." She tried again to reach for the door.

George strode forward, closing the door as it pulled open. "Can I ask you to stay inside please, ma'am? I'll let you know when it's safe to go outside."

"But-" Rachel pulled again at the door. George held firm, then locked the door and took the key. "I can't let you go out, ma'am. It's just too dangerous."

Realising that she wouldn't be able to get out of the lodge through the front door and determined to dig a little deeper into George's activities, she relented. George sighed with relief as she took a step back, but his smile evaporated when she asked, "So, the wolves, when did you start bringing them back onto the island?"

His frown deepened and a red flush began to creep from his collar. She watched his eye movements, they flickered to the left as he opened his mouth, a sure sign he was about to lie. "Wolves? There ain't no wolves on Volkolak."

"No? But I thought I heard them—up in the forest."

"That's just the dog that feller was talking about."

"Oh, but I thought I heard more than one."

Maintaining his composure though she could see that he was struggling, he replied, "There ain't no wolves on Volkolak! See that pelt up there," he pointed to the mangey grey pelt hanging above the door. "That there is the female wolf that tried to kill my son. After that, I made sure every damn wolf on this island was put to rest. There ain't no wolves on Volkolak! And if there are, they won't be alive for long."

With the man's detestation of wolves clear, Rachel dropped her questioning. If there were wolves on Volkolak, which now seemed unlikely, then George had nothing to do with it. Perhaps he was telling the truth, and it was just a dog that was making the racket.

A flush had risen to George's face, and he suddenly deflated as though popped. "I'm sorry, miss. I didn't mean to shout; it's just that when that she-wolf got my boy ..."

"I understand. I'm sorry that I brought it back to your memory."

"That's okay, miss. I've been thinking on it a while these past days."

"Oh?" she waited for him to continue, but after a moment of staring at her, his mouth slightly open, he snapped it shut, and reached for the mobile on the desk. In the next moment, a boat landed at speed on the beach, saving him from the embarrassment of ending their conversation with an excuse.

On the beach, the boat's driver jumped ashore, then ran towards the lodge, obviously in a state of excitement. George pushed past Rachel, unlocking, then throwing open the doors.

"Michel!" he called to the running man. "What is it?"

"A body!"

"A body?"

He clambered up the steps. "Yes, a body. I dragged it out of the water about an hour ago. I've called the Coast Guard."

"Where? Where's the body?"

"In the boat." He gestured back down the beach with his thumb.

"You brought it back here?"

"Well, what the hell else was I supposed to do? Ain't no one else for miles around."

"Sure, but … hell! Let me see."

George ran down the steps, his heavy weight making the old boards bow, and despite his warning to stay inside, Rachel followed. The crisp Alaskan wind bit at her neck, and she shivered, wrapping the fleece a little tighter, pulling the sleeves over her hands, and ran to keep pace with George.

"I told you to stay inside."

She ignored him and continued to the boat. "Who is it?"

"How would I know?"

The younger man jogged beside her, grabbing her arm to slow her as they drew near the boat. "It's not a pretty sight, ma'am."

"I can stomach it," she replied. "I want to see who it is. It might be-" her words were lost as a pair of dulled blue eyes stared from the bottom of the boat. Without colour, the man's dead-white skin was a sharp contrast to his dark hair and beard. "Jean-Luc!" she whispered, then louder, "It's the man with the wolf ... from the aeroplane. He's French."

"Aye, and he's dead too. And what's this about a wolf?"

"He had a box. There was something alive in it. It howled, so I know it was a wolf. That's how I know you're importing illegal wolves onto the island, which is why I know that the hunters who went up to Eagle Point this morning weren't hunting bear."

She shrivelled at the look of contempt on George's face.

"That's a lie!"

She grew bold, watching each nuance of reaction. "Well, then, it was meant for the Institute."

He paused, his contempt deepening, and replied with a stony, "There ain't no institute on Volkolak. Christ, woman! We've been over this."

"There is."

"There ain't."

"Yes ... there is!"

"I've called the Coast Guard," Michel butted in. "They've confirmed they'll retrieve the body."

With terse irritation, George said, "Cover him over; he can stay here until they arrive."

"Sure, but-"

George waved a dismissive hand then strode back up the beach, threw open the lodge doors, and disappeared.

Rachel turned her attention to Jean-Luc laying in the bottom of the boat. "I've never seen a dead body before. He kind of didn't look dead, apart from his eyes, if you look at them you can tell," she rambled.

"It's the water—it's so cold it keeps them looking fresh, unless the fish start taking a bite."

As Rachel scanned Jean-Luc's corpse with fascination, Michel dragged a tarpaulin from the one of the other boats. He unfolded it with Rachel's help, and together they placed it over Jean-Luc's body "That'll keep the sun off him, and the flies."

"What about the bears?"

Michel's eyes locked to hers, held them for a second longer than necessary, and then he replied, "Bears too, at least until the Coast Guard get here."

The body covered, and walking back to the lodge with Michel, Rachel experienced a frisson of attraction she hadn't felt since she'd first laid eyes on her second to last boyfriend Alistair Lawton. They'd met at a friend's birthday party held at the local rugby team's clubhouse. He'd been chatting with a group of large men; all rugby players they had the strong shoulders, wide backs, and muscular thighs that really got Rachel going. Alistair had been the tallest, and her knees had trembled as their eyes met across the bar and he'd held her gaze before holding up his pint in a silent 'cheers'. They'd bumped into each other an hour later outside the toilets, struck up a conversation, and she'd taken him home. They'd made passionate love until the early hours and then every night for the next month, spent whole weekends together, only leaving the bedroom to shower or eat, until he'd grown bored, stopped answering her texts, and then married a slimmer, blonder, younger woman six months later. Looking across at Michel now, he had the same broad shoulders, slim waist and strong thighs that Alistair had, but with the added advantage of having all his own teeth. She hovered as they stood in the entrance.

"Do you fancy a coffee?"

CHAPTER TWENTY-NINE

Crouched on the crest of the rock, Katarina squatting beside him, Max waited. The disembowelled body of the man killed earlier in the day lay close to the cave's entrance, its entrails intact, a first feed for the woman placed by its side. Max watched in fascination as she jerked, her body changing with each spasm. Further from their den, still slumped in the clearing where he had found him with his arms around the woman, lay the second man. Reeking of disease, Max had silenced his scream with a single swipe that tore out his throat and left his poisoned blood to sink into the earth.

The older man was for tearing, and biting, and swallowing. Max had torn out his stomach, throwing it into the ferns, then clawed hands had reached deep inside, the blubber a thick white edge along the tear. Organs encased in fat, he had eaten his liver first, then the kidneys, leaving the heart for Katarina, growling a warning as she reached for the intestines, snapping his jaws to make her obey.

At the cave's entrance, the second female jerked, her muscles in spasm as the poison from his bite seeped into every cell, metamorphosing, tearing at muscles, breaking fibres, renewing cells. Muscles grew, and cartilage stretched, morphing into the image of himself. Fangs elongated; sharp incisors that would rip and tear. Legs strengthened, calves bulked, thighs of carved alabaster became shaded with hair, the mound of her sex bulged, the damson bud disappearing beneath curling hair. He jumped from the rock as she grew still, her transformation complete, and waited for her to wake when he would claim her.

Katarina followed, curling an arm around his thigh, stroking the soft place between his legs. The stink of her pussy rose to his nostrils, sweet and ripe, and so, so fucking delicious. He snickered. Fire already lit between his legs, he sunk long talons into her hair, forced her to her knees, and took her as she howled with pleasure.

When second female woke, she scrambled to the cave's entrance then crawled inside. Max followed.

CHAPTER THIRTY

Fire crackled in the hearth, the heat pushing back the odour of mildew and fusty fabric that pervaded the lodge, and Rachel sat across from Michel, glass of wine in hand, holding herself in a position she hoped hid her overly generous midriff. She and Michel had hit it off, and he was smiling as he took a sip of his beer. George eyed them from behind the bar as he polished a glass for the fourth time.

"He's watching us," Rachel said in hushed tones.

Michel glanced over at George.

"Don't look, he'll know we're talking about him then!"

"George loves to gossip," Michel smiled from behind his glass. "He'll be going back into the kitchen to tell Carmel all about it."

"There's nothing to tell."

Michel raised a brow. "Then why don't we give them something to talk about?" His tone was conspiratorial, his smile broad.

"Such as?"

"Well, this for a start." He leant over until she could smell the wine on his breath and placed warm lips on hers. She made a small gasp at his touch as tingles shot between her legs. He sat back in his seat, understanding the effect of his kiss. George held the glass mid-air, his mouth ajar. Rachel giggled. "Won't you get into trouble?"

"It's the end of the season. I'm leaving here tomorrow. What can he do? If he wants me to come back, then …"

"Tomorrow?"

"Yep. This is just my summer job. I go back to Kodiak during the winter and teach kids to swim."

Rachel bit back her disappointment. She had only known Michel for a few hours, but there was familiarity and ease in their time spent together. "Well, that sounds great." *Dumb!* They sat in silence, Rachel enjoying the heat and warm glow emanating from the log burner before her mind settled on the reason she had travelled to the island. Taking a chance to dig for information, she said, "I came here to find out what happened to my friend, but so far nothing."

"Chris? The guy who drowned?"

"Yes! Did you know him?"

"Sure, he was here for a few days before he went camping on the other side of the island. I gave him a few pointers on survival, you know, how to set up camp and get a fire going. He'd watched a few tutorials, but if you've never been camping before, watching a few *YouTube* tutorials just won't cut it."

"Do you think he drowned then?"

"I guess so. What else?"

"Well, something happened to him on the beach. He sent me a video, he was being stalked by … something … some strangely deformed … well, it looked like a woman, but she was so covered in hair and had enormous teeth."

"Sounds like George's ex-wife!" Michel laughed. George picked up on the mention of his name and threw a slitted glance to the pair.

"He heard you!" Rachel whispered with a laugh.

"Okay, I'll be quiet. So, you think this hairy woman attacked him?"

"No, but he was scared, and he said …" she checked over to George who now had his back turned to them and then disappeared into the kitchen, "he said in his video that George was a liar, and they were all in on it."

"In on what?"

"I don't know. I thought perhaps he was smuggling in some rare animals, or wolves."

Michel swallowed.

"What? What is it?"

He leant forward, all humour gone, his eyes sharing a truth. "Well, since you mentioned wolves, I have heard howling in the forest …"

"Really?"

His eyes widened, and he nodded an affirmative.

"So, you think there are wolves here? George said there weren't any, but I knew it! I knew there-"

Michel burst out laughing. "Of course there are no wolves. There's just a pack of dogs that's gone wild. We had a couple of dogs go missing a few years ago, some pedigree Labradors a couple of hunters brought to the lodge. No one ever found them, and now this howling's started, I think they've got their own pack of little pups and grand pups out there."

"That's not what George-"

"Listen, Rachey babe, there aren't any wolves on this island. George hates them. If there were, he'd have killed them all already, and hung up their pelts to prove it."

Disappointed that he hadn't agreed with her about the wolves, but even more disappointed that he would be leaving tomorrow, she stroked his knee, eyeing him from behind her glass as she took another sip of wine. He returned her touch by stroking her thigh then refilled her glass. After another hour of talking beside the log burner, Rachel was a third of the way through her second bottle when Michel took her hand and led her upstairs to the bedroom.

An hour later, and the sex had been ... good, although Rachel had had to do much of the work, and Michel's ardour had quickly disappeared as soon as his own needs had been met. With a promise of more later, she lay with a deep and unsatisfied ache that she hoped Michel would help relieve at some point during the night. She didn't feel that she knew him well enough to ask for him to 'finish' the job; it would be impolite to demand.

As the wind howled outside, her thoughts turned back to George and the lodge, and she decided to share her suspicions. "This place," she gestured to the faded wallpaper and threadbare carpet, dim in the bedside light, "it looks shabby, like it's been neglected."

"Yeah, times have been tough for George and Casey."

"Casey?"

"George's ex-wife. She left during last season. Carmel is his new wife. She was here when I arrived. I guess he got married in the spring or something."

"I hate to ask, but do you think she's a mail-order bride?"

Michel pressed his lips together, curling them over his teeth as he suppressed a laugh. "Yes, I do. It's so obvious, isn't it. I mean, where did he meet her? He hardly ever goes off the island, and when he does, it's only for supplies in Kodiak. He's always on the internet though."

"I bet he bought her. And I bet he bought her at the same time as he bought that new boat, and his car, and ... has he got a new laptop recently? That one in his office is a top of the range MacBook Pro, they cost around two thousand dollars."

Michel whistled. "Expensive."

"It is, and so are the surveillance cameras that have been set up, yet this place is falling down around his ears."

"So, what're you saying? That George has come into some money recently?"

"Yes, that's exactly what I'm saying, and it has something to do with Chris' disappearance."

Michel frowned. "How do you figure that out? Perhaps he won the lottery and just hasn't had time to start doing this place up? Carmel has done wonders downstairs."

"Sure, but I think it's more likely that he's done some deal, maybe agreed to something illegal. That's why Chris died, because he found out. The institute-"

"Ah, it's all so far-fetched, Rachel. Your friend Chris was an amateur adventurer. He just didn't have the skills to survive." She remembered the box of food left in the tent and the other 'luxury' goods that any serious survivalist would never have brought along. "Alaska is an unforgiving place. The weather can turn within minutes and on the day that Chris disappeared, a storm blew in no one with any sense would have been out in. I warned him, Rachel, I told him that there was a storm coming, but he wouldn't listen to me. He was on skid row, he told me, and going out into the wilds and surviving the harsh weather would help get his career back on track. Don't ask me how that works, but he was certain it would. Desperation made him rash, and inexperience mixed with desperation is a dangerous combination, and I think that's what killed Chris. There was no reasoning with him, even George advised him against it, but to be honest, none of us realised just how harsh the storm would be."

"I don't think he would have gone onto the water if it hadn't been for that creature on the beach. It tracked him through the woods and scared him into the boat. But whatever it was, it wasn't like anything I've seen before. At first, I thought it was a hoax, but the prosthetics were too good not to be real. I'm still not sure what I saw, none of it adds up. It was standing on two legs, but had this huge jaw and massive teeth, and it was covered in hair."

"Sounds like a bear to me. A bear on the attack will stand on two legs."

"Sure, but it wasn't hairy enough to be a bear."

"Could have had mange? Some of the bears had it last year."

Embarrassment slid over Rachel. Michel was absolutely right. In her mind's eye, the creature standing on two legs could have been a bear, the shot was unclear after all. Her brain befuddled with alcohol, her memory merged with this new image, and she became unsure. "Damn! I wish I had the video to show you. I'm sure it wasn't a bear, well, I was sure, but now that you've explained it like that ..."

"It could be?"

"Yes, I guess." In her mind the image of the hairy woman was now a mangey bear. "You're probably right."

"So perhaps ... your friend just had a very unfortunate accident?"

"I guess."

A finger trailed around her nipple. "And maybe, Chris being so desperate, capitalised on its appearance, and exaggerated the story in his video. He would have been terrified, bears are dangerous, and he had no experience, but adding the 'George' factor just made it all so much more intriguing?"

Rachel's thinking became unclear, confused by Michel's reasoning as he stroked her tingling flesh. Increasingly aroused, she lay back on the pillow. In the distance a howl cut through the night. She sat up, tingling flesh forgotten. "But that," she said jabbing a finger towards the window, "is not something I'm imagining."

Michel sat up. "It is not. It's that dog they're looking for." He laughed, pulled at her shoulder, then pressed it back to the bed, and slid his leg between hers.

"The institute-"

"There isn't an institute."

"There is ..." Michel kissed her throat. "Peter mentioned it ... when we were stranded ..." His kissed lower, across her chest, and then to her belly. *Here it was ... at last.*

"Nope, there's no institute on the island, Rachel." He kissed the sensitive skin below her navel, then flicked at her bud with his tongue. *Yes! He **was** going to be a gentleman.* He raised his head. "I'm a bush pilot, I've seen the entire island from the air, and if there was an institute here, I would have seen it." Michel straddled Rachel's hips.

"But the men in black uniform?"

Michel scooted up to her chest. "Hunters."

Rachel's hope weakened. "They said they were Special Ops."

Michel's excitement was obvious. "Maybe the institute is off-shore then?"

His shadow fell across Rachel's face – *Her hope was lost. He was not going to be a gentleman* - and pushed his hips forward.

"Offshore? But they took Peter, and there was something in-" Rachel's flow of words became garbled as Michel filled her mouth.

CHAPTER THIRTY-ONE

Peter woke, disorientated and unsure of where he was. It took a moment for realisation to hit then, with a sinking in his belly, he took his glasses from the bedside table, and checked the clock; three-fifteen am. He flopped back on his pillow, knowing that sleep would elude him. The minutes passed as he stared at the ceiling, his eyes adjusting to the light, unease suffusing every cell of his body. Closing his eyes, he was taunted once more by images of Laura: her face smiling at him as she turned from the altar, newlywed, the joy in her eyes unmistakable as she walked out of the church, her arm hooked with Max's, Laura dressed in evening finery at another awards ceremony, Max on the stage receiving his award for his breakthroughs in stem cell therapies. The memories flashed and pulsed, pushing at each other: Max taking his first steps into Kielder Institute, Max's face drained, and ridden with guilt as Peter opened the door to Marta bending over him, her shirt open, her breasts pushed to his shoulder, Laura offering her point of view in one of his seminars, Laura sitting across from him in Starbucks showing him her engagement ring, Max's face contorted in pain as his body succumbed to the virus. The memories jostled and pushed, refusing to fade. *Laura ... Laura ... Laura. Oh, sweet Jesus, save me!* Her contorted face, unconscious in a drug induced sleep, but still, gut-wrenchingly, recognisable, covered in dark hair that swept from her temple to her cheeks to her chin, and the elongated jaw, incisors grown sharp, ready to jump from the box, and bite down into his flesh, tearing into muscle and bone the moment she woke. He shuddered, turned in his bed, opened his eyes, then sat.

He had to see her.

The walk to the laboratory was surprisingly easy and comfortable. The doors swung open at the touch of the identity card that had been supplied during the afternoon, and the corridors were lit with a low light, and the air was warm. He flashed the card at the locked laboratory door; a light flashed green, and he was inside. It was not quite the state-of-the-art facility Marta had promised, but it was functional, warm, and secure; a place he could easily work in although every fibre of his being wanted to resist the temptation to delve deeper into the project. It was grotesque, unethical, that was all true, but it was also utterly fascinating, and Marta was right, they were pushing the boundaries of what was scientifically possible, and that, Peter realised, was a scientific aphrodisiac, and made the project 'sexy' as some of his crasser colleagues would say.

He stepped inside, pushing the door to, and the overhead lights flooded the laboratory with light. Unlike the corridors with their warm glow, this one was stark white, illuminating every corner of the space.

Laura remained in the box at the centre of the table. He had wanted to place her in the larger cage but keeping her beneath consciousness made it far easier to take her temperature and bloods and enabled him to gauge her menstrual cycle. From the information he had, she would be ovulating in another seven days. However, that was according to the human female's cycle, and Laura was no longer purely human. He made a note to research the menstrual cycle of dogs and wolves, both domestic, and wild, and turned with a startled yelp as the door opened.

"Sorry, Doctor Marston, but I saw that the light was on ..." Kendrick, the soldier from Marta's office, and the one who had rescued him from the beach, stood in the doorway, fully dressed. Peter fidgeted with the cord of his dressing gown.

"I needed to take some more observations," he lied.

"I couldn't sleep," Kendrick returned.

"Me too," Peter admitted with relief; he was not the only one struggling. He returned to Laura in the box, Kendrick joined him. Both men stared down at the comatose woman. As Peter reached in, Kendrick drew his breath. "It's perfectly alright, she is absolutely harmless in this state. I have given her a large dose of a sedative." His fingers brushed long chestnut hair away from her cheek. Gold glinted at her ear. He fingered the lobe.

"An earring?"

"Yes," Peter replied, stroking a thumb over the gold earring. It dangled by a single link from a diamond stud. "It's a honeypot. Max used to call her his little bee because she made everything so sweet. They were a birthday gift from him the day after they married."

"You were that close?"

"Yes, I taught her at university, and obviously worked with Max. They were good friends."

"Must be tough ... seeing her like this."

"It is. I've been working on a cure, but my efforts have been severely limited as I've had so little access to materials and information, but now that I'm here ..."

"I don't think Doctor Steward is interested in a cure."

Peter stroked the unconscious face. "No, she's not."

"Obviously you know that the plan is to breed them."

Peter nodded.

"And implant some device in the embryos, in-vitro. Katarina told me, though she wasn't supposed to, that Doctor Steward is working towards creating some sort of dog soldier. Katarina was having real trouble with the whole project and talking about handing in her notice before ... before she was killed."

"She may not be dead."

"No, but she might as well be."

Peter noticed the emotion in Kendrick's face and wondered just how close he had become to Katarina.

"It's like something out of a sci-fi film – fucking fucked up – they'll be half bot-half man-half wolf."

"That would be a third man, third wolf, third bot."

"Whatever, it's still screwed up. It's all fantasy though; I can't see it ever really becoming a reality. You know, Marston ... I've seen some shit in my life, but this ... this has got to be the most disturbing."

Peter nodded, still staring down at Laura's hair-covered face, then asked, "So why are you here? Why are you working on this project?"

Kendrick stared straight into Peter's eyes. "I get to be in charge. And the pay's good." There was no sense of shame, or struggle with morality in his gaze, and Peter, remembering his conversation with Marta and how the promise of publication in respected journals, and the temptation of a professorship, along with the massively increased salary, had been the driving force that broke down his own defences, realised, to his shame, that he and Kendrick were really no different; both had sold humanity out to self-interest.

CHAPTER THIRTY-TWO

The scent of her ... the One ... Laura .... the most beloved ... was lost among the stench of decay and, mouth-watering, blood-full life that rose through the forest, and Max's nose rose to find it, the pain of grief riding him in waves. She was locked away with *them*, the Screamers, the men that shot pain, and broke bones, destroyed flesh. Anger burned in his belly, and he threw back his head and screamed his rage. He would take her from them, tear their flesh from their bones, rip their veins ... he snickered ... spray their blood. Another howl, a frenzy of anger that suffused each particle of his flesh. Her name repeated: *Laura ... Laura ... Laura.*

Behind him the Red One crouched, tearing at the flesh of the man ... fat man ... Max cackled at the memory, of how his chin had disappeared into his neck as he'd screamed, the scream cut short as claws had gouged through his neck, ripping it apart, the blood spraying high into the trees. The Red One had dragged the fat man back to the cave, an arm missing where She, the Katarina, had ripped it from its socket. Max cackled. He would rip them, rip their arms, and their legs, stop their screams with teeth clamped around their open jaws, crunching down on bone until it splintered. He would take back his Laura ... the most beloved ... Blessed be the One. He tore at his own flesh as rage whirled, scratching talons along his chest. Blood trickled through dark hair as his frustration turned in on himself. The blood oozed, slowed, then stopped, the torn flesh mended.

The stench of their fear, the men with his Laura, carried on the breeze through the forest. It was stronger now, but Max waited. Soon they would be ready, but the time was yet to come.

He licked at the wind; it carried the taint of others, their sweat, and their sweet perfume, mingled with the stench of sour decay. He growled. The Red One rose from his crouch, jabbering as he sniffed at the air. Katarina cackled. The second female, the Small Dark One, rose and sprinted to his side, crouching beside his leg. Katarina clawed at her, pushing her away. Bared teeth snapped, and Max snarled a warning. Cowed, the females stood at his side, the smaller one yapping her excitement. Max jumped from the rock, down to the earth, and disappeared with a sprint into the forest, excited for the hunt. They followed as he darted between the trees, at his shoulders, falling behind, passing between the trunks, jumping worming roots, never faltering as he picked up his pace, arms sliding to and fro in a steady rhythm, legs powerful and pumping without fatigue. Excited yaps filled his ears, and he snickered, a small cackle at the joy to come; the gnashing, and biting, and tearing, the soft flesh parting between his jaws, the delicious meat, the hot blood that would trickle down his throat.

As the trees thinned, he slowed, and listened to the sound of the sea as it lapped its waves against the stony beach. The women stood at his shoulder. The second woman sniffed at the air, the stench of rotting was rich, and began to follow its trail. He allowed her to leave the group but watched her progress.

She skirted the building, ignoring the doors that would take her to the Screamers, and followed a scent Max had already noticed; beyond the house and its living, breathing prey ... their food, their sustenance, their drink and their meat – thank you lord for what we are about to receive - Max snickered - was the stench of death, of rotting offal and faeces, and fish. He allowed her to follow the scent but turned his own attention to the house.

The building below was dark, no light inside, but higher up a light shone as a hazy rectangle, brighter where the fabric was parted. The voices behind were muffled, a man and a woman. Below the window was a box; its surface chilled his feet as he jumped to it. Closer, only feet from the window and his prey ... *Oh, thank you Lord, you are my bread, you are my wine*. He muffled a small cackle, licking his lips as his mouth watered at the thought of sinking his teeth into warm, moist, screaming flesh ... *Lord, Thou art my shepherd* ... The noises inside were familiar; a rhythmic banging and creaking, the woman moaned her pleasure, the man grunted his. Excited, Max grasped the pipe that ran at a diagonal across the wall, pulling himself up to the window - *I trust in you, to provide* - another snicker and saliva drooled between bone-white and pointed teeth. The noise of their rutting grew, and he drew level with the window, long talons sinking into the wooden frame, the ache at his groin sadistic and twisting, his need not to be ignored.

Muscular arms pulled him up and he watched as the man thrust, the woman, blonde hair spread over the pillow, eyes closed, mouth open, throat exposed, breasts full and bared to the room. Max licked his lips, the need to fornicate as strong as his need to sink his teeth into her throat and drink from her life blood. The male was strong; broad shoulders were carved with muscles, arms wormed with throbbing, pulsing blood as he rutted, his buttocks twin mounds. Max watched with fascination as the man pulled back, the muscles of his back rippling, the wings of a tattooed eagle flapping with each thrust into soft flesh. Strong, lean, and muscular. Max gnashed his teeth; the man would be his, one of them, to follow where Max led ... *thank you Lord, those who believe shall not go without* ... a low snicker. He would follow where Max led, to tear the One from the men with fire. Below him the second female yelped. Leaving the rutting male and his mate until later, he jumped to the ground and ran to Katarina and The Red One beside the boat. The Small Dark One yelped again.

A deep and throaty growl rose to a roar and then a lumbering and massive form lowered its head and charged. The Small Dark One ran at the bear, but it slapped her to the ground with one swipe of its massive paw. She writhed as the bear reared to its full height and screamed as its claws sliced into her chest.

The bear's roar filled Max's ears, and the stench of its breath filled his nose. It lumbered towards The Red One and Katarina. Hackles raised, they backed away from the boat where Katarina had pulled off the cover. The heavy stench of death and rotting flesh rose to mingle with the dank odour of the bear. Max sprinted forward, placing himself between Katarina and the bear. The Small Dark One yowled. The Red One snapped its jaws.

The bear reared again, towering above Max.

The stench of decay clung to the bear, the corpse's torn white flesh hung from its jaws. Max raised to his full height, lips pulled back in a snarling growl. The bear landed with a thud, growled, then reared on its back legs again. Katarina yowled, jumping, skittering, and gnashing her jaws. In the next second, the bear threw itself forward, sharp claws swiping through the air, ripping through Max's torso. The bear's massive weight threw Max to the ground. It followed its advantage with a pounce, landing both paws on Max's shoulders; huge jaws clamping around Max's jaw, ripping at his cheeks, spiking through to his oesophagus.

Suffocating under the heavy weight now on his chest, he hauled for breath through a punctured windpipe. Releasing Max's head, the bear slashed at his torso, gouging his ribs, and cutting at his innards, puncturing his lungs. An agony of pain ripped through Max, but with one desperate swipe, he plunged sharp talons down the centre of the bear's chest, slicing through fur and skin, tearing the fabric of its body from its sternum to its navel and then, as the bear released its grip around his neck, to its ball sack. With a squealing grunt, the bear swayed, pulled back, then dropped to the ground, its innards bulging through the opening, held back only by the membrane that covered them. Behind, the females jostled and yipped, jumping forward to stab at the bear with their talons. The Red One jumped to the bear, tearing at its throat.

Blood seeping from his wounds, Max retreated to the side of the boat. The females rushed to the bear, pulling at its innards. As the membrane broke, the stomach fell to the beach, sliding and spreading with an undulating roll over the stones. The bear jerked with a spasm, its eyes reflecting the moon as it stared. It grunted, panting as the females snapped and snarled, pinching at each other, one pulling the other from its body. The

Red One reached into the cavity, and pulled out the liver, the females grabbed and grasped for its kidneys.

As the bear took its final breath, and the females cackled and snickered, digging and pushing, and biting and tearing, Max sank against the side of the boat. The stench of the man inside, his face destroyed by the bear's teeth, his side torn to reveal festering organs, rose to mingle with the particles of Max's own blood as it ran from his wounded throat through the hairs on his shoulders and chest, to drip onto the stony beach. The pain was an agony, but as the minutes passed, the wounds began to heal. The puncture hole in his lung closed, the fractured ribs knitted, and the gaping hole in his throat, and the gouges in his cheek where the bear's claw had scored the jawbone, sealed.

The others fed, and as the Small Dark One grasped for the heart, Katarina slapped her hand away, tore the organ from the cavity, and presented it to Max. He bit into the flesh, the bear's blood joining his own as it slid down his throat. At the house, lights appeared at the high windows and then the lower rooms brightened, but the house remained silent, and the doors closed, and then the building disappeared as an intense white light flooded the beach.

The bear's heart, half-eaten in his hand, Max limped to the others, grunted at them to follow, then led them through the woods, and back to the cave.

CHAPTER THIRTY-THREE

With Michel's naked hips pressed up against her buttocks, Rachel stared out onto the beach from behind the gap in the bedroom curtains. As the yowls, and screaming growl erupted, the hairs on her scalp crept in a painful contraction and she shivered.

"There's someone on the beach! I can see them." Peering closer to the window, her breath steaming the pane, she wiped away the mist. "There's more than one, I'm sure of it."

"I can't see anyone. The cover has come off the boat though." Michel's voice held a note of dread. "I knew we should have tied it down."

"The cover? The one over Jean-Luc?"

"Yes. I just hauled it across. I meant to go out and secure it later, but ..." he stared through the glass, "someone distracted me."

Rachel riled. "So it's my fault!"

"Hey, don't get on your high horse."

"But someone's been murdered!"

"How. He's already dead." Hands cupped Rachel's breasts, and Michel nuzzled into her neck. "Do you know what I think has happened?" he asked between soft kisses at the nape of her neck.

Rachel cast his reflection in the window a glance, and then turned her attention back to the moonlit beach. There were too many shadows to see clearly. "No, well, I guess I do, but go ahead."

"Well, I think a bear came sniffing around Jean-Luc."

Rachel pulled a grimace, wrinkling her nose as though that would stop her hearing the next part of his explanation.

"And it started to eat him, and then another came along, and before you know it, it's picnic time for Mr Fuzzy and his friend."

"God, that is a disgusting thought. And, Mr Fuzzy?"

"Yeah, just what I used to call my bear."

"You had a bear?"

"Sure, didn't you? I used to sleep with mine."

"Sleep with your bear?"

"Yeah, but ... but not in a weird way."

Realisation dawned. "Do you mean a ... stuffed bear."

"Yes, of course! What? You thought I meant a real-life bear? Who in their right mind would sleep with a real bear? They may look cute and all, but they're goddamned dangerous!"

A flush rose to Rachel's cheeks. "We should go and take a look."

"Nope! No one in their right mind goes out in the dark to track down a bear." Michel pressed up behind her and her attention wavered as his excitement became obvious. Her body responded with a deep ache that still hadn't been satisfied and all thoughts of the disturbance outside, and the hideous wails, screams, and growls, disappeared. Jean-Luc was dead anyway, and the Coast Guard would be collecting what was left of him tomorrow. She twisted to face Michel and his excitement, and they fell together on the bed, devouring each other with open mouths.

FROM THE SAFETY OF the veranda, George had flooded the beach with light and caught a glimpse of something hobbling towards the forest. Back in the office, he picked up the phone and dialled the number for the Institute's director. The phone cut to dead after the third ring. "Goddamned liars!" Tomorrow he would be paying the Institute a visit.

CHAPTER THIRTY-FOUR

As sunlight filtered in through Rachel's window, and Max curled behind Katarina on their bed of ferns deep in the cave, the air just west of Volkolak filled with the distinctive chop, chop of the US Coast Guard's MH60 Jayhawk helicopter.

The journey out of Air Station Kodiak had been uneventful, but as the helicopter approached the wilderness lodge, and the wide expanse of stony beach that curved along its front, the brow of US Coast Guard, Joshua Bartholomew wrinkled with a deep frown as he attempted to make sense of the sight on the beach. Two boats sat high on the pebbles, one had an outboard engine, the other was half-covered with a flapping piece of blue tarpaulin. Both appeared to have been neglected for some considerable time.

A corner of the blue tarp flapped like a dying fish as the wind caught it. The area around the boat was red. As the helicopter hovered to land, the view became clearer. Blood and gore were sprayed around the boat and smeared down its side. A trail of blood led away from the beach and into the trees, passing what could only be a very large bear laying stretched out on its side. Surrounded by pools of blood, its belly was concave, and something straggled from its belly, but before he could register what it was, the blue tarp flapped open revealing its cargo, the body of a man, half-eaten.

"Holy ... what has happened here?"

"Straight out of a horror flick!"

"Carnage! Just carnage!"

"Looks like a bear got to our guy before we did!"

Five minutes later, Joshua, and his crew, were inspecting the remains of the bear, and the drowned man they were charged with collecting.

"Definitely don't need to medevac this one!"

"You don't say!" Boyd laughed.

"He is one hell of a mess!"

"Is it our guy?"

"I think so. Where's the lodge's owner?"

"Wade has gone up to the lodge to find him."

"I guess someone didn't think to tie this sucker down," Joshua said reaching for the blue tarp. "There's no evidence that it has been slashed to gain entry. The bear just pulled it off."

"Easy pickings!"

"Ughh!"

"The bear's dead though. I guess the owner took a dislike to it chowing down on Mister Macron."

Joshua moved from the boat and focused instead on the bear's mutilated body with relief; at least it was just an animal, seeing a man's flesh torn, even if he was already dead, and perhaps because he was already dead, was too hard to stomach. His belly gave a queasy roll, and he gagged back the retch that was twisting at his gut. The stench was abominable.

"Stinks like it shit itself."

"I think it did!" He agreed, "but I don't think that the owner had anything to do with its death. Look at the state it's in! Its intestines are pulled out from its belly. See how the belly sags?"

"Yeah?"

"Well, I've seen that before."

"Yeah?"

"It's been disembowelled. It looks just like the cows my Gramps slaughters. He hangs 'em up, slits their bellies, then lets the innards just fall out. The belly's empty then, just like this bear."

"Well ... then where are they? A bear this size's gotta have a whole lot of intestines in there, plus internal organs. If-"

"Looks like someone took them down the beach."

Joshua followed the man's pointing arm to a smeared trail of blood that snaked towards the forest.

"That's not right! Who in their right mind would take the intestines out and cart them down the beach?"

"I don't think it is a who, more of a what."

"What the hell kind of animal would do that?"

Joshua continued to follow the trail. Ahead of him, Craig turned and shouted, "Looks like we've got some footprints here too."

"What kind of animal?"

"Well ..." he squatted to inspect the marks. "You'd best take a look for yourself."

Stepping beside Craig, he crouched beside a clear footprint that extended across two flat stones. The heel was rounded and narrow, the foot long and widening towards the toes. The flat rock stopped where the toes should be, and the small stones beneath were smeared with blood. "They're human, right?"

"Well ... they do look human."

Boyd joined them. "I think you're right."

"What the hell has gone on here?"

"We need to talk to the owner."

Half an hour later, Joshua made preparations to move what remained of Jean-Luc Macron whilst Kyla, the only female member of their crew, photographed the scene. George Wilson, the lodge's owner had finally arrived. Out of breath, and with his face flushed red, he carried himself with a defensive air.

"It's one hell of a mess."

"It sure is. What happened here, Mister Wilson?"

"Bear! What else?"

"Well ... there are human footprints around the boat, bloody footprints that lead into the forest."

A flicker of fear crossed George's face as he glanced at the forest. "That can't be right. I've told my guests to stay inside, and there's only me and Carmel ..." his voice trailed off.

"And?" Joshua prompted.

"And nothing. Damned bears! I need me some more hunters to get their numbers down. I'm going to have to call in the Department to get them culled otherwise. Right now, I'd appreciate it if you could get Mister Macron off of my island. My guests are starting to get a little antsy."

"Well, the State Medical Examiner-"

"I ain't waiting for no Medical Examiner! That body is stinking this place up, making it dangerous around here. I don't have nowhere suitable to keep it."

"I was going to say the State Medical Examiner's Officer, back in Anchorage, will want a full report. We'll have to take photographs, make notes ..."

"But the guy died at sea!"

"Sure, but we still need to make our report. And then we can bag him up."

"And how long's that gonna take?"

"As long as it does."

CHAPTER THIRTY-FIVE

As Kyla focused down on the face of Jean-Luc, and George continued to bluster about the bear and its stinking carcass, Rachel opened her eyes to light flooding in through the curtains left parted as she'd looked onto the beach last night. Throwing off the bedcovers, she moved to the window to get a clear view of the boat in daylight. She noticed the uniformed men first, and then the red mess around the boat. She pulled the curtain at an angle across her naked body and stared with disbelief at the carnage.

"Michel!"

Michel made no reply, and she realised that she was alone. "Damn!" He had left her without saying goodbye, and there wasn't even a note on her pillow. Disappointment enveloped her. "Bloody men!"

Head thumping from lack of sleep - Michel had just kept going! - and too much wine, she made her way to the bathroom. The scent of Michel, and their lovemaking, still clung to her and she took a final deep breath of the odour before taking a hot shower and soaping every inch of her body. Teeth brushed with the complimentary toothpaste and brush Carmel had supplied, she pulled on yesterday's jeans, top, and fleece, and made a mental note to swallow her embarrassment and ask Carmel if she had any spare underwear—hopeful that some knickers had been left behind by previous guests.

Relieved to feel fresh, and now in full control of her faculties, she took the complimentary pad and pencil from the bedside table, and made her way to the dining room, starving after her night of passion, and hunger induced by lack of sleep. The lodge was silent, and even when she sat at the table set with breakfast cutlery, no one appeared to take her order. She sat and made notes as she waited: the facts she knew, what she suspected, and a list of suspects and or witnesses. Five more minutes passed and, wondering if she had somehow misunderstood the protocols of American breakfasts, she left the room.

The entrance lobby was also empty, the silence of the lodge exchanged for the deep tones of men's voices, and a putrid odour. She covered her mouth and nose with her sleeve.

"Miss Bonds," George rounded the corner as she took the last riser down to the beach. "You may want to stay inside today."

Moving her sleeve from her nose, she replied with what she hoped was a professional air, "Actually, I'd like to take a look around. Jean-Luc isn't the only man to have died in the vicinity of Volkolak Island in the last week."

George's frown was instant. "Mr Macron died in a plane crash, Miss Bonds."

With deliberation, she said, "But Chris didn't." She watched George's response with a trained eye and tried to appear natural.

"You are correct, Miss Bonds. Mister Miller sadly lost his life at sea."

She decided to ambush him; his response would tell her more than his words. "After he sailed from your lodge ... in your boat."

"Well ... yes, that's true, but I fail to see-"

"The Institute, George. Tell me about the Institute."

"Well, it ... I ..." His jaw snapped shut, his eyes focused over her shoulder, and he walked away.

"The one on the island, George," she called after his back. "The one ..." her words faded as the doors swung shut behind him. Several uniformed men followed George into the lodge, and she caught 'check the woods', 'looked human', 'lethal predator', and 'coffee first'. Remaining on the beach was a uniformed woman taking photographs around the boat. She decided to take the opportunity of speaking to the woman alone, and perhaps questioning her about Chris, after all, it was the US Coast Guard who were alerted to his disappearance and then called off the search. The putrid stench intensified as she approached the boat. The woman's skin was sallow beneath her summer tan, and she greeted Rachel with a smile that was more of a grimace. "Stay back please ma'am. This is a crime scene."

"But he's dead!"

"Yes, ma'am, he certainly is. But as his body has been desecrated, we're having to treat it as a crime and take down all the evidence."

"Desecrated?" The word seemed ill-fitting, reminding Rachel of graveyard robbers and grotesque perverts with a penchant for death. Only last year, one of her colleagues, Brian Smiley, had covered the story leaked from a friend in the police force about the local funeral director and his penchant for necrophilia. He'd hugged the story to himself for several days, sporting a self-satisfied grin each time he'd passed her - they had a less than friendly rivalry - then crowed when he'd handed her the story of Mr Dalby's sexual molestation of the dead, ten minutes ahead of going to print. The story had been sensational, truly scandalous, and picked up by the national redtops and even a couple of broadsheets. *The Sun*, having gained access to photographs, had run with the headline, 'Cross-Dressing Zombie Bride.' And printed a picture of Mr Dalby dressed as a bride in full, and drag-queen style make-up, arm around a corpse in black tie and tails. Despite the pixelated face of the 'victim', the paper had had to print an apology. When Brian had been promoted ahead of Rachel, despite her seniority and longer time served at the paper, Rachel had decided that this time, 'for certain', again, that she would look for another position, or even another career.

"By who?"

"The bear." She pointed to the hummock of brown and glossy fur at least twenty feet from the boat, then returned to Jean-Luc, pointing her camera at his torso, and adjusting the focus to take a close up. Rachel winced as the woman stepped on a bloodied stone, noticing the smears down the boat's side. As the Coast Guard continued to photograph the ruined body, Rachel focused on the smear. Hair had caught in splintered wood. Making an effort to seem interested in the body, she took a closer step and reached for the hair as the woman turned her back. With quick movements, Rachel left the scene and made her way to the bear. Once close enough to the animal to compare them, she held the hair in a pinch. The coarse hairs were at least two inches long, some black, some a dark copper, and others a deep chestnut. They reminded her of pubes. She took a sniff, and instantly regretted the pungent stench that invaded her nostrils, dropping the hairs in disgust, but quickly bent to retrieve them.

"That's tampering with evidence."

Startled by the smooth baritone at her shoulder, she twisted, and her view was immediately blocked by a muscular chest only inches from her face. The next moment, as she craned her neck to look at the man berating her, and their eyes locked, was the most intense of her life, and the desire that overwhelmed Rachel's senses was so strong it took her breath. Stunning too, and absolutely amazing, was that his reaction mirrored hers. Never in her life had the need to consume another human bitten her so hard. Sure, she had fancied men in the past, felt that twinge of desire at the sight of a particularly sexy male, but this reaction was innate, instinctive, and on a whole different level of absolute, all-consuming need. As they stood with eyes locked, the entire world dropped away, and all that remained was his face, and his immense, and powerful presence. Staring into his eyes, she lost herself completely. Silence sat between them, a delicious chord vibrating with ... what? Love at first sight? Lust? A soulmate?

The man was the first to break the silence with a distracted, "It's evidence."

She returned his mumbled words by holding out the hairs and simply saying, "They're pubes". Her shock was instant, and she jerked her hand away, closing her fingers around the hairs, embarrassment stabbing at her cheeks like hot needles. "Sorry!"

"What?"

"Sorry! It's just ... they look like pubes." She opened her hand, a flower opening its petals, and held the 'pubes' to show him. "See!" She took the hairs in a pinch of fingers and held them to her nose and sniffed. "They smell like pubes too."

"Did you just ..." His face crumpled in a grimace. "Did you just sniff those pubes?"

Realising her faux pas, the flush that was rising spread like a fire from her chest to her neck and joined the heat on her cheeks. She stared at him, a rabbit caught in headlights, her mind refusing to string together any sensible kind of sentence.

"I ... No! they just *look* like pubes. I ... hell!"

A broad smile broke out across the man's face. She laughed with relief. "Sorry!" she blurted again, then glanced at the dead man in the boat. How in God's name could she be flirting with this man over an eviscerated bear whilst the body it had chewed through rested only feet away? *Have you no shame!* Her mother's voice rang in her ears. Her cheeks, already hot, became fiery. *No, mother. I'm just a whore.*

She offered him the pubes.

"That's okay, I'll let you keep them."

"I don't want them! I was just comparing them to the bear. They're not the same."

"Oh?" He took a step forward checking the hairs in her hands and then the bear's. "Look like dog hairs."

Dogs again!

"Or a wolf?"

"Yes!"

"You think they belong to a wolf?"

"I don't know, but they are kind of coarse, maybe coarser than a dog's?"

"Perhaps. Although I don't think they're connected to this ... crime."

"Oh?"

"Nope. No dog, or even wolf, could have done this to the bear."

"Then what do you think killed it?"

"We can't say for certain, but the only thing on this island that could damage a bear to this extent, is another bear."

She glanced at the footprint. "But that's a human foot."

"It does look like one, ma'am, but sometimes what we see deceives us. Until an expert has taken a look at the evidence, then we can't say for sure."

"So, it could be human?"

"I can't commit to that, ma'am."

"But if it is human, then that means I was right, and someone was murdered."

"Sorry?"

"Last night! I thought I saw a man running into the woods, but Michel ..." she slowed, telling the Coast Guard that Michel was in her bedroom last night, would be awkward. She chose her words carefully, "After I heard the noise, I looked out of the window to see what was making all the noise. It was horrendous, like someone, or some *thing*, was being murdered, truly awful, it reminded me of the foxes at home, or the cats when they were having a fight, only ten times worse-"

"Miss?"

"Sorry! I'm rambling. Well, I thought I saw a man running, but it was dark. My ... one of the staff convinced me that it wasn't. He said it would just be a bear."

"And you didn't think to come out and check?"

"Yes! Yes, I did, but Michel, the member of staff, said it was too dangerous."

With a glance at the bear, the Coast Guard agreed. "The member of staff was correct. The Alaskan bush isn't the place you go out into during the night to check on terrifying noises." He paused, then asked, "And where were you when you saw, or thought you saw, the figure running."

Rachel turned to point to her room "There."

"So, in your bedroom?" His brow furrowed, and he shielded his eyes with his hands as he surveyed the side of the lodge.

"Yes. But it was too dark. It must have been at least two am."

His voice took on a more serious tone. "And you say you were looking out with the member of staff?"

Rachel's cheeks tingled. His blue, and very attractive, eyes bored into hers. "Well – *damn, she would have to admit it!* – yes, he was in my room …"

Never had she felt so ashamed as in that moment.

"At two am?"

Sink hole! Someone open up a sink hole beneath her feet! Heat radiated from her cheeks, and her stomach plunged as she noticed emotion flicker over the man's face. He was disappointed!

"I see." He crossed his arms, and she noticed the bulk of his muscles, the worming veins across large hands, his height as he towered over her, and the breadth of his shoulders, his feet were massive in his boots.

You know what they say about men with big feet, don't you Rachel?

The tingle on her cheeks was accompanied by heat. *Big willies?*

No, potty mouth! Big shoes.

For crying out loud! Shut up!

"So," she continued in an attempt to focus her mind and appear professional although that boat had already sailed, "the footprints here suggest that a man did run across the beach and into the forest." Her cheeks burned, and she knew without looking into a mirror that her whole face had flushed a deep red, perhaps even puce. Why did he have to be so damned good looking? She always went to pieces around attractive men! "Which means ..." She attempted to regain her equilibrium and improve the man's opinion of her. "I think we should follow the tracks into the forest." He raised a brow in what she hoped was admiration.

"We?"

"Yes. I'm an investigative journalist and I intend to follow this story and help discover the truth of what has happened here. Last week, my friend went missing from the cove around the other side of the island, and then Jean-Luc had a very suspicious package, and now-"

"Chris Miller? The guest who died in the boating accident?"

"Yes, he was an actor, making a film about surviving in the wilderness, and I'm not convinced it was an accident."

"That's not something I can comment on, ma'am."

"But you will be tracking the footprints into the wood, won't you?"

"Well-"

At that moment, Carmel thrust a mobile phone at the Coast Guard. Behind her, George was running across the beach. "Please, you read this!"

The Coast Guard took the mobile and read the screen. "SOS!!!!! Trapped at Eagle Point. Attacked by wolves! Jerry and Suzy dead. Caleb dead. Please save me!" He scrutinized the screen. "This came in yesterday! When did you see the text message?"

"Just now." George said, his face flushed, his heavy frame heaving. "There must be a delay somewhere up there." He pointed to the sky. "Wifi's been playing up."

The Coast Guard reached for his radio.

CHAPTER THIRTY-SIX

Joshua beckoned for the other men, and two females, to gather around. The journalist appeared to be a little unstable, and he paired her with Wade, a reliable older man whose head wouldn't be turned by her allure. With her gently rounded curves, obvious even beneath the thick fleece and overly tight jeans, she was just the kind of woman Joshua loved to stroke his hands over. He'd been surprised at the wave of jealousy he'd felt as she admitted to being with a man last night. It was ridiculous! He didn't even know her, but on first sight, he knew he wanted to 'know' her, and know her in a deeply satisfying carnal way. He focused on giving instructions to the men, making efforts to retain his professional demeanour, and ignore the increasing need he had to be close to the woman.

She'd said her name was Rachel. That she was British was obvious from her accent, and he had a little trouble understanding some of what she said, particularly when she started rambling in that ditzy, confusing, way. She seemed nervous, and on edge, but who could blame her? She'd come to try and discover more about her friend's disappearance, gone through the trauma of a plane crash, been stranded on a freezing Alaskan island, and then subjected to the horrifying sight of a dead man half-eaten by a now grotesquely disembowelled bear. The scene was horrifying, but the sight that had triggered warning bells in his head was the broken trellis at the side of the lodge and gouged wood beneath the bedroom window that Rachel had pointed out as hers. Something, very possibly the animal that had killed the bear, had climbed up the lodge wall to her window.

Rachel had insisted on joining them despite his objections, and Michel, the man she had admitted to being with the night before, had also insisted on coming along. Joshua noted with some satisfaction, and then anger on her behalf, that Michel seemed more interested in ogling Kyla's ass than talking to Rachel. Her efforts at engaging him in conversation were met with lacklustre interest, and Joshua realised that Michel was a hunter, already looking for the next adrenaline rush, and tracking a new target.

Pebbles crunched underfoot as the group moved from the beach and into the woods. Expecting the trail of blood to peter out within a few feet of the bear's body, he was surprised, and a little disconcerted when it ran almost vertically from the body to the first trees, and then into the forest proper. As they moved further between the trees, the spatters of trailed blood pooled, the creature perhaps injured and stopping to rest. The blood loss continued as spatters, with large droplets becoming smaller until finally only a spot appeared here and there. The trail lost, he picked it up again by following snapped twigs, and trampled undergrowth. After at least forty-five minutes of walking through the forest, they reached a clearing. Joshua could find no sign of which way the wounded animal, or animals, went next.

"Is there any point in going on?" Boyd asked as Joshua checked for clues.

"Of course there is! George said that the group went to Eagle Point."

"Then we should have started the search there, we could have found them by now."

"We followed the route they took!"

"It's been a day and a half. If wolves got them, there won't be anything left to find."

"There'll be bones."

"The woman could still be alive."

"If she survived outside all night."

"Wade's right. She could be alive. We need to keep looking."

Another hour passed without any sign of wolves, or the hunters they'd attacked. In the distance the promontory of Eagle Point burst from the green forest and jutted its jagged blackness to the sky.

"Pipe down, guys. We're nearly at the point."

"Can we rest a minute?" Rachel asked.

Cheeks flushed, hot beneath her padded, tightly fitted jacket, she looked unused to the exertion, and he agreed.

"Thanks!" She walked ahead to where a cluster of smooth and rounded stones sat surrounded by large ferns and took a sip of water from a cannister.

A sour aroma tickled his nostrils. "Anyone else get that?"

Craig followed his lead and sniffed. "Yeah, kind of ... shitty."

"Like wet dog."

Rachel sniffed. "Pubes!"

"What?"

Her face flushed a deeper puce as Boyd snorted with derision – for some reason he had taken against the woman – but Joshua understood exactly what she meant; the smell was the same as the pinch of hair she had pocketed as they'd spoken beside the mutilated bear. "Can you pass me them?"

She dug in her pocket and pulled out the mess of hairs. He took a sniff. His nose wrinkled. "She's right!"

"Pubes? You've got to be shitting me!"

"No, they're not pubes ... they just look like pubes ... these were taken from the boat back at the lodge. The scent is the same."

The pinch of hairs was passed around the group, each member nodding their agreement.

"Stinks!"

"Pheweee! That is powerful."

"Where's Kyla?"

Joshua scanned the group and then the surrounding forest. The woman was nowhere to be seen.

"That bush pilot's gone too."

Silence fell among the group. Joshua recalled Kyla's unprofessional giggle as Michel had whispered in her ear. He'd cringed, noticing Rachel's frown of hurt, and decided that at the earliest opportunity he would remind Kyla that she was on duty, and that behaviour commensurate with her station as a member of the US Coast Guard was expected at all times, even if she did have the hots for the guy.

"I bet she's with Michel!" Rachel blurted, echoing Joshua's thoughts.

Relieved that none of his crew had voiced what they were all thinking – they were a team, and no one would talk another member down in front of a member of the public – he said, "They've just fallen behind." As he asked Wade to check back along the route, Michel appeared, fumbling with his trousers' zipper.

"Where is she?" Rachel blurted.

"Where is Kyla?" Joshua directed the question at Michel with a steady glare?

Michel returned his stare with a shrug, then said, "She had to pee. I left her squatting behind a shrub." The man's laugh grated on Joshua's ears. A pout sat on Rachel's lips, and he couldn't tell whether the flush on her cheek was from the exertion of walking up an increasingly steep incline – given her Rubenesque figure – or from embarrassment that her beau was no longer showing interest. He settled for both. Checking back down the track, he thought he saw the top of Kyla's head appear from behind a shrub, but it disappeared, and she didn't emerge from the path. He called her name. She made no reply.

"She's probably taking a dump!"

Ignoring Michel's coarse remark, Joshua said, "I just saw her ... so where is she?"

THE STICKY SCENT OF the woman's genitals clung to Max's tongue. She had tasted ... divine ... ripe. Catching her had been easy. She hadn't even known he was there, and he'd waited until the last drip of urine had landed on the soil, clamped one hand around her mouth, thrust the other between her parted legs and clasped her to his chest. He'd carried her, slipping silently through the trees, away from the hidden man who had watched her squat until the urine had flowed, and the others waiting further up the hill. He licked the palm of his hand where her juices had smeared, yearning to take it into his mouth, and force his tongue into her dark place. The scent of ovulation was strong. He would take her when she woke. With the marks of his bite deep in her shoulder, her lips cut and bloodied from his kiss, her legs were splayed, the pink bud of her womanhood peeking from between the slit of hairless skin. New growth was already forcing its way across her mound, replacing the unnaturally cropped bristles with long and curling dark hair. He bent, licked the bud, inhaled her scent to his memory, scooped her back into his arms, and ran with her through the forest.

AFTER HALF AN HOUR of searching the immediate area and finding nothing, they returned to the point from which they had started beside the cluster of boulders, and Joshua declared Kyla officially lost. Michel had shown him the place where she had relieved herself. The evidence was there, the dark forest floor darker where urine had soaked into the soil, and droplets sat on the broken fronds of a young fern, but there was no evidence of Kyla, or that a struggle, or attack, had taken place.

"How could she have got lost? The path is so obvious."
"Perhaps she saw something and went to investigate."
Joshua tried his radio again, but she made no reply.
"Try her mobile."

Joshua scrolled through his contacts and dialled her number. It rang. Kyla's voice answered yet again and asked him to leave a message. "Hey! It's Joshua. Call me as soon as you get this message ... OK? Damn!" Call ended he searched over the heads of the group, hopeful that he would see her making her way towards him. The forest remained still. He wiped at the sweat beading on his brow.

"Josh, we should get back. Get someone out here to search for her."

"But we're already here! We are the ones to look!"

"I'm not going back without her."

Joshua checked his watch. Just after noon. At this time of year, twilight settled in around 7pm, but they needed to be out of the forest way before that, to be safe. Apart from the lack of supplies, they hadn't come equipped for a night out, or even the dip in temperature that the evening would bring. "God damn it! Kyla!" he shouted. "Where the hell are you?"

A bird catapulted from a tree close by and fluttered into the sky. He noted the opaque caste of the sky. Blue earlier, it was now a pearlescent grey. "Storms coming!"

"A storm?"

"Yep! By the look of that sky."

All eyes turned upwards.

"We should turn back."

"But we can't leave her here."

Beyond the boulder where Rachel had sat, a pathway seemed to have been trodden through the undergrowth. Stepping over a large boulder mostly buried in the earth, Joshua noted the broken twigs and snapped ferns, the squashed stems where something weighty had trodden them down. Through the trees, a steep and rocky outcrop rose to create a wall of stone. At the top was a promontory that would make an excellent place to look out over the forest. "Something has been this way." He fingered the rifle slung across his front.

"Perhaps what took Kyla?"

"There's no evidence that anything took Kyla."

"Apart from the fact that a woman who has spent her whole life tracking animals through woods like this has disappeared without trace!"

"Perhaps she just went back?"

Boyd snorted. "No way would Kyla go back! She lives and breathes being a Coast Guard."

"She could be injured?"

"Perhaps we should go back? I mean …"

"No, let's continue forward. I want to get to the top of that rock and take a look out over this place. If Kyla *is* injured, she may have lit a fire to help us locate her."

"Why would she light a fire?"

"It's something I remember she said once. She got lost in the woods as a kid, so she lit a fire, and the smoke helped her parents find her."

"Smart kid."

"She's a smart woman."

Mumbled assent passed through the group, and they all agreed that Kyla was probably fine and, whatever had happened to her, she was more than capable of getting herself out of a sticky situation. Joshua listened to the men's talk with rising concern. Everything they said about Kyla's abilities and experience made him believe that something terrible had happened to her. How could she have gone missing? It was impossible that a woman with such experience would disappear without trace, she had either been attacked by something, or fallen, but they would have heard her screams if she'd fallen or been attacked—surely! He turned from the group and stepped further up the steeply rising pathway leading them to the base of the rock. It jutted almost vertically for at least thirty feet. Saplings and ferns grew from rocky outcrops. "It's a dead end."

"But the path leads here. You can see the tracks." Rachel pointed for a newly broken twig and a freshly trampled fern.

"We could have done that."

"We could, but is one of us bleeding?"

Joshua swung to Rachel. In her hand was a long and curling frond. Snapped at the middle, it hung broken, its stem crushed and smeared red. "This looks to me," Rachel said meeting his eyes, "as though something with blood on its foot has stepped on it."

"Then they must have come this far and turned back."

Rachel took a step past him, scouring the rock, and pointed to a place where it had sheared leaving a jagged shelf at eye level. "There's blood here too. And," she reached into the crevice and tugged, "and hair." She pulled a tuft from the rock. "It's the same! Whatever was at the beach, climbed up here!"

Joshua peered to the top of the rock, a goat, or a seasoned climber could manage the cliff-like promontory, but there were no mountain goats, or seasoned climbers, on Volkolak. "Can I see the hair?"

"They're the same ... aren't they?"

The hairs were the same coarse mixture of black, copper, and deep chestnut. "Yes, I think they are."

"So ..." her eyes wandered to the rocky outcrop then turned back to meet his with a flicker of excitement, "whatever was on the beach, went up there?" She craned her neck to follow the rock face to its summit.

"Perhaps."

"You sayin' that whatever killed that bear on the beach was here, and climbed that?" Boyd pointed to the vertical rock face.

Joshua nodded.

"Ain't no bear that could climb that!"

"A wolf perhaps?"

A hand rested on his shoulder, and Craig, a broad-shouldered man who stood several inches above him, pointed upwards. "Tell me I'm not seeing that!"

Alerted by the anxiety in the man's voice, Joshua followed his pointing finger. The group quietened to silence as each of them peered at the rock. About ten feet from the top, was what looked like a bloody handprint.

"Is that a handprint?"

"Where? Show me!"

"I see it."

Joshua's belly knotted as the track of whatever climbed up the rockface became clear; a partial footprint, a palmprint where a hand had clasped the rock, the wisp of hairs that had caught.

"That's not a bear, or a wolf. That looks human to me."

"No human could have climbed that."

"Sure they could."

"I'm going to take a closer look." Joshua returned to the base of the rock, placing his hand where he believed the man, or creature, or whatever it was, had placed its hands. There was nowhere for him to gain a foothold at that level. "Give me a push up," he commanded. Boyd stepped forward, lowering his shoulder for Joshua to step up on. He hoisted himself to the ledge, noticing the scratched marks that corresponded with fingers where the hand would have gripped the rock. He made his next move to climb up the rock but had to stretch his arm to its fullest extent to even touch the next handhold. Realising climbing upwards was impossible, he jumped down. "There's no way I can climb that."

"But it went up."

"None of this makes sense."

"None of it is helping us find Kyla."

"Or Sam."

"I'm going back down."

"We can't leave her out overnight!"

"We don't have a choice. It's not safe for any of us to stay here longer. We're not equipped for it and there's a storm blowing in." Josh made eye contact with each of the group. "Agreed?"

With mumbled agreement the men turned to set off back down the hill, following the narrow track through dense woodlands.

As they turned, the leaves of nearby trees shivered, and the creatures that had watched from among their branches, leapt to the ground.

CHAPTER THIRTY-SEVEN

The narrow track opened out to the less densely overgrown area of forest, and a rustle to Rachel's right was followed by creaking and the snapping of twigs. Leaves shivered on a nodding branch and a squirrel glided to a neighbouring tree. It landed, chittering in a fury, and a flurry of red fur. *Stupid squirrel!*

"This forest gives me the willies."

Boyd threw her a frown.

"It gives me the creeps," she translated.

He fingered the strap of the rifle slung across his shoulder.

"I guess we're all on edge," she tried again.

"Sure."

"Or is it that you're just pissed off about something else?" she prodded.

"For crying out loud, woman!" he hissed. "I'm trying to listen. You just don't know when to stop, do you!"

"Sorry for asking!"

A thud followed by a grunt drowned out Rachel's words and her jaw snapped shut as beyond Boyd's angry face, Joshua disappeared beneath a mass of muscle and fur and snapping jaws.

"What!"

Boyd swung his rifle at the writhing mass. He fired, hitting the creature that had Joshua in its grip, but it made no impact, and Joshua's scream of terror was quickly silenced as he was dragged into the undergrowth. Gunshot fired again as Boyd followed the disappearing shape, then swung the rifle in an arc, checking between the trees.

"He's gone!"

"Get after it!"

Three men pushed through the undergrowth, but there was no sign of Joshua or the hideous creature that had attacked him.

"What in God's name was that?"

"Had to be a bear!"

"That weren't no bear."

Rifles swung, following any movement. A scream erupted and the guard at the back of the group disappeared, yanked through the bushes.

Uncomprehending fear was etched onto each face as Boyd shouted, "Get behind me!"

Taking backward steps from the scuffed earth and bloodied foliage where Joshua had been attacked, a tree shivered, and a flash of brown was accompanied by a thud as another creature hit the forest floor unseen. As the men swung to locate the creature, it landed on Michel's back. Sharp claws dug deep into his chest as fangs sank into his neck. Boyd fired. The bullet missed, and bark splintered at the beast's side. Fangs anchored into Michel's flesh, its face contorted into a threatening sneer as it dragged him into the forest.

"Christ's sake!"

Shock erupted as angry shouts.

"Did you see it?"

"Where the hell did it go?"

"It ate him! It fucking ate him!"

"Shut up!"

"Did you see it? It was a woman!"

"No fucking way that was a woman!"

"It had titties!"

"There are two! That one was different from the one that got Joshua!"

"Oh, Jesus! Mary mother of God what the fuck is going on?"

"Shut up!" Boyd repeated. "And listen!"

Silence fell among the group, and the noise in the forest ebbed to nothing.

"That's what I saw on the beach!"

"Shh!"

"It's what was in the box!"

"Christ sake woman," Boyd hissed. "Shut up!"

She quieted, focusing on the noise of the forest; branches cracked as the trees swayed, leaves whished as wind blew through them, and someone screamed.

"Joshua!" The agony of his cry melted into Rachel's bones.

His cries were followed by an unearthly howl and joined by another voice. The noise bounced off the trees and grew to a cacophony that came from every direction. Shadows thickened beneath trees as dark clouds shifted above the forest. Ferns and mosses darkened against blackening trunks, and the cries and howls faded then stopped. Rachel's heart tripped a hard and painful beat.

"Have they gone?"

Ignoring her, Boyd circled, twisting three-hundred and sixty degrees with his rifle at his shoulder, the barrel pointing into the trees, his finger resting on the trigger. In silence, he beckoned for them to move on. They walked in silence, each man alert and continuously scanning the surrounding forest as they made their way down the hill. As minutes, then an hour passed, the forest became a repeating pattern of trees, moss, ferns, and undergrowth with the only indicator of progress back to the lodge, the steep decline of the land.

They continued to walk until the sound of running water indicated a stream ahead. "That stream goes all the way down to the lodge," Rachel informed Boyd. "All we have to do is follow it down and we'll be safe!"

Encouraged by her words, the men picked up their pace.

"There's a birdwatching hide around here too, and a lake."

"Okay, but let's just focus on the stream and getting to the lodge."

"I was just saying! Perhaps-"

"Ain't nowhere safe from those monsters."

"Let's just get back to the chopper."

"Will you take me too?" Thoughts of leaving the island on the helicopter were a huge relief, but her mind tripped back to the bear on the beach. Convinced that the figures she had seen running back into the forest were the same creatures that had killed Joshua, Michel, and Wade, her mind flowed freely as it compared the images of the bear with what she imagined had happened to them! *What was the word for it? Disembowelled? No, the other one. Ev ...* "Eviscerated!" Her churning mind vomited the word.

"What?"

"You got Tourette's lady?"

"Shut the hell up!"

"Sorry!"

Rachel's mind continued to churn. She was now certain the creatures that had attacked them in the woods were the same that had killed the bear, and perhaps the female that had attacked Michel was the same as the one in Chris' video. That they are not wolves, not any kind she had seen before, was also certain. A word crept into her mind that she pushed away. *Ridiculous!* She tried to focus on the facts once more; one of 'them' had been in the box on the beach. The men who had come to rescue her had taken it and Peter, ergo they had specifically come to retrieve Peter and the box, and not the plane's survivors. Peter's destination had not been the lodge, ergo, he was somewhere on the island with the box, and its contents. *Werewolves. No!* Peter was a scientist who worked with animals. He had slipped when he had mentioned the Institute, and had failed to cover his tracks, which meant he was in on it too! *Werewolves! No, Rachel. Yes! No!*

"Werewolves!" She clamped her jaws together. *Idiot!*

"What?"

"They're werewolves. The creatures that attacked Joshua and Michel are werewolves."

Boyd shook his head and Craig frowned then looked away.

"Okay, so not the kind that can be killed by silver bullets, but didn't you see how much like people they looked?"

"It looked more like a sasquatch."

"There are scientists on this island! Peter was one of them. He's involved too. They're experimenting on wolves. Perhaps they're splicing their DNA with humans. They're doing it in Japan! A scientist called Nakauchi is doing it! He's creating animal embryos that contain human cells and then placing them into a surrogate! The government gave the go-ahead this year." Boyd's glance at her was scathing, but she continued. "Oh ... my ... God! And they're planning to transplant the organs that grow in these hybrid animals into humans! What if ... what if that's what the Institute is doing? Growing animal-human hybrids? And do you know why there is so much resistance to it?

"My God woman, shut up!"

"No, listen to her."

"Because, obviously there are massive ethical considerations, but what they're really afraid of is that the human cells might stray beyond the development of the targeted organ, and travel to the developing animal's brain, and affect its cognition, how it thinks!"

"Seriously? They're doing that?"

"How do you know all of this?"

"Yes, they are, and I know because I was doing research into it last year. I'm an investigative journalist."

"She could be right."

"Quiet!"

"Listen up, lady. There ain't no such thing as werewolves, and there ain't no institute on this island. I've been hunting for the past twenty-years or more, and what I saw was some sort of a bear. Sure it was mangey, and kind of skinny, but it was a bear all the same."

"But you saw it! That wasn't a bear. No way."

"It weren't no werewolf!" Boyd insisted. "Now, pipe down and let's get out of this forest."

"It could be some sort of fucked-up hybrid! The woman could be right."

As Boyd shook his head and told the group to 'Quit talking!' once more, a piercing yowl erupted, so close that it that scratched at Rachel's eardrum. In the next second a figure landed in front of her, cutting her off from Boyd. Towering above Rachel, the male, obvious from the naked genitals dangling from a mass of swirling pubes, stared directly at her. Boyd screamed unseen as she locked eyes with the muscular beast. Craig was toppled from his feet, landing with a thud as a large female straddled him, naked buttocks pushing down against his belly, her claws holding his arms to the floor. Rachel backed up as the huge male advanced. The grunt of Craig's struggle, and Boyd's screams, filled her ears, but her focus was on the beast in front of her; she recognised him. "Joshua!" The beast's eyes flickered, and a clawed hand reached forward. In the next second, he was thrown to the ground as another male bowled into him, landing with enormous force against his side. Joshua slammed into a tree with a grunt. As he recovered, the new male leapt forward, pinning Rachel to the ground. As its jaws opened to bite into her, it was dragged back and thrown to the forest floor.

The creatures turned on each other and as the two huge males rolled on the forest floor, clawing, biting, and tearing at each other, Rachel realised she was alone. Boyd and Craig had been attacked and the only evidence they had been with her only seconds ago were the remnants of Craig's torn shirt and Boyd's rifle. As the males continued to thrash and snarl, she grabbed Boyd's rifle and crawled commando-style into the undergrowth.

To the background of vicious growls, thuds, and grunts, Rachel crawled through the scrubby trees, ignoring the branches tearing at her face and catching on her clothes. Fingers wrapped around the rifle's barrel, she focused on the forest ahead, heart ripping in her chest. Somewhere ahead was the stream that ran down to the lodge.

Heart hammering, she was unaware that the angry grunts and thrashing of the huge males had stopped. She powered forward, jumping roots and broken branches, sliding down steep embankments, desperately searching through the trees for sight of the stream. With ears full of her own rasping breath, the pulsing of her blood, and feet pounding against the forest floor, she was oblivious to the yelp then loud cackle that rose to a crescendo and ended in a howl. Sweat trickled down her back and beaded at her forehead.

Ahead was the stump of an overturned tree, its roots overhanging the pathway. She recognised it as the one they had passed on the way up. Somewhere along here, Michel had said there was a birdwatcher's hide, and that half a mile east was a lake. Dismissing the hide as a safe place, she continued her descent, expecting a clawed hand to grasp her at any second.

Branches crack behind her and, turning to look, she landed with a thud as her foot caught on a thick tangle of roots worming across the forest floor. Pine needles and grit sloughed into her mouth, splitting her lip, and the putrid stench of faeces filled her nostrils. Paralysed as the noise of thudding feet approached, she was unable to scream as steel fingers locked around her ankles and pulled. Twigs, bark, and last year's hardened pine needles scratched her belly as her jumper rode up, and she was pulled into the undergrowth.

A hand slapped across her mouth and then the light disappeared.

CHAPTER THIRTY-EIGHT

Thudding feet passed by, but the hand remained clamped around her mouth. Pinned to the floor, Rachel's eyes adjusted, and she realised that the darkness was a rough cloth through which she could see light. The hand across her mouth felt gritty, but devoid of hairs. As the thudding feet disappeared, the cloth was pulled from her face and was replaced by a pair of green eyes peering out from mud and mascara-caked lashes. A mud-covered finger pressed against lips also smeared with mud in a plea for Rachel to remain silent. She nodded and the woman slowly removed her hand though her finger remained at her closed lips.

Rachel opened her mouth to speak, but the woman shook her head. Slowly pulling her to sit, the woman motioned for her to be still, then reached into the pocket of her hunting jacket, pulling out a handful of mud. She smeared the mud over Rachel's hands, neck, hair, and then clothes, dipping her hand back into the pocket and returning with more mud. As the minutes passed and the sound of the creature's yelps, cackles and howls grew distant, the woman motioned for Rachel to follow.

They crept through the woods, treading slowly between the trees until they reached the stream Rachel had been so desperate to find. Instead of following it down the hill, the woman led Rachel across it to the watcher's hide. The entrance to the rectangle of slatted, weather-blackened wood was hidden behind a zigzag of shrubs. With a slow hand, the woman reached for the handle, opened the door, and pushed Rachel inside.

The interior was dark, lit only by what light seeped in through the closed shutters, but she was instantly aware of a man in the corner. She stopped at the door, grasping the frame.

"Go in!" the woman whispered.

"Come in!" the man said in a familiar - Wolverhampton! - accent. "And close the door."

With a shove from the woman, Rachel stepped into the hide, peering into the corner. An oblong shutter opened, the shadows retreat, and light illuminated the man's face.

"Chris!"

"Shh!"

"Indeed!" he replied in a whisper.

"Sorry! Oh ... my ... God! Chris!"

"Rachel?"

"Yes!"

"Bloody hell! What are you doing here?"

"Come to find you!"

The woman closed the door.

"What is that smell?"

"She landed in bear shit!"

"Jeez! That is ripe."

"Chris ... how ... when ... what ..."

"Where?" Chris laughed. "Slow down, Rachel. I'll tell you everything I know."

"What the hell is going on?"

Gentle pressure pressed down on Rachel's shoulder. "It's alright Rachel, just calm down."

A sob was quickly silenced as the woman pulled Rachel to her chest in a motherly gesture. Taller than the petite, mud-covered blonde, Rachel had the uncomfortable sense of being an overgrown schoolchild, ungainly next to their smaller, more attractive, mother; it was a familiar feeling. A gentle pat on her back brought on Rachel's tears. "Shh, there, there now. There now," the woman crooned. "It's alright. Everything is alright." The gentle and giving kindness was not something Rachel was familiar with.

Minutes passed as Rachel gathered her senses, and her mind settled into cohesive thinking. Chris stood motionless, so unlike his on-screen persona, as he watched across the lake. He and the woman moved with quiet steps around the hide and even their breathing seemed gentle. Over the next minutes their story unfolded.

The woman was the Sam who sent the text begging for help, the only surviving member of the hunting party. She had watched as her husband had been torn apart by a monster, and the woman he was groping taken into the woods. Chris had said 'karma' after Sam had described seeing her husband practically eating her best friend's face and sliding his hands down her panties. Rachel had nodded, one ear listening to the noises beyond the hide. "And the other man, Caleb?"

"I didn't see him being killed-"

"But you know he's dead?"

Sam nodded, and tears welled in her eyes as her face screwed up with the painful memory. "I was crouching in the undergrowth when the creature came past me. If I'd put my hand out, I would have touched him."

"How come he didn't know you were there?"

"An old trick ... I covered myself with mud, it's like a camouflage. There was bear shit too, I think that helped. Anyway, the creature was dragging poor Caleb behind him."

"Was he dead?"

She nodded, holding back the tears. "Yep! I got a look right into his belly as he passed." She stopped a moment. "All his clothes were ripped and there was just this big hole."

"Nasty!"

"I know, right!"

"That's what they did to the bear. They attacked Joshua ... but he's one of them now."

"Joshua?"

For the next twenty minutes Rachel explained exactly what had happened, how the plane had crashed, and the bear had eaten Jean-Luc's corpse. The bear had been killed by what they thought was another bear only it wasn't, and there were bloody human footprints into the wood.

"So ... they ... the wolfmen were at the lodge?"

Rachel shuddered. "Yes. I knew I'd seen something that looked human run back into the forest, but Michel convinced me that I hadn't. And do you know, at each turn of my investigation, he put me on the wrong track."

"Investigation?"

"Rachel's an investigative journalist for the paper back home. I sent her the video of the woman on the beach."

Turning to Chris, Rachel asked, "How did you survive? It's a miracle."

"Indeed!"

Chris pointed to the lake. At its centre was a small island, and on that another hide. On the shore was a rowing boat. "They don't like water, Rachel. And I'll tell you how I know ... On the beach, before I left, the woman crept as close as she dare to the water, but she wouldn't get too close. When my boat capsized, I made it back to the island, but she was still tracking me. I made it back to shore and the stream that cuts through the hillside saved my life. I was terrified Rachel! As I made my way up the hillside, she tracked me on the other side of the stream, and I couldn't understand why she wouldn't cross. And then I realised; she had stayed away from the water on the beach, and now wouldn't cross the stream even though it was narrow enough for her to jump! It was a revelation; she was terrified of water, and that saved my life. And then I was lucky. I found the lake, and the boat moored to one of the fishing pegs and rowed out to the island."

"And then you met me." Sam nudged his shoulder.

"Yep, and then I met you." Chris returned the warmth of her smile.

"Then why are you in the woods now, and not on the island? It's not safe!"

"Indeed, it is not! But we've got to get off the island. We can't stay here forever."

Outside a howl split the air and was joined my another, and then more, until the hill came alive with wailing.

Sam and Chris exchanged a look of understanding. "There are more now!"

"Indeed, there are!"

"Joshua's one! The big one attacked him and dragged him into the woods."

"Did you see the others die?"

"No, I only saw them being bitten, but the attacks were so savage that I thought they must have been killed."

"You were right then, Sam. Their bite is contagious. They are werewolves!"

"I said they were!" Rachel blurted. "I said that exact word, but the others just looked at me as though I was a lunatic!"

"Shh! Try to keep your voice down."

"Sorry!"

"How many do you think there are?"

"There's the woman in the pink shirt. A huge male and we think two females. How many US Coast Guards were there?"

"Five, one woman and four men, plus Michel, the bush pilot from the lodge."

"And you know that Joshua has been infected, so there are perhaps nine now?"

"And there's one at the institute. It was in a box on the plane when we crashed. It washed up on shore and they took it away, with Peter."

"Is that what those buildings are?"

"You've seen it?"

"Yes, it's close to the beach on the other side of the island; a cluster of buildings that look a lot like containers that have been slotted together. They're clad in wood so kind of camouflaged."

"Michel lied! He said he'd seen the entire island by air, and that there weren't any other buildings on it. It must be where they've taken Peter, and the box." She shook her head. "Damned lying snake!"

"And you think one of the creature's was in it?" Sam asked.

"Yes, I'm sure now. At first, I thought it was a wolf. Then the soldier told me it was a dog, but it stank like they do, and it had those ... those godawful red eyes."

"The eyes *are* horrific."

"Yeah, it's like they're full of congealed blood."

"Much as I'd like to sit here and chat with you guys about just how gross the creatures are, we need to make plans to get back to the lodge," Sam said. "Chris and I have discussed this, and we believe the best plan is to follow the stream back down. We'll only be safe once we're at sea. If memory serves, there are two boats on the beach-"

"Three."

"Okay, three."

"One's got Jean-Luc's remains in it, and another has no engine."

"If Jean-Luc was bitten, do you think he'll become one of them?"

"A zombie werewolf?"

"Well ..."

"Stuff like that is just for books and films."

"Sure, but there's werewolves on the island—they're real."

"He was already dead, Chris. I really don't think he'll rise."

"Just a thought."

Sam raised her brow and gave him a nudge with her shoulder. "I do love his sense of humour! Now, back to business. We launch the boat with the engine."

"If it's got petrol in it ... they kind of look as if they've been there a while."

"Sure."

"There's a helicopter now—the Coast Guard arrived in that."

"Can you fly a helicopter, Rachel?"

"... No, but ... I was just saying ... it's something we could try."

"I can."

Both women turned to Chris with disbelieving eyes.

"Are you shitting me again, Chris?"

"No! I admit, I'm not much of a wildlife survivalist, I'm more of a camper-"

"I'd say you're more of a Glamper!" Rachel said, remembering the tent and the luxury items it held.

Chris laughed. "Indeed! But I have had a few lessons. My nan bought me some for my twenty-eighth birthday. The pilot said I was a natural." Rachel raised a brow, but quickly hid her disbelief. "It's true! ... It is."

"Okay," Sam said, "Well, a few lessons are better than nothing, but I still think our best chance is to get one of the boats launched. We know they hate water."

"And if that doesn't work, then we launch the helicopter."

"I doubt the keys are in it ..."

Hope disappeared from Chris' eyes. "You're right, it was a stupid idea."

"No! No, it was a great idea. I just can't see it working out, that's all."

"I'm an idiot, Rachel. You know it."

"No, I don't know it. You've managed to survive being tracked by one of those monsters and survived in the Alaskan wilds for a week! I would say that's pretty amazing."

Chris' smile returned. "It is, isn't it."

"It is, and just think of all the publicity afterwards! My God! You'll be able to write a book, be on breakfast telly, teatime telly, they may even give you your own show."

Chris' smile slipped and he gave Sam a quick glance. She had turned to look out through the oblong opening to the lake and its hide, and Rachel's nose for secrets, honed by her journalistic training, told her that they had done more than just survive together. She scrutinized Sam, then Chris for the seconds when they were unaware of her gaze, then said. "When are we leaving?"

CHAPTER THIRTY-NINE

As Sam, Chris, and Rachel smeared their skin and clothing with more of the stinking mud from the wet land around the lake, Joshua stood impaled against the root-ball of the upturned spruce that Rachel had recognised less than an hour ago. Great hanging tendrils of woody roots and clumps of enmeshed soil hung above his head. He grunted as he pulled himself from the broken root that had speared his side. The gashes left by the creature that had bitten him were already healing, their pink sides knitting together beneath flesh now covered with long, dark hairs.

The air in the forest was alive with scent, and he was aware of each strand of curling stench, each sticky particle as they trailed among the trees. The pulse of life was strong, living in the pumping blood of a thousand creatures, but the desire to drain it was stronger. He swallowed, licking a rough tongue over newly sharpened teeth. Bone white daggers sat at the side of his mouth ready to sink down into the flesh that his body craved. The blood from the male had trickled down his throat and into his belly, igniting a need that burned like a fire in his mouth until every nerve in his body was alight with the need to gnash, and grip, and tear, and swallow.

Rachel ... Rachel ... Rachel ...

The creature's bite had taken him by surprise, the dark silhouette jumping from the trees before he had a chance to even register it was there. ... *Rachel* ... Knives had sliced down through his flesh, grazing bone, pinning him to the ground, and he'd watched Rachel's horrified eyes as he'd sunk to the floor, and the thing had ripped at his neck. He'd felt the tongue flick against his throat, licking at his lifeblood as she'd screamed his name. Blackness had closed in around him and then he was in an agony of writhing and deep pain that seared the core of his being, melting his very bones. Gripping him in a vice, throwing him in jerking spasms as they tore through his flesh, his body had bent, and turned, and reformed, the flesh tearing, paring, then creeping back along the bone, and covering new growth.

The sound of *everything* had come to him then: the scratching of mice, the grunts of rutting boars, the beating heart of deer, and the smell of the Others, their sweat, their hair, the sticky, sweaty heat between their legs. They had crouched, and watched, snapping, pulling each other back as one stepped beyond the other. The male had slapped at the largest female, forcing her back behind him, keeping her in place.

Rachel ... Rachel ... Rachel ...

The word pulsed in his mind, and he craved to sink his flesh into hers.

His eyes had grown accustomed to the red glow that made everything bright and seen, and he had followed them, followed their scent, hungry for blood, hunting. Snickering, they had found their prey, and he had seen her again, the woman who had called his name. The male had waited, urged him to attack the man, but every part of his body, his teeth, and the ache between his legs, wanted the woman. Cells, though transformed, still carried the memories of desire, and that desire had become a burning flame that only She could put out. The male had wanted her for himself. Joshua had nearly died to stop him.

Rachel ... Rachel ... Rachel ...

Nose to the air, he searched for her scent, but caught only the stench of wild boar and bear, and the female tracking him. He crouched. She pushed out from the shrub. He snarled. She returned his snarl and they circled. The scent of her dark place was sticky, and his need to fornicate grew. She took a step to him, locking her red eyes to his, touching between her own legs, then grasping between his. Throwing her to the floor, he thrust into her dark place. Ecstasy rode him, and she dug claws into his buttocks locking his hips to hers. Blood seeped from the wounds.

An angry howl erupted in the distance, and the female pushed him away. She flipped to a crouch, then sprinted to the Others, disappearing into the forest as Joshua's seed swam past the alpha's rapidly growing foetus, anchored in the lining of her womb.

Hunger for flesh returned, and he could think of nothing but the sweet curves of the woman ... the Rachel ... to hold her tight, to drink her blood, to lick her dark place, to take her breasts in his mouth, *to have and to hold* – he snickered – *till death us do part*. He sniffed at the air, catching the particles of her scent, then sprinted down the hillside, away from the howling alpha male, and towards the need that consumed him; to own the woman ... the Rachel ... her body, her soul, mated for life, till death.

CHAPTER FORTY

As Joshua was driven through the forest by his need to own Rachel, Max sat on the promontory above the cave and filled his lungs with the crisp air that bit at his skin and howled. Harsh and sorrowful, it was a call for the Others to join him.

A large male, the blue shirt of his uniform torn where bone and muscle had grown, twisted, and transmogrified into his new form, stepped out from the tree. Eyes gleaming darkest red, he snapped his jaws, tormented by the irresistible hunger for blood and flesh. As he stood several feet behind Max, another male joined them, gun belt still girdling his waist. Within a minute, the Others had gathered until the pack was ready. Crouching, and snapping, they sniffed at the air, tasting the excitement to come. Below, in a clearing, flesh and bone waited to be torn. It hid among the wooden boxes, behind a tall fence, and with them was the Laura ... the One ... the She. Her name repeated in his mind ... *Laura ... Laura ... Laura ...* and then the anger surfed his memories: She running, keeping pace, her arms pumping in time to his. Beside them the Smalls, their smalls, born beneath a moon welcoming his sons into the forest. Memories flashed, broken, disjointed: they'd squirmed from between her legs, breaking through the dark red caul, to lie curled on the bed of ferns; She ... *Laura!* ... cradling them to her breast ... Max nuzzling into her neck, his need for her sex, to feel her warm and loving legs wrap around his waist, stronger than ever ... She running ... the smalls playing, climbing on his back, jumping from his shoulder, sharing their first kill ... the spike in Laura's neck ... the Smalls lying in an unmoving tangle of arms and legs, white fangs bared in open and soundless mouths ... his arms paralysed, his voice silenced as the third spike speared his chest. Anger riled to rage, and he howled, jabbing an arm at the wooden boxes. The Screamers couldn't hide from Max. The forest filled with yaps, and snarls, and they ran as one down the hill.

The male with the gun belt still tied to his waist reached the fence first. Sprinting down the hill, he jumped from a rock and up to the fence. It threw him back, and he landed with a hard thud and lay still. The stench of singed hair caught in Max's nostrils as a second male was thrown back from the fence. Wires sparked with an irritated buzz. A female, her blue shirt torn from hem to collar, jumped from a tree, and grasped the wire. Her body jerked in a juddering dance as she clung to the fence. Smoke and the stench of burning flesh rose as a tendril onto the air.

A crack screamed against Max's eardrum and Katarina jerked as bullets sprayed into her body. With an angry growl, Max darted forward. Pain ripped into his bicep as a bullet caught his arm. He snapped at the air. Another crack and pain seared his leg. He grasped for Katarina, pulling her into the forest.

The first male was already at the treeline as Max hauled the female behind a tree. The second male, the Red One, tried to stand as bullets hit into the ground beside him. Shouts from behind the fence were followed by silence and then a whistle, and the Red One's head disintegrated in a spray of blood and bone across the forest floor. His body slumped to the ground, chest flat against the soil, arms and legs jerking, his neck a bloody stump. Behind the fence a shout of, "Got it!"

Max yowled, and jumped back into the forest, hiding behind the trees. Watching the male, he expected him to rise, but the body remained still, the blood pumping from his jugular in irregular bursts, stopping as his heart died.

The excited noise of the men behind the fence grew silent as Max crouched with the Others, Katarina clinging to his side, the blood where the bullet entered her thigh, and another on her shoulder already slowing. She squatted, delved fingers into the wound, and pulled out the metal. Grunting at her, shoving her then jabbing at his own leg, she dug fingers into his flesh. Max growled, snarling at the pain, snapping his jaws at Katarina. She cowered, her fingers deep in his flesh, but scooped beneath the bullet. Her finger slipped from the hole, the bullet cradled in her talon. He grunted, as it dropped to the floor, and returned to watching the men behind the fence. And waited.

CHAPTER FORTY-ONE

With faces and hair thick with mud, Sam, Rachel, and Chris made their way to the side of the stream and tracked its progress down the hillside. Though her heart pounded with each step, Sam kept a stern face, cajoling Rachel, and Chris, to keep going. Rachel had been the hardest to get out of the hide and had clung with fingernails digging into the wooden frame before Chris had managed to talk her round. Now, half an hour later, she was much more relaxed, though, understandably on edge; it was the only way to be, being complacent would get them killed.

They had initially walked in silence, but now Rachel was talking a little too freely, although keeping it to a whisper, about a sluttish guy called Michel, and the US Coast Guard she'd fallen for over the corpse of a Frenchman. Life, Sam mused, was bizarre.

'I think he was the one, Sam, and now,' Rachel sobbed, "he's a goddamned werewolf! It's just not fair."

Unfair seemed a ridiculous concept to use in this context, and Sam riled to the woman's self-pity. "Oh, Rachel! Really! Now, come on. Life isn't fair. None of us have it easy."

"Always look on the bright side," Chris added.

"That's right. Now, stop getting yourself down, and just focus on getting down this hill."

"Life's a piece of shit," Chris sang, "when you look at it!" He sniggered at some unfathomable joke, then shrugged his shoulder and mouthed 'What?' as Sam silently berated him.

"Chris! Sam's having a moment here!"

"Indeed, she is. Indeed."

"Rachel, Joshua may be gone, but you've got your whole life ahead of you."

"But it was so intense!"

"Sure, I get it." She threw a glance at Chris, but he was checking out the trees to his left. "I've felt something similar too ... recently."

"With Jerry?"

"Pah! Not that goddamned snake! ... Sorry. I didn't mean to ... No, not Jerry. I did love him though, once, but the man was ruled by his dick, and that ain't something any woman should have to put up with."

"I guess the monsters did you a favour then."

Sam laughed. "That's kind of brutal, Rachel, but yeah, I guess they did."

The girl made a short gasp and then repeated 'sorry' at least four times, before saying, "God! That was so crass of me."

"Don't worry, honey. Forget it. It was harsh but true."

"Rachel always did have a knack of putting her foot in it! Ay, Rachel?

"Indeed!" she replied.

Sam slipped an arm across the girl's shoulder. A howl erupted in the distance. The girl stiffened. Chris scoured the trees.

"They're on the other side of the island."

"Near the institute."

Although some of the tension left Sam's chest, she remained alert. They may be on the other side of the island, but that was no indicator of safety; those things could run like the wind.

Another twenty minutes passed, and the stream took a sudden dip and disappeared beneath the rock. Increasing her pace, sweat began to form at her hairline; she hadn't realised that their line of safety would be broken. Ten minutes later, it reappeared, and she relaxed again. They had walked for as nearly as far as she'd travelled with Jerry, Caleb, and Suzy, so the lodge couldn't be much further.

Another howl, again from the far distance, but close by a branch snapped, and she turned with horror to the bending of a tree. Noticing her sudden movement, Chris and Rachel stopped to follow her gaze. "Don't stop. Just keep going. We're safe, just remember that. It won't cross the water."

Rachel made a mewling sound, and Chris' attempt to speak stuck in his throat.

"Just keep walking, focus on going forward."

Thudding feet landed somewhere among the trees.

"When we get to the beach, run to the sea."

Another mewl from Rachel.

"Got it," Chris confirmed.

Minutes passed, and the thudding of feet had disappeared, though the cracking of dried twigs and branches underfoot was more regular, and closer.

Rachel froze. "I can't stand this! Where is it. I want to see it."

"Rachel!" Sam hissed, bumping into the woman. "We've just got to keep moving. I'm sure the lodge is just down here.

We're going to run into the sea—remember. We'll get the boat, and then be safe." She prodded Rachel's shoulder.

Crack!

All heads swivelled to the noise as a huge figure landed on the other side of the stream. Rachel screamed.

Please, Lord, don't let the water disappear again. Please! Aloud Sam said, "Just keep moving." With quick strides, she passed Rachel and Chris to lead from the front.

The creature snapped its jaws, keeping their quickened pace with ease, the contours of its huge muscles obvious even beneath the covering of dark hair.

"It's Joshua!"

Sam turned to scrutinize the monster. Massively broad and muscular shoulders sat above a narrow waist, and it was easily as big, if not bigger, than the male that had killed Jerry. Though the hair was black.

"What ... um ... did Joshua look like?"

"He was beautiful. Kind of like a cross between Jason Mamoa and The Rock."

Sam understood the attraction, and as the creature continued to stalk them beside the water, she could see the remnants of the face that had entranced Rachel.

"It is him!"

"You may be right, Rachel, but-"

"It is! I just know it."

"Well, he does seem particularly interested in you."

"He does?"

The stream began to dip, and with it, Sam's gut.

"Just keep walking."

Ahead, instead of disappearing as Sam had feared, the stream widened and in the next minute, the shore came into view. Mobile in hand, she made a last effort to contact the lodge and beg for help.

CHAPTER FORTY-TWO

Max waited.

As time passed, and the light around him grew dim, bright light shone through the fence, and the men and buildings disappeared behind it. Trunks cast dark shadows as the light caught on their bark, the floor silver. Max waited until the forest beyond the light was deepest black.

Movement at the gate. He sniffed, taking in the particles of their stench, the sourness of their fear, and the oil … petrol … diesel. An engine growled into life. Voices mingled with the noise. A man shouted. Another returned his call. The leader calling his pack. The heavy clink of metal was followed by scraping of metal against metal. From the light, a truck rolled. Metal clinked, rolled, then clanked, and the buzz of the fence continued.

Max waited.

The sky above was spattered with light. The forest was black. The Others waited too, their excited chitter interspersed with hisses as they grew impatient, but he wanted them to be hungry, desperate for the warm lifeblood of the Screamers inside the fence. Their offal … their liver … their life-giving kidneys. Memories of flesh sliding down his throat, the blood warm, trickling down his chin, intestines slipping across his chest as he bit through them, roused his hunger. He pushed the need down, scratching long talons against a trunk—they had to wait.

Minutes became hours and the noise of the engine returned. He growled, kicking at a large male as it lay curled, its arm around a female. He kicked again. The male growled. Max returned the growl, pouncing on the male, biting down on its throat. The male lay still, the female lowering her eyes, submitting. Max growled again, pulling another male from his crouch. The engine grew louder as the pack assembled. Muscular and alert, yearning to gnash their teeth and tear at flesh, they stood ready, and waited at the edge of the light, unseen. As the vehicle approached, and the grating metal screeched in his ears, Max gave the signal, and the beasts, driven by the need to tear into flesh, burst from the shadows, and descended on the truck as the gate opened.

"FIRE!"

As the horde of wolfmen descended from the trees, and the empty truck sat idling at the gates, Kendrick gave the order for his men to fire. This time, at Dr. Steward's insistence, there were no bullets. The electrified gate, which had been opened partially to give the impression that it was allowing the vehicle access, slammed with a grinding of gears and clash of metal.

"All secure," the guard called as the men positioned across the entrance opened fire on the advancing horde. Each one a highly trained marksman, some with sniper experience, focused on an individual and fired. As soon as one dart was fired, the spotter passed a loaded rifle, reloading the first.

Within seconds, each of the wolfmen had been hit, and their terrifying onslaught slowed to a stumble. Only one managed to make it to the fence, and she was thrown back to the forest floor by the explosive force of the electric shock riding through her body at a current that would kill a normal man. As the volley of shots slowed to zero, silence fell, and the only sound Kendrick noticed was the heavy breathing of the man beside him.

"How many did we get?" Night vision goggles on, Kendrick counted the glowing orange shapes beyond the gate. "Hot damn!"

"Is that them all?"

"It matches the list of the infected and the missing."

Gillespie whistled. "We are on fire!" he exclaimed.

"Je-sus! That was A for fucking awesome!"

"Did you see them go down? It was like they were running in slow motion."

"Did you see those titties jiggle?" Johnson snorted with laughter.

"Shut it, Johnson! You clown."

"Are they dead?"

"Why would they be dead?"

"Well, we pumped them full of enough anaesthetic to kill an elephant."

"Three each, that's the minimum. If some are dead, then that's the price Steward will have to pay."

Johnson nodded. "Psycho bitch."

"Watch your language, Kipper. There are ears everywhere around here."

Kipper scanned the other men. "Them?"

"Who knows. Just do the job you've been assigned and keep your trap shut." Kendrick climbed down. "We've got an hour before they need another dose." He said as the men gathered around. Behind him a truck backed up. Inside, a container had been converted into a cage. "Check that each one has at least three darts that have been fully emptied. If not, give them another shot. Now, to it. We've lost ..." he checked his watch. "Precisely three minutes and ten seconds so far. Move it!" The decoy vehicle was pulled into the compound, and the men threaded through the small gap left open between the gates. "Anyone not back here by twenty hundred hours precisely, will be locked out, and shot."

In the next twenty minutes, all the wolfmen were dragged back inside the compound and thrown up into the cage.

Unseen, beneath the decoy car, Max gripped the metal undercarriage, and waited.

CHAPTER FORTY-THREE

Marta sat straight in her chair, a cup of black tea cold before her. She fingered her pen, pressure along its barrel making the tips white. Kendrick stood before her, greasy sweat glowing at his forehead. The pungent aroma of stale sweat hovered around him, polluting her perfumed space. The self-satisfied grin on his face scratched against her nerves.

"I told you that I wanted all of them brought back alive. Not with their heads blown off." He made no reaction to the terseness of her voice. That irritated her too.

"That order came after we used those bullets. The other ammo had no impact. My men did their best to protect the compound, and you, Doctor Steward."

She sat back in her chair. "It wasn't Max you killed ... was it?"

A flicker of reaction. "No."

"But you have him?"

"We have all of the wolfmen that are alive on the island sedated. We haven't been able to identify them all ... yet."

"I need to know that Max is among them." She could hear the wheedling in her voice. The pen bent beneath her fingers.

"He will be."

She locked his gaze for emphasis. "I want the evidence, Kendrick." He returned her gaze then dropped it. "Understood?"

"Yes. But ... how exactly can we identify him among the others?"

"How? He's the alpha."

"But they all look very similar ... Most of them are very muscular. There are differences in colour of ... coat, and obviously gender, but other than that, they look the same. Does he have any identifying marks?"

"He has a tattoo. On his left buttock."

"... I see."

"Go look, then!"

With a stiff bow as though he was still in the army, Kendrick swivelled on his heels and left the room. The band of tension across Marta's shoulders increased, and the headache she medicated against that morning returned. "Now see what you've done, Kendrick," she said to the empty room. "You've made me feel unwell." She rubbed fingertips at her temples then sat back in her chair. The leather padding was comforting, but her eyes burned with tiredness; since Max had escaped, she had barely been able to sleep.

Her telephone rang. 'Blake Dalton' was printed on the screen and the pain in her stomach twisted; their last conversation hadn't been easy. She allowed it to ring several more times before answering and, after the initial greetings, sat back to listen. The pen snapped in her fingers, and she threw herself forward. Tea spilled as she knocked the desk; *they've pulled the plug! The senseless, blinkered idiots had cancelled her project!*

"They've already begun collecting the stronger specimens from Kielder."

"What the hell! What the very hell!"

"It's out of my hands, Marta. I told you before that our sponsors were getting tired of waiting, and this current security breach-"

After a sharp intake of breath, she said, "It is all under control! Max has been captured. We can see this as a success, Blake. Max was allowed to roam free for a short time during which we monitored his every move, and then brought him back in. The tracking device worked perfectly, as did the retrieval protocols. Max will be back, sedated, secure, and ready to continue trials within the hour. In fact, there was no security breach, this was all a planned exercise."

"Planned?"

"Yes, planned," she lied.

"And Katarina?"

The growl of anger erupted from her throat before she had a chance to bury it down.

"I'm guessing, that wasn't planned."

"Who told you?"

"All security breaches are logged, Marta."

"Kendrick! The bloody toad!"

"What? Did you think that we wouldn't find out? Max escapes, kills one of your staff, and disappears into the forest? It's Kielder again, Marta, and you know how that ended."

"It's not Kielder. We learnt the lessons from that catastrophe."

"Nevertheless, Marta, you've been relieved of your post."

They haven't shut it down! "But ... this is my project!"

"And one you obviously cannot handle."

"Of course I can handle it. Max is being returned as we speak."

"And the others?"

"It has to be Kendrick! He's your spy, isn't he!"

"That is irrelevant, Marta. All that *is* relevant is that you have lost control and the project is going to be closed down, at least in Alaska."

"What? So where will they be doing the research? Is it Peter? If it is that snivelling wretch …"

"No, Marta. It's not Peter."

"But I bet you'll take him with you, won't you! Where are you taking him?"

"I'm not at liberty to say."

"What about us, Blake?"

"Us, Marta?"

"Yes, us, you and me, we've spent … time together."

Silence and then, "Marta … the age difference …" A huff was followed by an excruciating silence, then his voice took on a colder tone. "It was you who called us 'colleagues with benefits', Marta."

Five years! She was only five years older! The pain of rejection was physical, and her anger reached a peak. She gripped a handful of hair, unable to form a cohesive sentence. "This was our project, Blake! You're the one who said that we should see Max's accident for what it was—an opportunity."

"Yes, and we did, but this thing is out of control. Corbeur is right, we need facilities that can hold the … subjects."

"Say it, Blake! Say it! They're wolfmen. Fucking mutant werewolves!"

"Calm down, Marta! I hate it when you're like this … There's no point in us having this discussion; a team has already been dispatched to retrieve the specimens that you currently have at Volkolak."

"Where the hell are you taking them?"

"Corbeur has arranged to have them shipped to a secure holding station."

"Where?"

"It's completely underground."

"Where?"

"More secure than any category A prison."

"Oh, for crying out loud, Dalton! Where is he taking them?"

"Ukraine."

"That corrupt shithole?"

He nodded. "It's the epicentre of biological experimentation and trafficking. Hell, you can even buy human organs and foetuses on demand. It's the perfect place to hide. Corbeur's in talks with some of the scrotes at the European defence agencies, they're very keen on developing biological weapons ... of this type."

"What about the Americans ..."

He snorted. "The Americans are already in Ukraine. The Nazis ain't got nothing compared to what's going on under their watch. Operation Paperclip was an astounding success," he said with a tone of pure cynicism.

Marta sucked air through her teeth with rising ire. "Well ... you're not taking Max!"

"Of course we're taking Max. We can't leave any specimens behind; the project is to be eradicated from the island, and you said it yourself, he is the perfect alpha male."

"Well, you're not having him. I'm going to keep him."

"Now you're just being stupid. You can't keep him. You can't even stay on the island."

"You can't have him, Blake. Corbeur can't have him. He's mine!"

"Marta? For crying out loud woman, what are you going to do? Take him for walks? Teach him to do tricks?"

Marta snorted with anger. "Just watch!" Pressing the mobile's red 'end call' button she threw the phone across the room. "Just you watch, Blake. Just you watch." Heart pounding, nausea swirled in her belly, and she swayed, grasping hold of the desk, and waited for the moment to pass. She would show them; if she couldn't have Max, then no one could.

Turning back to her computer she accessed the files for the project. Copied them over to a secure, and highly classified, cloud storage facility and then deleted all the original files.

CHAPTER FORTY-FOUR

The truck had rolled to a stop within the compound and parked among a collection of other vehicles. Max had waited, clinging to the metal undercarriage until the voices of the men had quietened, and their stench had thinned, and they were no longer near. He crawled from beneath the truck, darted to the shadows and scoured the area. The forest sat beyond the fence, and slits of light shone from the buildings. He crept beside the walls, reaching up to see inside. Some of the rooms were empty, in others they walked, and sat, and laughed. He snapped his jaws in silent rage. The urge to bite down through flesh and bone, and tear their limbs drove him onwards, but the need for Laura was stronger, and he crouched to pass the sitting, laughing, sour-stinking, blood-full men.

A door opened, a Screamer shouted then laughed, and Max squatted in the shadows, watching as two figures emerged, then walked away. Keeping to the shadows, Max sprinted along the wall, and entered the building.

CHAPTER FORTY-FIVE

The lab door opened as Peter retrieved the thermometer. Wiping residue from the glass stick, he checked the temperature, then disposed of the tissue in the bin. Kendrick strode forward, his face stern.

"Is there a problem?" Peter asked as he entered Laura's temperature into his notes.

"I need to identify the alpha male among the animals we just brought in."

Peter stopped typing. "Max?"

"That's correct."

"That should be easy, his DNA markers have been logged." He gestured to an open laptop on the far worktop. "They're on the files-"

"I need a visual identification."

"Well, he's the alpha-"

"Sure, but they all look pretty much the same, especially when they're out cold."

"How many do you have?"

"Nine, including three females."

"Well, you can tell by their-"

"Yes, I know that! It's the males we're struggling to identify. Marta said Max has a tattoo on his ass. I've got to check it out."

"Ah!"

"Exactly, so I need your help. I'm not prepared to get that close if there's any chance they could wake."

"So you need me to ensure that they are under sedation?"

"They're already sedated. I need you to make sure they don't overdose, but yeah, I need them comatose Doctor Marston. Pretty much dead, if possible."

"Of course. I'll prepare the injections now."

As Peter began to collect the vials of anaesthesia, Kendrick's phone rang. With a quick glance at the screen, he muttered, "Marta! Which of my balls does she want to break this time?" then took the call, turning to the wall to speak.

Kendrick's words 'pretty much dead, if possible', repeated in Peter's mind and a thought began to form as the man continued his increasingly heated conversation. If Marta wasn't prepared to put an end to the project, even though the horrors of Kielder seemed to be recurring, then he would. As Kendrick continued to talk, he began his search through the cupboards for the vials he was sure would have been shipped, along with the contents of the labs at Kielder; Marta would be a fool not to make sure there was a good supply of the drug. He checked through the cupboards that lined the wall then the tall cupboard in the corner. Increasingly frustrated, he slammed a cupboard door shut.

"Need any help!" Kendrick asked as he finished his call.

"No!" He grabbed a sealed box from a cupboard. "I've got what you need right here." With a smile, he tore at the box.

Placing handfuls of vials into a separate container, he handed them to Kendrick. "Use the Z-track method. Instructions are in this file." He handed a black plastic file across to the man. "One vial each should do it." As Kendrick left, he turned his attention back to Laura. She shifted in the box. He checked his watch. Time for another shot. Once administered, her breathing slowed again to a state of subconsciousness only just above that of a coma. He stroked her cheek, seeing through the grotesque deformities that had transmogrified her face, to the woman she had once been. "It's the kindest thing, Laura." He stroked long hair back from her brow. The golden honeypot and diamond at her ear glinted in the overhead light. "You'll see." Reaching to the cupboard he pulled out the box from which he had taken the vials for Kendrick. The box was marked with 'Beuthanasia D-Special.' He read aloud, "Contains pentobarbital and phenytoin. Warning: for canine euthanasia only ... That's the one," and placed the vial on the table beside Laura.

CHAPTER FORTY-SIX

"Marston said to use the Z-track method. From what I can tell, that means just stabbing them in the ass and pushing the plunger down." He demonstrated by stabbing the filled syringe into the first animal's muscular buttock. The creature made no movement, gave no sign it was aware, and Kendrick pushed the plunger down. He threw the syringe in the sharps bin and tore open another before filling it with fluid from another vial. "See! Easy." Holding the second syringe, he turned to the gathered men, "Now, it's your turn. Get these critters sedated pronto."

Four men each took a syringe, filled it with fluid from the vials, and injected a sleeping wolfman. Only the two females remained to be injected when Kendrick noticed that the first wolfman he had injected had stopped breathing. He moved in closer, watching for the rise and fall of its chest. It was completely still. "Shit!" he whispered, his expletive drowned out by the chatter of the men and clink of syringes and vials as they disposed of the poisoned receptacles. The two females received their injections.

"All done!" Kipper called as Kendrick held a hand above the wolfman's mouth. The air was cold beneath his palm. "Shit!" Louder this time.

"What is it?"

"This one's dead!"

The men turned to look. Kendrick checked on the second male he had injected. It too was still. He reached across, pulled its eyelids apart. The pupils did not contract. "Shit! This one's dead too." Checking around at the other creatures they had brought in from the forest only hours ago, he realised that each one was dead.

"They OD'ed?"

Kendrick moved from creature to creature, feeling for a pulse, sliding eyelids open. "Damn! Damn! Damn!"

Kipper picked up one of the remaining vials. "I guess that's 'cos we just killed them. This is dog euthanasia."

"What!" He snatched the vial and read the tiny print on its side. "Beuthanasia D. Special ... for dog euthanasia only. What the hell!" He stared from the vial to the dead wolfmen. "Marston!"

CHAPTER FORTY-SEVEN

The last hour of walking had been an agony as the creature had continued to track them beside the river, but when they had finally reached the inlet where the lodge sat, they had emerged to a hail of bullets as Carmel had opened fire on the beast.

Chris pulled at the outboard engine again, his face flushed pink with effort. The motor whirred but didn't start.

Joshua squatted at the edge of the forest, protected from Carmel's bullets beside the deeply furrowed and wide trunk of an ancient poplar. Pushing Chris aside, Sam took the pullcord. The engine made no effort to start.

"God damn it! Damn thing has seized."

Mobile now in hand, Chris began to video the beach. "It's been neglected, probably out of petrol."

Joshua stood and watched.

"We filled him full of bullets. How come he's still alive?"

"He's a werewolf. Only a silver bullet can kill him."

"There's no such thing."

"Well, what else? Sure as hell looks like a werewolf—half man and half wolf, that's just what he looks like. Bit of a cross between Benicio Del Toro's version in the Wolfman, that was made in 2010, and Kate Beckinsale's brother in Van Helsing."

"Much as your knowledge of the movies fascinates me, Chris, can we please stay focussed! We've got to get off this beach before he gets any closer."

"But he's scared of the water. You can tell that."

"Or before any of the others find us."

The waves pushed the boat against the shingle. "Damn!" With a leap, Sam returned to the water, and pushed the boat. "We're going to have to paddle."

Joshua took two steps onto the beach.

"He's getting lairy! Look at him!"

Broad-shouldered and muscular, Joshua was magnificent even with his bastardised face.

"He wants me!" Rachel whispered.

"What did you say, Rachel?"

"He wants me!"

"Yeah, to eat!" Chris quipped.

"No, he really wants me."

Rachel stood in the boat, causing it to rock. Sam pushed it into deeper water, the cold sea bone-achingly painful.

"Sit down, Rachel!"

"No one wants me, Sam. Not my boss, not my mother, not Alistair Lawton, not Michel … All I've ever wanted is to be wanted."

"You're talking like a crazy woman, now sit down, or you'll fall over the side."

She stepped to the side of the boat. The edge dipped to the waves.

"Rachel!"

Joshua took another step forward, an arm outstretched. Carmel fired a shot.

"Stop shooting!" Rachel called.

Joshua stood with arms open.

"See!"

"Rachel!" Sam shouted. "Sit the hell down!"

Jumping into the water, Rachel flinched at the cold, then strode against the waves and up the beach.

"Oh, my Lord!"

"Rachel!" Chris shouted, peering from behind his mobile. "No! ... Oh ... my ... God!"

"He'll kill her!"

"Silly cow!" Chris stood as though to leave the boat, mobile still focused on the beach.

Sam grabbed his jacket. "No! You can't follow her!"

"Get the hell back here, Rachel Bonds!" he called.

"Rachel! Don't-" Sam's words caught in her throat as Rachel stood only feet away from the creature that had been Joshua. It towered above her, its clawed hands ready to tear.

"Oh, my God. I can't look! It's going to eat her!"

In the beast's shadow, Rachel offered a gesture of embrace. It pounced, wrapping huge arms around her middle, scooping her into its arms. Fangs bared, it lifted her to its jaws, and bit. She screamed, writhed, and then became limp. Throwing back its head, it lifted Rachel to the sky like a trophy, and carried her into the woods.

"This is sensational!"

"Did you get it on video?"

Chris thumbed his mobile screen. "I sure did."

Sam placed an arm across Chris' shoulder staring after the disappearing figure of the beast and his bride, as water lapped at the boat. "Get paddling, honey, and let's get the hell out of here."

CHAPTER FORTY-EIGHT

Peter stood over Laura, a Beuthanasia D-Special-filled syringe in hand. Watching the rise and fall of her chest as she breathed, a tear sat at the corner of his eye. He lifted her arm, searching for a well-defined vein. The clack of heels sounded in the corridor, and then the lab door swung open. Marta strode into the room, obviously flustered. "Peter!"

Startled, he dropped Laura's arm.

"Peter!"

"Yes?"

"Where is the live virus?"

"Live virus?"

"Yes! I've been searching for it for the last hour."

He nodded to the glass-fronted chiller on the counter. "In there." He placed the loaded syringe beside Laura as Marta took the tray of vials, then searched for an insulated, protective carrycase. His curiosity roused, Peter asked, "Where are you taking those, Marta? You do realise how toxic they are?"

"Yes, of course I do!" she snapped back.

"And that they need to remain at a controlled temperature."

"Yes! What's your point, Peter?"

"Well ... I'm wondering where you're taking them. What's going on, Marta?"

She huffed like a petulant child. "Titan Blane have shut us down!"

Peter stared at her, incredulous.

"I know! How very dare they!"

"But what about Laura, and Max?"

"Max has been recovered. Dalton is sending a team to retrieve him and ship him to Ukraine."

"Ukraine?"

"A secure military facility. I know! All those lies!

"And what about Laura?"

"And Laura too, I presume."

"No!"

"That is exactly what I said, Peter."

"No, the whole project has to stop!"

"You can't stop it! They're on their way ... Listen, Peter, Titan Blane and Corbeur have handed the project over to the Europeans. The breeding programme is a failure. But we don't need the breeding programme now we have the virus isolated. I've arranged transport off the island. I'll be leaving within the hour."

"But what about Laura?"

"We don't need Laura. Or ... Max. We can use fully grown men. Willing soldiers, or convicts on death row, maybe political dissenters! I don't care where the subjects come from, as long as they are healthy and strong."

Peter's face was set to stony, Marta plummeting in his estimation.

"Come with me, Peter," she continued. "I've already arranged to co-operate with the Americans. They have secure, state-of-the-art facilities, military facilities, not like this Mickey Mouse operation."

Peter remained silent, and stroked Laura's arm.

"Well ... what do you say? You know I need you on board."

"No! It stops here, right now!"

He picked up Laura's arm and guided the syringe to a wide blue vein.

"What's in the syringe, Peter?"

"Beuthanasia D. Special."

"Seriously, Peter!"

"Yes, Marta. I can no longer stomach this horror. What you've done to Laura is abominable, what the Europeans will do to her is beyond endurance."

"I haven't done anything to her, Peter. Max turned her into this ... monster." Marta peered into the box, her eyes narrow, lips pursing. "Fine. Kill her then; she never was good enough for Max anyway."

"And you were?"

As Marta attempted to reply, her words were drowned out by the piercing noise of the alarm. Unsettled, fear melded with Marta's anger, and for a moment she appeared startled, but quickly gathered her senses, and said. "Kendrick has it all under control," then slammed the lab door shut. The noise of the alarm lessened to an irritating whine.

"What does that mean?"

"It means that I have every faith in him. He dealt with the earlier attack masterfully, and retrieved Max, and the other infected males and females."

"How many?"

"... several."

"How many?"

"At least ten, or so."

"A repeat of Kielder then!"

Marta sighed. "That's why we're on an island, Peter."

"And its inhabitants are expendable." A dry statement.

"It was the safest option."

"Until it wasn't."

"Yes! Fine then! ... Until it wasn't. But the programme failed regardless of security measures. In trials, the technology was successful, and we were able to control the behaviour of the subjects, but we wanted to create something better, in-vitro implantation using Max's own stem-cell research. It would have given us the absolute control we needed. Max was the perfect specimen to produce the embryos."

"But Max wouldn't co-operate."

"Correct."

"Katarina was right! He's not just a savage beast! There's still something of Max, the Max we knew, and loved, left. I've read Katarina's notes, she was convinced that was the case, she was certain that something of his old self remained." He grabbed a folder from the counter. "Here, I printed this off. See!" He stabbed a finger at the text. "Here, and here, and here! Max showed signs of improved cognition. He was communicating with her at the access panel, for God's sake, accepting her touch, trying to speak to her, holding his hands in supplication!" He swallowed, fighting back a tear. "The man was begging, Marta. Begging!" Marta's eyes focused on the wall behind his shoulder, her jaw tight. He continued. "Katarina noted that when she mentioned Laura, tears actually formed in his eyes." A flicker of spite shone in Marta's eyes. "He's not just an animal that you can use for experimentation, he's not just Subject Alpha 1! He's Max Anderson, husband, lover, brother, son, colleague, father-"

Marta's eyes glowered as she interrupted. "Are you referring to the pups he sired?"

"His sons, Marta. They were his sons."

"Are."

"They're alive?"

"Yes. Unless you've already killed them." Peter's jaws clenched. "Oh, yes, I've seen your little trail of horror. I know that you were about to end Laura's life too as soon as I walked through that door, so don't come the Mister-high-and-mighty-holier-than-thou with me!"

Peter mentally scanned the adults and juveniles, males, and females, he had injected with the euthanising drug. "No!"

"Yes! I had them shipped over at the same time as Max. And now the whole family is here!" She laughed. "So, you can't accuse me of being a home-wrecker." She cackled, then snorted with derision, and slipped the strap of the bag of live virus across her shoulder. "I have to go, Peter. Last chance! Come with me."

Ignoring her plea, he asked, "Which room are they in?"

"I have no idea."

The alarm continued to wail, and Peter turned from Marta to the laptop on the counter. With the bag of live virus secure, she left the room. Noise, and the acrid aroma of smoke, filled the space as she opened the door. She turned. "If you change your mind about your future, then meet me on the quad. The helicopter will arrive in thirty-five minutes."

Peter moved to the laptop whilst Marta hovered in the doorway.

Furious fingers tapped at the keyboard as Peter accessed the project's files.

Marta moved away. "Thirty-five minutes, Peter. And they're in Room 7!"

Folder located, Peter read the information:

Subject: 12 A.1 - Romulus
Legend: Sire – Max Anderson. Dam – Laura Anderson
Age: Juvenile. Approximately 9 biological years.
Sex: Male
Status: In perfect health. Recommended.

Subject: 13 A.1 – Remus
Legend: Sire – Max Anderson. Dam – Laura Anderson
Age: Juvenile. Approximately 9 biological years.
Sex: Male
Status: In perfect health. Recommended.

He laughed despite the horror, naming the twins must have been one of Katarina's little jokes.

CHAPTER FORTY-NINE

Sweat beaded at Peter's brow as he wheeled the second cage into the room. He stopped to catch his breath as the door behind him swung shut, then coughed. Smoke from a fire somewhere in the building was curling poisonous tendrils through the corridors.

There were now three cages in the room: Laura and her twin sons.

After Marta's revelations that the boys were on the island, and that Titan Blane had pulled the plug on the Alaska strain of their operation, but were making efforts to continue elsewhere, Peter had an epiphany; he would release Laura and her sons into the wild. The island was the perfect habitat, and full of bears, deer, and other prey. Plus, once the Institute had been dismantled, and its staff relocated, it would be almost devoid of human life. Plus, plus, the water was an impenetrable barrier that they wouldn't be able to cross, and so the spread of the virus would be contained.

A tremor gripped Peter's hand as he grasped the trolley's handle and it slipped from the metal bar. He gripped it to his chest, pushing back the stab of confusion, and pushed at the trolley with his belly until all three cages were lined up. Behind him smoke had begun to seep beneath the door. Ahead was the door that would open into the compound.

He swallowed. He checked his watch. Fifteen minutes until Marta, and her helicopter, left.

With the catheter removed from Laura's hand, the drip, drip of anaesthetic had stopped at least twenty minutes ago, but she remained below consciousness inside her cage. In the other two cages, the boys crouched, staring at him with blood-filled eyes, their teeth bared.

He would have only seconds to escape from the room once he unlocked the cages. Lifting the bar of the external doors, a scream stopped him in his tracks. He listened, realised it came from across the hills, and continued to open the doors. The next minutes were spent pulling the cages to face the compound and the forest beyond its electrified fence. His plan was to release them and turn off the electrical supply so that they could escape into the trees, and then make his way to Marta. He checked his watch; eleven minutes to departure.

Laura's leg twitched.

A boy yapped and grasped the bars of his cage.

Peter unlocked Laura's cage. Her arm moved, clawed hand clenching.

The other boy tipped his head back and howled.

The tremor in Peter's hand grew violent. He reached for the clasp of the second cage, and the boy inside leapt forward, snapping at his hand. Peter took a step back, breath catching, a vice locking his ribs.

Smoke seeped beneath the door.

Time had run out.

"One ... two ... three!" He reached for the clasp of each cage simultaneously and flipped them. The first one opened. The other stuck. Needle-sharp incisors snapped at Peter's hand. He tried again, flipped the latch, and ran.

The door of the first cage swung open, followed by the second.

Smoke made the view to the internal door hazy, but he grasped for the handle. Behind him clawed feet skidded on the concrete floor and the room filled with growls and excited yaps. Expecting sharp fangs to sink into his shoulder, and claws to slice down his back, he grabbed the door's handle.

Pain tore through his shoulder and head as the door was thrown open and he was slammed against the wall. Aware only of being hauled up, he was thrown back into the room, skittling across the floor, and banging against a cage.

Max stood over him.

Peter scuffled back, arms crossed over his face as Max rolled his lips back into a snarl to reveal his fangs. "It's me, Max! It's Peter."

Max growled.

"I have Laura." He stabbed at the trolley. "I brought your sons."

Max snarled. "Please, Max! It's me, Peter! I was trying to help them." Catching sight of the dark centre of Max's blood-red eyes, he quickly looked away.

Paralysed by fear, he waited, screwing his eyes tight against the tearing horror he knew would come. Max sniffed, the heat of his breath hot against Peter's neck, then pulled back.

Silence descended as his sons took tentative steps away from their cages, sniffing the air, sampling their father's smell, activating their memories.

Max growled at the approaching boys and then a babble of incoherent noise erupted from his throat and the space erupted in a fury of yaps, growls, and hoarse barks that grated along disfigured vocal chords as the boys bounded to his side.

Laura sat up in the box and Max yowled, his voice laced with rage as she tumbled over the side and landed on the floor.

He roared, piercing Peter's ears, then took massive strides to her before scooping her into his arms. The boys quickly followed.

Scrambling to his knees, as Max cradled Laura, his sons at his side, Peter pushed the door open and stumbled out into the smoke-filled corridor.

MARTA PEERED THROUGH the helicopter's window. "Stupid man!"

"Pardon?"

"Not you, Peter. Max!" She continued to watch the treeline where Max stood with his sons, Laura in his arms, as the helicopter lifted. "... I loved him you know." Tears glistened in her eyes.

A strange kind of love, Marta! Peter remained silent, and instead watched the family disappear into the forest.

As the helicopter moved away from the compound, Marta dried her eyes, and reached for her mobile. "Drake, I have the virus. ETA is six hours."

Peter eyed the bag of live virus beside Marta and swallowed.

EPILOGUE

Thirteen months later,
Eagle, Colorado, United States of America

Enveloped in Jerry's huge cable-knit cardigan, her feet on Chris' lap as he took a sip of hot chocolate whilst massaging her toes, Sam reclined on the sofa, laptop on her knees. Logged into her bank account, she clicked the 'transfer now' button, and three and a quarter million of the $8,097,981 that had been paid out by the Institute, and Jerry's very generous life insurance, disappeared, transferred across the digital ether to the bank account of Carmel Wilson. 'Transfer Complete' appeared on her screen. "Yes!" She raised the glass of wine beside her monitor and spoke into the phone held against her ear. "It should be in your account now, Carmel."

A moment's silence, and then, "Congratulations, Sam! You are now owner of the Volkolak Island."

"Thank you, honey! I just couldn't stand to go back to working in a school, and you know I love the outdoor life."

"You live on island?"

"Yep, I sure will."

An odd mewl was followed by silence, and then, "I wish you good luck, Sam."

"Thank you, and listen, Carmel. Chris and I were so sorry to hear about George," Sam said referring to the heart attack George had suffered only six months after the Volkolak fiasco.

"His heart was too sad for leaving the island, his mind too troubled by the people who died ... Goodbye, Sam."

The phone clicked to dead, and as she closed the bank's tab on her laptop, the home page for the new website she was designing reappeared on the screen. With quick fingers she typed 'Volkolak Island Game Reserve' in the title field, and followed this with the tag line, 'The Ultimate Hunting & Survival Experience', before referring to the notes feverishly scribbled in a moment of epiphany:

> *Volkolak Island = Inhabited by a never-before-seen species of apex predator. Irresistible offer = the ultimate hunting experience.*
>
> *Target market = rich, big game hunters – millionaire/ billionaire hunting set – illegal trophy hunters = looking for next adrenaline rush.*
>
> *Hook = Volkolak Island, where the hunter may become the hunted. Have you got what it takes to visit?*
>
> *Potential clients? = Rick Delaney; Abdi Khaled, Alejhandro D'Angelo, Macy Bouvier. Big Game hunters to target = Jacklin O'Rourke.*

Volkolak Island

AS SAM TOOK ANOTHER sip of wine and composed the initial paragraph for her website, Rachel sat cross-legged on a mat of ferns overhung with branches in Volkolak's dense forest of spruce. A child suckled at her breast. With delicate pressure, she traced clawed fingers across the downy hair that covered his tiny cheek, then stroked the head of the older child asleep at her thigh. In the distance, a single howl was joined by others until the air filled with the call of the pack.

Underground Military Testing Facility, Ukraine

GABE WATCHED THE MONITOR with a sinking feeling in his gut as the creature swooped down. The target didn't stand a chance. He muted the sound as flesh ripped beneath razor sharp claws and 'it' bent to gorge.

"Begin deactivation, Carson."

"Yes, sir." Gabe suppressed the tremor in his finger with a deep breath and hit the button on the control panel. The grip of fear across his chest remained; he would never get used to watching 'The Team' in action. He took the warnings seriously: don't get sloppy, be alert at all times. Watching the monsters devour their prey - tearing at limbs and shredding flesh - was not something he'd ever be blasé about. Hell, if a mistake didn't kill him, then the stress of the job would. A trickle of cold sweat beaded at his temple.

Kendrick leant over his shoulder with a satisfied grunt. "Vicious bastards, aren't they."

"That is one hell of an understatement." Gabe stared at the crouched figure of the monster, its face buried against the neck of the writhing man.

"Twenty more seconds." Kendrick straightened his shoulder.

"Yes, sir." The tension eased across Gabe's chest as he began the countdown; twenty more seconds to let 'it' feed, then he'd deactivate the arse-wipe until next time.

Three ... two ... one, and he hit the red 'deactivate' button sighing with relief as the creature slumped, head lolling as it sat back on muscular haunches. Gabe checked its vitals on the monitor, watching as its heart rate reduced to a steadier beat and then slowed to a state of near deathly inactivity.

Kendrick patted his shoulder. "Good job, Carson." He walked to the door. "You know the drill; retrieval and lockdown, report to my inbox and copied to Doctor Steward by ten hundred hours."

"Yes, sir."

Kendrick gave a satisfied snort. "I think they're just about ready to go on Special Ops, don't you?"

"Yes, sir."

"Good ... Report. My inbox. Ten hundred hours."

Gabe gave a final nod to Kendrick as he left the control room and turned back to the monitors; the creature's heart rate remained slow, and its temperature had dropped. He reached for the phone. "A12 deactivated. Commence retrieval and lockdown."

He noted the time; just two more hours until his shift ended, and he could not wait. He'd have a cool beer, win his money back from Ridley, then crash.

THE END

What to read next

If you enjoyed *The Kielder Strain* and *The Alaska Strain*, try *Feeders*, a thrilling zombie horror.

Never Miss Another Book

Join me to receive updates of my latest novels, subscriber discounts, and early access to upcoming works: https://deadcitychronicles.substack.com/

About the Author

An English author, Rebecca lives with her children among the flatlands of the Humber estuary where Vikings and Anglo-Saxons once fought. Sometimes, on foggy mornings, the sounds of clashing swords can still be heard.

She writes post-apocalyptic thrillers and novels of horror.

Printed in Great Britain
by Amazon